Naperville

Chris Bittler

Cover design by Tracy Tomkowiak.

ISBN-10: 0989638413

ISBN-13: 978-0-9896384-1-8

To my Naperville associates.

CONTENTS

ACKNOWLEDGMENTS

Thanks to Dave for fixing the concept and letting me steal an old Chris and Dave sketch, Tracy for the amazing cover art, Bob and Lori for letting me sit in their camper all summer, and the judges of the Amazon Breakthrough Novel Award for choosing *Naperville* as a 2013 quarter-finalist.

* ON HAPPINESS *

The Wizened Security Guard held court in the Naperville lunchroom. His followers listened with rapt attention as bits of wisdom and hot dog spewed from his mouth. He was explaining the legal inaccuracies of *Matlock* when one of them burst forth with a question.

"Wizened Security Guard, you are so wise and stuff. Tell me: How can I be happy working in this corporation?"

It was Jerry from Facilities, whose skull had recently been fractured by a box of staplers and had subsequently taken to watching Tony Robbins videos.

The Wizened Security Guard smiled knowingly.

"You are wise to seek my counsel," the bearded sage replied. "I will gladly give you the secret of a long, happy career and ask for nothing in return – except your package of Ding Dongs."

The exchange made, the Wizened Security Guard sat up regally. Wisdom was in his eyes, and sesame seeds in his teeth.

"For a happy career, three things – and three things only – are to be avoided. Never drink coffee you can't see through, never use your sick days for being sick and never volunteer to organize a birthday party. Refrain from these abominations and you will be happy."

"I want my Ding Dongs back," said Jerry.

- Parables of the Wizened Security Guard
  Schaumburg Fragment, circa 2000 A.D.

CHAPTER 1

Avery viewed his empty binder.

"Well, everything seems to be in order on my end," he said, resisting the urge to rub his nose.

Mr. Jabra, the cherubic little man behind the desk, looked up and smiled. His eyes focused somewhere beyond Avery's right ear.

"Wonderful. All I need is the original request form."

Avery rubbed his nose.

"Like I've been telling you, it seems to be lost. That's why I'll accept any model – whatever's in stock – for this chair."

Mr. Jabra's gaze remained on the patch of air behind the visitor. "That is not a chair. It appears to be a trash can affixed in some mysterious fashion to a pair of roller blades." Mr. Jabra smiled again and straightened some papers.

Avery looked back at the binder, which, being empty, offered little in the way of advice. He had been going back and forth with Mr. Jabra for fifteen minutes and only now did it occur to him that the chubby, cheerful man had no intention of granting his request, had in fact probably just been toying with him. Avery's long, thin face registered successive waves of emotion: confusion, anger, defeat, anger, defeat, confusion. His straight red hair stood up like the quills of a porcupine in full retreat. His body jerked spasmodically, as if trying to escape from itself.

Mr. Jabra started to hum a bit.

Avery's frustration was a natural reaction to an insoluble problem, like some nefarious programming loop, because his brain knew three things to be true: (1) he needed a new chair, (2) the only way to get a new chair was to lie, and (3) he was a bad liar.

There was an additional truth known to both men: the old "chair" was indeed a trash can affixed in some mysterious fashion to a pair of roller blades.

Was it possible, Avery wondered, that in the entire Naperville Corporation there wasn't one extra office chair? He started doing the math in his head. *Sixteen stories tall, one hundred and thirty gigacubes from east to west, six feet per gigacube —*

Mr. Jabra stopped working and looked Avery directly in the left eyebrow.

"You have no clearance to be here."

"True," Avery admitted. There was no point in denying it.

"Can I give you a piece of advice?"

This was a positive turn of events. Perhaps the old bureaucrat had a heart after all.

"Sure. You see, I really need a new chair, and – "

"Run."

"Excuse me?"

"Run."

Maybe not so positive

"You called Internal Audit?"

"They'll be here directly."

Avery nodded, turned and pushed the chair-thing toward the doorway. The blades made steering all but impossible.

Outside, he struggled past the rows of work cubicles. No one even glanced up, despite his knit shirt which marked him as a stranger in Corporate Services, where short sleeves and a clip-on were *de rigueur*. In retrospect, the binder had been a mistake too: they all carried clipboards here.

He continued down the aisle. There was still nothing to indicate trouble. Perhaps Mr. Jabra had only been kidding.

Then the alarms went off and he knew he was screwed.

Every Naperville associate, from the Danville Terminus to the Davenport Wall, dreaded that undulating siren; it meant Internal Audit agents were approaching – and you didn't want to be wandering the corridors when that happened. Avery opted to pick up his chair-thing and run.

Reaching a row of residential cubes with floor-to-ceiling wall panels, he yanked on the nearest door handle and found it locked. He tried the next door, which bore a wooden plaque that read *Home Sweet Cubicle*. No luck.

"No solicitors," a tense, muffled voice said.

The angry whine of the IA cycles came from behind him, followed by harsh voices and a random scream. He ran some more. Unfortunately, the chair-thing was surprisingly heavy and Avery was surprisingly weak and he was forced to stop at the end of the aisle.

"You! With the trash can. Stay right there!"

An IA agent stood at the far end of the corridor.

Avery froze automatically. Naperville associates were conditioned since daycare to obey Internal Audit.

However, instead of marching down the corridor, the agents walked away. It wasn't until he heard the *whreee* of an electric motor that Avery realized they had gone back for their cycles. Mr. Jabra's advice came back to him. He ran.

Directly ahead was a set of white metal doors. Bursting through them, he was relieved to find a main thoroughfare – and a food court! Hundreds of associates were taking their lunch break, lining up at food stands or sitting at molded plastic tables.

It took Avery a few seconds to get his bearings. This food court was completely different than the one he was used to. Instead of a Weiner Hut, a Potato King, a Barley Burger and an Essbee's Diner, it had a Potato King, a Weiner Hut, an Essbee's Diner and a Barley Burger. There wasn't even a Soy R U – it was like being in a different corporation.

Above the din he heard the purr of the IA cycles. Avery inverted the chair-thing and placed it next to a potted plant. Being mostly trash can, it looked reasonably at home. Then he crossed to a Human Resources recruitment table, grabbed a brochure and held it so close to his face it was nearly wrapped around his head. It was a disguise that wouldn't fool a child.

The IA agents passed him without a glance.

Relieved, Avery exhaled.

"Are you interested in volunteering for the Quad Cities work site?"

He turned. A female recruiter had apparently been talking to him for several seconds.

"The brochure," she said, gesturing to the paper in Avery's hand as if he were a toddler. "Did you want to volunteer? It's important work and an automatic promotion."

Avery glanced at the brochure. He had certainly heard of the Quad Cities work site, a hundred gigacubes away at the west wall of Naperville. It was the final stage of the Transcontinental Corridor which, when completed, would create a self-contained office complex running from the Atlantic ocean to the new Pacific coast. The artwork showed two fat silver ovals laid east to west on a map of the old United States and connected by a tiny isthmus not quite in the middle like a dangerously-twisted balloon animal. Volunteers at the Quad Cities work site were said to be very happy and well-compensated, but since none of them ever returned it was impossible to know for sure.

He handed back the brochure.

"I've got to get back to my own job."

The sirens wailed again. Avery turned and —

"So, long story short — you didn't get a new chair."

"Plus, I forgot my chair-thing."

It was dinner time and Avery was dining with Sauder at their local food court in Customer Service, the one with the right eateries in the right order. He poked listlessly at a potato cube. Sauder could tell he was annoyed.

"It was a good story, though," she said a bit too cheerfully. "Especially when you got chased by Internal Audit."

"Thanks."

Sauder, her mind always torn between practicality and encouragement, added, "There are so many of these food court chairs — you wouldn't think Facilities would miss one."

"I tried that. They're tagged."

Dr. Bob, who had joined them uninvited, leaned in conspiratorially. "You know," he whispered, an inch of noodle dangling from his chin, "I hear that if you cover the tag in foil they can't trace the chair."

Avery gave his potato cube another nudge. "Aren't you the one who suggested I go to Corporate Services to get a chair? And how did that work out for me?"

Dr. Bob shrugged. The noodle dropped onto his sleeve. Dr. Bob was their superior, though not exactly their boss. With his wide mouth and large designer eyeglasses he looked like a cross between a Buddha and a helpful frog.

Bob was also not a doctor, Sauder had given him the nickname due to his penchant for offering compelling yet ultimately bad advice. Like when he had assured Avery he could get transferred to Premium Services even though no one from Customer Service had ever achieved such a promotion. Or when he claimed to have seen a polar bear through an exterior window. Or even the previous week when he had insisted Soy R U veri-steak patties were made from ground worms – as if anybody could sell a genuine worm burger for only five fun bucks!

Avery pushed his tray away. Suddenly, not all the insta-flav in the world could make his potato entrée palatable.

"Let's take a walk," he said to Sauder.

The couple headed, as they inevitably did on their evening walks, toward the sub-Dwight atrium. Avery struggled to keep up with Sauder, who, despite her short frame, tended to outpace him.

The atrium was fifty cubes across, with thoroughfares leading off in six directions. It narrowed with each descending floor and boasted a terraced garden of potted plants at the bottom, thirteen floors below. Sauder took a deep lungful of recirculated air and relaxed.

Below them, a quartet of young Risk Management cadets passed by in their jaunty dress orange uniforms, and two humorless Internal Audit agents in shapeless black suits were questioning a man clutching a file box. *Better him than me,* Avery thought. Across the way some wildly-dressed employees chatted over coffee at the Essbee's. Corporate Communications performers, Avery assumed.

"Remember when we were young and talked about joining a Corporate Communications Caravan?" Sauder said.

Avery nodded. It had been his dream since childhood. Traveling to all the distant departments of Naperville, perhaps as a singer, a juggler or even a motivational speaker.

"How stupid was that?" Sauder added.

That was Sauder: the practical one, the focused one, the one who was going to marry him. And not just a corporate domestic partnership either, but a religious ceremony in the Judeo-Catholic church she insisted they attend.

They continued their lap around the atrium, passing the WaltMart display window where freelancers modeled the latest crops, shorts and tees.

"I wish it were summer," Sauder said. "I think I'd look cute in those shorts."

Avery admired her silhouette from several feet away: hands on her hips, one foot thrust back as if she were about to bow. She was diminutive but gracefully formed, her dark brown skin smooth and without blemish.

"So buy some."

Sauder clucked her tongue at him. "It's too early for shorts."

"Why? The temperature's not going to change."

"Ugh. You know nothing about fashion. Besides, if I wait until summer, they'll be pushing the fall fashions and I can get my summer wardrobe cheap."

She marched on. He caught up with her in front of a cubicle décor shop, took her hand.

"I picked up a shower gift for Kensington and Queenie. Don't worry – I put your name on the card too."

"That's Saturday, right?"

"It's tomorrow night."

"Tomorrow's Friday."

"Not any more. Didn't you get the eh-mail."

Avery swore and took a small earpiece out of his pocket. "I turned it off when I went to Corporate Services. The Lowest Down again?"

"Yeah. He thought today was Friday instead of Thursday, so they moved the days up."

Avery was distracted, zipping through his messages. "But apparently I still have to put in a full day tomorrow." He jammed the earpiece back in his pocket.

"You know what the Lower Downs say: 'Passion and teamwork are more important than cold, hard facts.'"

"Fine for them, but I still have to – "

Sauder pulled him down and kissed him. It was warm and emphatic, but it was a good night kiss.

"Don't be upset. I'll meet you for lunch," she said as she pulled away. "We'll get some quasi-shrimp."

CHAPTER 2

He dropped Sauder off at her cube. It was still early, so he headed back to the food court. Dr. Bob was gone, which was fine; Avery had some genuine thinking to do. He ordered a powdered beer for three fun bucks and sat down at a quiet alcove. The court was pretty empty; most associates had gone home or to out to see the latest motivational media. The only people visible to Avery were an elderly couple nursing their coffees and some maintenance guy.

The beer was flat, so he added more sudz powder. It didn't help.

As Avery saw it, he had two problems. One was that he had yet to officially ask Sauder to partner with him. It was understood, of course – she was already planning the thing. And he assumed he loved her. Why wouldn't he? They had been together since daycare, when she used to protect him from bullies. She had it all planned out. They would move into a large partner cubicle (perhaps overlooking an atrium), have their children raised in one of the better daycares, go on their allotted two-week breaks each year to a WaltMart resort or the Vegas coast and spend their final years on vacation. So there was no real reason to hesitate. And yet.

The second problem – the bigger problem – was the chair situation. An associate without a chair was, well, a step away from being a freelancer – forced to wander from department to department making copies for food. Avery shuddered at the thought; he had enough trouble with the coffee machine.

Next to Sauder, Avery was probably the best customer service rep in sub-Dwight. He was friendly, understanding and, above all, fast. He did, however, possess one fatal flaw – a negative attitude. His director, Oic, could tolerate laziness, tardiness, sleepiness, even incompetence; but negativity was inexcusable. She kept Avery because he was competent (someone, after all, had to answer all those calls), but she made his life as difficult as possible. Not giving him a new chair was just an example.

Her official reason was that he had reached his associate chair shrinkage limit (two chairs per decade), but he was pretty sure she just didn't like him. Besides, the second one was just not his fault: those creeps in Premium Services had set it on fire.

He took another gulp of beer and accidentally belched. One of the elderly associates frowned.

And to top things off he had to work a full twelve-hour day in the morning – what was now a Saturday. At least he had a training session with the Weeds, he thought, which would kill a few hours.

As he considered these things the maintenance guy made his way along the edge of the dining area. He was bloated and old, with an unkempt salt-and-pepper beard. Facial hair was strange enough, but this person's attire was also unusual: a frayed black baseball cap, a blue long-sleeved dress shirt and midnight blue pants that were slightly too tight for his frame. No, definitely not maintenance.

Despite his girth, the man possessed a feline grace, which he exhibited as he tiptoed from rubber plant to vending machine in a vain attempt to remain hidden. Avery watched his progress. The man stopped at a trash can and pantomimed throwing something out.

Avery was considering calling Employee Assistance when, to his dismay, the stranger came over and sat down.

"Act casual," the man hissed, looking around quickly.

"Excuse me?"

"No, damn it!" the man said, half-rising from his chair. "I said *casual!*" His plastic chair, too narrow for his hips, stripped off his oversized flashlight as he rose. The elderly man gave them a disdainful glance. The stranger recovered himself – and his flashlight – and squeezed back into his seat.

"So. You need a chair."

9

"How did you know that?"

"I can probably hook you up," the man said, adding what might have been a wink.

"And you would be – ?"

"I'm a security guard." He rose and reached out his hand. "My friends call me the Wizened Security Guard."

They shook. The Wizened Security Guard squeezed back into his chair, producing an awkward squeaking sound.

Avery looked at the stranger. He had kindness in his eyes and dried milk on his moustache. The crown of his cap bore the faded image of a cartoon dog. His blue shirt, upon closer inspection, was wrinkled, unwashed and dotted with ketchup stains. Attached to his belt, in addition to the flashlight, were an ancient walkie-talkie and a large ring of keys and security cards.

He wasn't the Wizened Security Guard, of course. That would be like saying someone was Henry Ford, Ronald Reagan or some other mythic figure of the distant past, or, perhaps more accurately, like being the Tooth Fairy or the Boogie Man. Avery remembered whispered stories from his youth about the Wizened Security Guard, who stole from rich associates and gave to – well, it was assumed he gave something to the poor. The Wizened Security Guard was sort of an errant Santa Claus, except that instead of red he wore blue, and instead of leaving gifts he stole potato chips. Avery could imagine several ways this man could have earned the nickname.

"Wizened doesn't mean wise, you know – it means old."

"So I've been told," the guard said, wiping something off his shirt. "But I'm still smart enough to know where you can find a nice task chair."

"With arms? Fully adjustable?" Avery's interest was piqued.

"Oh yeah. All that stuff," said the guard. He took a moment to loosen the caps on the salt and pepper shakers. "Interested?"

"Well sure, I – "

Avery caught himself. This was just the type of person they warned you about in daycare: a temp, a floater, a black marketeer, possibly even a consultant. He decided to proceed with caution.

"I didn't think we had security guards anymore. Don't Risk Management and Internal Audit take care of security?"

"*Internal* security, yes. But we still handle the ingress and egress.

"Egress?" Avery lowered his voice. "You mean to the Outside?"

The guard nodded. "Look, I'd love to sit here and chat, but I've got rounds to make. You want a chair or not?"

"In exchange for what?" Avery asked, suspicious.

"Got any money?"

"All I have is twenty."

"What? Fun bucks?"

"What else would it be?"

"Right, right."

The guard shifted uncomfortably. A young female associate headed in their general direction and, seeing Wize, veered off forty-five degrees.

"Tell you what – I'll give you the new chair for your twenty, plus any unexpired food coupons you got."

Avery accepted the deal. They shook on it.

"So, where's this chair?"

"It's on my cart," the guard said, rising. "Come on. I'll even drop you back at your cubicle."

"Wait. How do you know where I live?"

"Security, remember?" the guard said, pointing to the cartoon on his cap. "It's perfectly legit, if that's what you're worried about. I'm dropping off some chairs for a buddy from the Docks and he gave me one for my trouble."

Avery pushed back his chair.

"Let's do it."

The guard rose and, after prying the seat from his ample derriere, led his new companion to a large portrait of Zig Ziglar half-hidden by a potted plant. After trying a half a dozen security cards, a section of the wall swung aside and they entered a smaller, older corridor. Parked on the opposite side was a maintenance cart. A new office chair, still wrapped in clear plastic, rested on the freight bed.

"Told ya," the guard said with a wink and a cough.

Avery stroked the chair lovingly. The fabric was drab gray.

"I don't suppose you have one in charcoal?" he asked.

Wize frowned. "Would you like to see the catalog?"

"I'm sorry. It's a lovely chair. I'll take it," Avery said.

"Hop in."

Avery did so. The security guard plopped down beside him with a wheeze. The cart groaned, listing dangerously to the left.

"Fasten your seatbelts," the guard called, and the cart puttered off at a snail's pace.

The hall, which Avery took to be a maintenance corridor, was narrower than the regular thoroughfare (only about eight feet wide), but seemed to run roughly parallel to it. They passed several boxes and pallets of supplies, but saw no one else. For a long while, both men were quiet – although whenever they intersected one of side passages leading off the right, the guard would give two quick rings of a children's bicycle bell attached to the steering wheel (he'd never ridden a bike, but had seen one in an old media of Sauder's).

The silence gave Avery a chance to examine the cart's unusual decorations. The dashboard and hood were plastered with bumper stickers. Some were for new WaltMart products (*Write from the Heart – the Plasma Retractable!*), while others seemed to bear subversive, though inscrutable, messages (*Competitive Salary Is None of the Above* and *If You Were Freelance You'd Be Home by Now*). A few bore pictures of bikini-clad women.

The security guard was weaving the cart from left to right for no apparent reason.

"So, what's a typical day like for the Wizened Security Guard?"

"Call me Wize," the guard said. "Pretty uneventful. Check the doors. Check the windows. You ever seen a window?"

"What – to the Outside?" Avery shivered. "No thank you." Naperville associates didn't go Outside, hadn't gone Outside since long before Avery was born. In fact, the further inside and down an associate could get, the better. It was not for nothing that the big bosses, located in a basement level in the middle of the corporate structure, were called the Lower Downs.

"Interesting view," the guard said, swerving to crush a disposable cup. "But mostly I just check on things."

There was a squawk from Wize's walkie-talkie., followed by a garbled voice:

"U-S-Eight, U-S-Eight. Unit One to Unit Two. Over."

Wize grabbed it.

"This is Unit Two. Over."

"Report of birthday celebration at sub-Morris 8. Thought you'd want to know. Over."

"Have to pass. I'm over in sub-Dwight. Over."

"Roger, Unit One. Be advised celebration includes ice cream. Over."

Wize eased up on the pedal.

"Please verify ice cream. Over."

"Affirmative. Mint chocolate chip."

"Roger. Proceeding sub-Morris 8. Over!"

The guard set down the walkie-talkie and hit the gas.

"You don't mind if I make a pick-up, do you, son?"

CHAPTER 3

Mr. Hon was a Lower Down and tried to look the part. Tall and fit, with only a touch of gray in his temples, he wore the vertical striped shirt with solid white collar that was the mark of his rank. He wasn't the Lowest Down (though he hoped to be), but as head of Internal Audit he was pretty low.

"What is it, Snoop?" he asked.

"We've located him, sir. The Wizened Security Guard himself!" The junior executive spoke without turning from his bank of monitors. His real name was Esselte, but he had acquired the nickname for obvious reasons.

"Outside agitator, you mean. Put him on the main screen."

"Sorry – no visual yet, sir. Radio signal puts him a 500 cubes due east of sub-Morris."

"Party?"

"Seems likely, sir."

"Mr. Bush, send an IA team. Order them to track and contain, but not to confront," he said. He examined the screens, as if expecting to see his invisible prey. "After all these years, we may finally have that fat lunatic."

"So you've seen it, then?"

Avery and Wize were speeding down a narrow side-corridor at what Avery felt to be a dangerous clip. His analysis was regularly confirmed by the large number of storage boxes that were nudged, knocked over and occasionally crushed as they flew by. Wize, preoccupied with searching for the correct exit to the main hallway, barely heard the question.

"Eh?" he mumbled.

"The sky. You've seen it?"

"Hell yeah. Lots of times. I'm nearly two hundred years old, you know."

Avery let this comment pass. Wize was obviously taking his nickname too seriously. Nobody in Naperville lived past 120.

"What's it like?" he asked. "The sky, I mean."

"Magnificent. Vast. It's miles above your head, you know. And blue as a robin's egg – but then you've never seen one of those either." He continued his count. "Nineteen, twenty – almost there."

Avery thought he could imagine it. Like most associates, he had been to the massive WaltMart Real Nature Park in the LaSalle-Peru Recreation Unit: a two-square-gigacube labyrinth of rides, shops and attractions. The most memorable was, of course, a visit to Huck Finn Rock. Located in the very bottom of the atrium, Huck Finn Rock was the one place in Naperville you could touch the actual earth – or at least rock and river. Entering and exiting the exhibit was a big deal in itself, what with the extensive decontamination and cavity search. But for the ten minutes you were inside, it simulated being Outside.

What Avery remembered most was the sky. It was powder blue and sixteen levels above – the full height of the corporate campus. If one lay in the right place, they saw nothing above them but sky, which is to say nothing at all. He and some friends dared each other to lay there for a full minute; Avery was the only one who succeeded. It gave him an odd sensation somewhere between his chest and stomach that was equal parts fear and exhilaration.

Of course, he had never seen the real sky. The Outside air was known to be toxic and the few remaining Outsiders were thought to be savages at best and subhuman at worst. Besides, he had everything he needed in Naperville.

Avery's reverie was shattered by a cry from Wize.

"This is it – happy birthday!" the hefty guard yelled.

To Avery's dismay, the cart headed right for a set of double doors. Instinctively, he held his arms in front of his face as the vehicle burst through. People scattered, throwing folders and cups of coffee in the air.

"Wize!" Avery cried as he tried to keep his balance. "This is a working suite, not the hallway!"

"Shortcut," Wize said matter-of-factly. "But if it makes you happy I'll slow down. Don't want to lose the element of surprise."

Wize swerved the cart down a row, then steered it at a leisurely pace along a wall. A serious young woman poked her head out of her cubicle and frowned as they passed.

"Delivery!" Wize called back.

An oblivious supervisor yelped as they ran over one of his wingtips.

"Maintenance!" Wize explained with a grin.

Avery heard happy, off-key singing in the distance.

"Hmm, we're a little early, but I think we can pull it off. Just follow my lead."

They pulled up about ten feet short of where the walkway stopped and a wide opening in the cubicles began. Avery could hear the familiar buzz of associates getting an unscheduled break. Wize squeezed out from behind the wheel, much to the relief of the cart's suspension system.

"Act normal," the guard said as he skipped forward.

They came upon a group of forty or so associates milling about a large table. Most were waiting in line as a few women busily sliced, scooped and distributed sheet cake and ice cream. Some people hung back around the periphery, chatting, while a few men – the first to be served – were wolfing down their treat.

"Who wants an end piece?" asked a tall, cheerful female server.

"Me, me, me!" yelped Wize, swooping in and grabbing the plate.

Before the woman could object, the trespasser cut her off.

"But before we dig in, my friend here has something to say."

He pushed Avery forward. The group, anxious for sweets, glared at him.

"Um, howdy!" he said uncertainly.

Wize stuffed his mouth with icing and gave Avery an encouraging shrug.

"So, um, how old is she today?" Avery asked, breaking into what he hoped was a smile.

The woman cutting the cake stopped mid-slice.

"She?"

"The, uh, birthday girl."

The scooper woman's eyes narrowed. "You mean Harry?"

"Sure. Harry." Avery looked around nervously. "It's a little joke we have. I call him The Birthday Girl."

The crowd closed in around him, menacingly. One man (apparently Harry) stepped in front of him.

"I've never seen you before in my life." he said.

"Heh. Old Harry," Avery said, putting down his cake. "I told you we joke around." He looked to Wize for help, but the guard had moved to the other side of the table and was picking up the sheet cake.

"Who are you?" the scooper demanded.

Avery felt a bead of sweat forming on his forehead.

"Well – look at the time," he mumbled, looking at an empty space on the wall. "I'd better get going." He cast another pleading glance at Wize, who was walking backwards with the cake in the direction of the cart and silently mouthed words that looked to be, *Get the ice cream.*

The bead of sweat was becoming a small stream. Avery shouted, "Have a great weekend," and ran after Wize.

The crowd might have chased them, what with the missing cake and all, but Avery's farewell threw them into a conversation about whether it was Thursday or Friday. Apparently some of them hadn't read their eh-mail from the Lowest Down's office either.

The cake thieves, meanwhile, had boarded their conveyance and were making their getaway.

"I can't believe you didn't grab the mint chocolate chip," the guard huffed as they burst through another set of double doors. "That's the main reason I came."

Avery reached over and slammed his foot on the brake. The guard twisted half around to make sure the cake wasn't damaged.

"Hey – what was the idea of leaving me like that back there? I thought they were going to attack me!"

"Relax. It was a diversion. You grab their attention while I grab the cake. You grab the ice cream while they chase me."

A hundred replies rushed to the front of Avery's mind and cancelled each other out, leaving the weakest of all to stumble off his tongue. "I don't even like ice cream."

Back at the party, a small software programmer scooped up a bit of icing from the table and licked it off his finger.

"This is the worst Thursday ever," he said.

"Friday," the server corrected.

"Why so glum, chum?"

Avery and Wize were now cruising down the side aisle of a large department whose inhabitants paid little attention to the oddly-paired duo.

"It's nothing," Avery replied glumly. "It's just — have you ever felt that your life sucks?"

"No, but then I'm not you," Wize said, wiping his mouth with a Happy Birthday napkin.

Avery glanced at a motivational poster as they glided by: "Happiness is a JOB REQUIREMENT!" He was past thirty and nowhere near the level of achievement the standardized tests had predicted for him. On the bright side, where there was a new, fully-adjustable task chair there was hope.

Wize suddenly cocked his head as if catching a scent. Avery's heart skipped for a millisecond for fear they would be crashing another, possibly less friendly birthday party. Then something locked his left forearm in a vice-like grip. The security guard, he realized, was much stronger than he looked.

"You notice anything odd about that group down there?" Wize nodded at a side aisle to his left.

Avery looked over at the next two intersections. There was nothing unusual: rows of gray cubes, a few random associates, and a maintenance crew traveling down a parallel aisle about thirty yards away.

"I just see a few janitors pushing a cart."

"They're moving pretty fast. Isn't that suspicious for a maintenance crew?"

Avery considered this.

"Maybe they're about to raid a birthday party," he said.

"No. If there were food in the area I would know about it."

Avery laughed. "So, what? You think they're following us?"

"One way to find out," Wize said, hitting the accelerator.

They sped past one aisle, then slowed to a stop at the next. Sure enough, the maintenance team (a short man, a tall man and an average woman armed with a utility cart, a mop and a broom, respectively) rushed into view and continued forward. The short man, however, spotted Wize and signaled his co-workers to return. The three then milled about, trying to look nonchalant. The tall one pushed his mop half-heartedly across the worn carpeting.

"Don't look," the guard said under his breath, "but look."

Wize backed up the cart so it could not be seen by the crew in the parallel aisle. He waited a few seconds, then raced it past the next aisle, stopping at the one after that. After a few seconds, the crew dashed into view at their end, the tall guy crashing into the woman and the short guy crashing into him.

"A maintenance crew," Wize spat. "Guess they don't think much of me in Internal Audit."

"They've spotted the crew, Mr. Hon."

"Dang!" Hon cried, with an eye on the office swear jar. It was half full of funbits, mostly his. "And still no IA squads in the area?"

"Closest are Rambler and Bash. About five minutes away," Snoop replied.

Hon sighed. "Tell those maintenance morons to close in. Hopefully our team will get there before they piss all over themselves."

"That's a funbit!" cried Snoop.

"Why would janitors be chasing us?" Avery asked.

The maintenance team was still keeping pace with them.

"They must be temping for Internal Audit."

Avery shivered involuntarily at the thought of his near escape from the IA agents. If they had captured him – well, every associate had heard horror stories about that secretive department: the abductions, the torture, the black marks in your employee file. And that was if you were innocent.

"And it's not us they're after – it's *me*," Wize said as he sped up the cart. "Not that it matters at this point."

Avery shook his head erratically. "I don't want to be tortured," he said.

"Eh – you get used to it."

Avery monitored the maintenance crew, sneaking a peek at every intersection. Each time, the trio would stare back intensely. After a few such exchanges, he noticed that there were only two – the tall one was gone.

"Hey – !"

"I see it," Wize. "They're trying to trap us."

He grabbed a canister from his belt and gave it to Avery.

"Use this on him."

Avery was about to ask who *him* was when he saw the tall guy up ahead. Taller and even more gaunt the Avery himself, the man raised his mop menacingly.

"Get him, boy!" Wize cried. He steered the cart to the left of the attacker, putting him on Avery's side. Unfortunately, they sideswiped the cubicle wall, slowing the cart to a stop. The tall guy swung his weapon down on Avery, hitting him square on the shoulder.

"Ow!" Avery cried instinctively. Then, realizing the lightness of the blow, he straightened. "That barely hurt," he told Wize.

"Get him!" Wize repeated as he tried to back up the cart.

Avery raised the pepper spray canister and fired.

"Oh! Holy Providence, that stings!" he said.

"Turn it around, genius."

The tall guy, seeing his advantage, began raining blows down on Avery.

"Stop it," Avery cried. "That's really irritating!"

He finally managed to spray the tall guy full in the face, just as Wize maneuvered the cart free of the wall and drove forward. Avery gave the disoriented janitor a shove as they glided by, sending him reeling against the wall. He bounced down the aisle like a pinball, then fell into a cubicle with a crash. A woman screamed.

"Nicely done," Wize said.

The victory was short-lived, however. Ahead of them, the other man barred their path.

"Short guy!" Avery cried.

The short guy looked much more solid than his vanquished partner. Plus, he was armed with some kind of chemical dispenser. A large canister was strapped to his back, connected by a hose to a nozzle. With one hand, he held the nozzle; with the other he was pumping vigorously on a plunger to pressurize the device.

"I don't like that," Wize wheezed as he cut a sharp left down a side corridor.

But there at the very next intersection stood the third maintenance worker. She was unarmed, save for a long broom. Legs apart in a judo stance, she snapped the broom head off over her knee, then snapped the remainder in half. These two pieces she brandished like short swords.

"I really don't like that," Wize noted, putting the cart in reverse. He then swung it into the original corridor and headed back toward the short guy.

"What are you doing? You could have turned the other way."

"No time," Wize explained. "We have to get to the maintenance hallway and that means going through Shorty."

"But he's got chemicals," Avery said. He cringed, thinking back on stories about IA squads. "Maybe even napalm."

In reply, Wize reached down under his seat.

"Take the wheel and head right for him," he ordered.

As Avery steered the cart, Wize stood up, holding a large, heavy blade that looked like a sword with a bolt at the end. Avery realized it was from an industrial paper trimmer.

"Yeee-hah!" Wize cried, swinging the weapon carelessly above his head.

The short guy looked up and stopped pumping. His eyes went wide and he froze in place. The cart breezed by without incident.

Moments later, the judo woman flew around the corner in pursuit. She gave the short guy a disapproving look.

"I've wet myself," he mumbled.

Wize had now resumed driving duties. Avery, turning around, spotted the judo woman.

"I don't think we can scare her," he said to Wize.

"I've got a better idea," he said without looking back. "Climb in the back. When I give the word, release our cargo."

Avery crawled into the cargo area, despite the swiftly advancing pursuer. Wize took several quick looks back to gauge her progress. Avery waited nervously.

"N-n-n-now!" the guard cried as they reached a patch of tile flooring.

Avery pushed the sheet cake off the back. The judo woman tried to jump over it but her foot caught an edge and she tumbled to the floor in a mess of icing.

"Bulls-eye!" Avery cried.

Wize frowned. "I meant the chair," he said.

Just then deafening sirens went off. The main lights dimmed, replaced by flashing red emergency blinkers. Avery paled, knowing what it meant.

"You hear anything?"

"You just passed gas."

"No. Not that. It's like a – "

Sirens blared.

"Internal Audit," Wize concluded, frowning.

Several cubes behind them, two heavily armored scooters crashed through a pair of glass doors and raced toward them. An unlucky woman who didn't move quickly enough was slammed to the floor by the first scooter and run over by the next. The riders, dressed in thick black jumpsuits and unshaped cloth hoods, drove forward.

Wize's cart, which apparently had a hidden overdrive, was already accelerating. Avery grabbed his seat with both hands before risking a backwards glance.

"They're gaining on us," he reported.

Directly in their path, some twenty cubes ahead, was a set of swinging warehouse doors.

"We should be able to make it," Wize said. "Keep your head down."

Avery assumed the doors led to the maintenance corridor, but he was unsure how getting there would rid them of the IA squad. He lowered his head and looked back. The agents had stopped to pummel a bystander. One agent seemed to want to continue jabbing the convulsing victim with his stun rod. The other, though, was pulling him back to the scooters.

"Do they hurt people for fun?" Avery asked.

"That's how they get the job."

Wize raced the cart through the double doors without slowing down, then turned right. The vehicle tilted uneasily on two wheels.

"Now what?" Avery asked.

"I've got a secret weapon." Wize said. "Right up ahead."

Wize had resumed his abnormally calm demeanor, which for some reason gave Avery an irrational sense of security.

Wize stopped the cart by a set of oversized lockers.

"They'll be here any minute. Quick – get the weapon from that middle locker."

Avery jumped out and yanked open the metal door.

"I don't see anything."

A hand pushed him from behind and the door shut on him.

"Hey! What are you – ?"

"Seventeenth floor," said Wize, his voice fading.

Avery waited for the cycles to come and go before he crawled out of the locker. He wasn't sure where he was, but he guessed it was a long way from sub-Dwight. He had no chair, no chair-thing, not even any fun bucks. Still, as he wandered home he was thinking about Wize's last words: Seventeenth floor.

Naperville only had sixteen floors.

CHAPTER 4

In a small but private office in sub-Dwight an extremely short, moderately pudgy, exceptionally nervous woman drummed her fingers on the surface of her credenza. She was, in fact, quietly singing the word "credenza" to a popular old tune called *Bonanza*. Over and over, and without even realizing it, she repeated the same phrase, humming the parts she couldn't remember:

I've got a thing, da da da, da da dum . . . credenza!
Dum da da dum, da da dum, da da dum,
It's a credenza too!

Oic hummed a lot while at her desk. She believed that it helped her think, though usually it had the opposite effect. In this instance, she was also singing because she really liked her credenza. It wasn't a great piece of furniture, being the same powder-coated aluminum and melamine material that made up virtually all the workstations in 15,000-square-gigacube, sixteen-story office building that housed the Naperville Corporation. No, the special thing about the credenza was that she had one.

Oic was a Director of Customer Service, one of only a few hundred in the entire corporation, and that entitled her to a private office, complete with a bookcase, two guest chairs and the aforementioned credenza. She had worked hard to advance to the position. True, she was at fifty-one much older than her peers, but a promotion was a promotion and a credenza was a credenza. And she had both.

I'm a credenza too!

Not that it was an easy job. There were weekly reports to file, the constant pressures from the Lower Downs, and the endless days of meetings that she could no longer sleep through now that she was a director. There was her staff, with its endless list of requests, complaints and questions. As if she cared about such things. Her job, as she saw it, was to keep her job, and that was difficult enough.

Just thinking about her employees annoyed her. She drummed harder.

Dum, da da dum, da da dum —

Oic (or *Oink*, as she was called behind her back) knew her people made fun of her, thanks to her administrative access to IA's surveillance devices. *She doesn't know the first thing about customer service*, they would say, or, *Oink wouldn't know a customer if one dropped on her fat head.* The latter insult hurt as she was sensitive about her weight.

Well, maybe it was true. She didn't really know who the customers were, or why they called so often, or for that matter why they were always so angry. But she knew who *her* customer was — the Lower Downs. And what the Lower Downs wanted was clean reports and a trim budget. Oh — and also not to be bothered by actual customers. Yes, if there was one unbreakable, immutable law in her department it was to never, under any circumstances, let a customer gain access to someone who could actually help them.

She remembered the last time that happened, and an involuntary shudder raced from her skull to her coccyx. She let out an expletive:

"Cre-*den*-za!"

On this particular Thursday — er, Friday — Oink had a lot on her mind. Orders had come from below for yet another round of transfers to the Transcontinental Merger Project in the Quad Cities. That meant cutting a CSR, yet still handling the same number of customer queries. Even Oink could sense that her unit was stretched to the limit. She had already suspended all vacations and breaks, but it seemed that her team couldn't handle any more calls. Still, she had confidence the Lower Downs knew what they were doing; that's how they got to be Lower Downs.

I've got a thing, and a thing and it's called —

But who to cut?

With a tap of the biscuspids, she called up her security screen and started flipping through live shots of CSRs. It was late in the day, but several associates were still at their workstations. Stephanie, Konica, Bill, Dr. Bob. She turned them over in her mind, examining them like doughnuts in the commissary. None of them great employees, but all of them showed up and didn't cause trouble. She loved the quiet ones.

She flipped to a short, dark-haired girl – Sauder – who was typing away on her virtual keypad. *Probably daily tallies,* Oink thought. On the shelf behind her, amongst the binders, were several books. Real ones. With titles like *Pre-Capitalist History* and *The Great Merger: Disney and WalMart.*

Oink remembered that Sauder was a history buff, a frivolous hobby, to be sure. Sauder was intelligent and driven and had quickly risen to Senior CSR. Oink wondered if she might be a threat.

She continued flipping through workstations, but many were empty. She was eyeing her empty bookcase through the translucent screen and making a mental note to bring in some motivational knickknacks from her home cube when Avery popped up.

He was wandering around his cube, obviously looking for something. Finally, he turned a file box on its side and sat on it.

Now here is a layoff candidate, she thought. Losing his chair again was an embarrassment to the unit. And missing that day's training session was even worse. Sure, there was no way he could have made the meeting, since the day was moved up at the last minute (the Weeds themselves hadn't even made the meeting, what with their commute time from the Moon). And, sure, Avery was her best employee, which is why he handled the training in the first place. But if someone had to be put on permanent vacation –

Dum da da, dum da da –

And what was up with these Weeds, anyway? Good workers, by all accounts. Great over the phone or eh-mail, but in person – creepy. Was the Lower Downs' ultimate plan to close Oink's unit, or the entire department?

The thought made her stop drumming and humming. Would they put Oic herself in charge of those inscrutable plant-people? Would they transfer her to the Moon?

She resumed her drumming.

No, she thought. They wouldn't waste the oxygen. And no matter what happens to the department, they never lay off directors.

"After all," she said aloud, "anybody can do work, but it takes a special person to make the reports look good."

Leaning back in her faux-ergonomic chair, Oink allowed herself a smile. Stacks of folders sat in front of her, as they always did, stuffed with material just waiting to be transformed into colorful charts and optimistic conclusions. Her job, at least, was secure. Once again, she had hummed and drummed her way through some quality analytic thought. Unconsciously, she burst into song:

Dum da da, dum da da, dum da da dum
I'm a credenza too!

Several floors below, in the sub-basement, a fit, white-haired man with an artificial tan sat behind a real mahogany desk. This was the Lowest Down, the CEO of the Naperville Corporation, one of the hundred most important men on the planet. The lives of millions were affected by his every decision.

He was bored.

The far wall was covered floor to ceiling with monitors. The Lowest Down's eyes rested on one in particular which showed a short, squat woman, a customer service director, who was – humming?

He exhaled loudly and threw his hands out to demonstrate his consternation to the empty office. He absent-mindedly ran a hand through his silver hair.

There was a knock at the door. The Lowest Down took a brush out of his desk drawer and ran it carefully over his head before telling the visitor to enter.

"Lowest Down – I think this will dazzle you!"

It was Leonard, the 4Em consultant.

The man behind the desk frowned. He hated these 4Em people, and didn't trust them. They were a kingdom unto themselves – literally – in their geodesic dome covering what once was Minnesota, and the Lowest Down wondered if the cold had driven them crazy. This man, for instance, had undergone several procedures to give himself the physical characteristics of some kind of spotted cat. Black and yellow fur covered most of his body, and he was showing the beginnings of long whiskers around his dark nose.

Leonard seemed unfazed by the Lowest Down's lack of enthusiasm. He set a flat rectangular object on the desk and stepped back as it activated itself. The object unfolded twice and projected a holographic image between the two of them.

"As you can see, Lowest Down, we've simplified the design of the Grand Atrium per your instructions. Many of the flourishes have been reduced, without losing the overall grandeur. Sort of the African Zen school, if you take my meaning."

The Lowest Down eyed the image without expression. To him, it looked the same as before: a glass train station.

"Looks great," he said. His eyes wandered to a monitor showing a supply clerk slumped over his desk.

Maybe he's dead, he thought hopefully.

"We think Naperville will find it much cheaper to build," Leonard continued.

"Naperville doesn't care if it's cheaper, so long as it's quicker."

"Of course."

The Lowest Down surveyed the strange visitor's wardrobe, which included a frayed baseball cap, insanely oversized plastic frame glasses and a bright yellow wool scarf that reached the floor. He wondered if such affectations were a sign of, or merely a substitute for, creativity.

"Thanks for bringing it by," he said at last. "I'll sign off after Facilities gives it the once over."

"Very good, Lowest Down," Leonard said, stretching across the desk to fold up the imaging device.

The Lowest Down frowned. "Oh, and Leonard – in this corporation, we wear pants."

After the consultant had excused himself, the Naperville chief leaned back in his chair and thoughtfully tapped his teeth. The Grand Atrium was to be the final piece of the Transcontinental Merger, a project as ambitious as it was difficult. After decades of competition and outright war, three major corporations (four if you counted the barley pushers in Overland Park) were joining together to create one unified campus from the Atlantic to the new Pacific coast. Some of the other Lower Downs viewed the merger as a dangerous move. Their two partners were, after all, much larger and probably had aspirations of taking over Naperville. But for either to do so would incur the wrath of the other. It was a situation the Lowest Down felt he could manipulate to his benefit.

The Lowest Down knew that there was little real benefit to the corridor. It wasn't wide enough by half to handle the volume of freight between corporations. But it was the grandeur of the thing. It would give American business a brand presence it hadn't had in centuries. *Hell,* he thought, *the Chinese will be able to see it from space!* The timing was also important: it was due to open in two short months, on the 300th anniversary of the completion of the Transcontinental Railway.

The Lowest Down tapped his teeth again.

Of course, all that assumed they could get the damned thing done.

Mr. Hon, sitting in the Lowest Down's waiting room, looked up as Leonard scurried out. Eh-mails signals didn't reach this office. The sofa was hard and angular. There was nothing to do but worry. It was intentional.

Still, he couldn't imagine he was in any kind of real trouble. IA had eliminated a dangerous agitator, and that could only be viewed as good news by even the most cynical leader, which this Lowest Down certainly was.

He was just nodding off, his head, bobbing forward, when the office door opened.

"Hon," the Lowest Down said. It was flat and matter-of-fact tone, as if the man were reading it off a file.

Hon didn't wait to be called a second time; he rose, straightened himself and walked briskly into the office.

All the screens in the Lower Down's office were blank, save one. It showed the Wizened Security Guard's reckless escape to the roof. Hon watched the replay. Wize raced his cart up the ramp, then leaped out and let it roll back down. This stymied his pursuers long enough for him to push open the rusty double door that led to the Outside.

"No body?" the CEO said, not looking away from the screen, where the Wizened Security Guard was squeezing his large torso out into the fading daylight.

"Um, no, Lowest."

"No pursuit to the Outside, then?"

"No, sir. The agents were, ah, reluctant."

"Hon," the Lowest Down said as he turned toward his subordinate. "You're an idiot."

"Yes, sir." It was best not to argue.

"On whose authority were you pursuing this man?"

"Sir, he's a known Outside element, sneaking around the campus for who knows how long? It's part of our mission to find and apprehend such people."

"Exactly! And did you apprehend him?"

Hon sighed. He was going to get chewed out whether he deserved it or not

"Obviously not, sir. But he's as good as dead out there – "

"He practically *lives* out there!"

Hon paused. "You think he's escaped!?"

"I'm counting on it."

Hon waited, trying to look suitably chastised. Of course he knew this rebel security guard was alive. His people were trying to track him down as they spoke. He just hadn't seen any reason to bother the old man – or the associates – with the truth.

"What are your orders, sir?" he said at last.

"IA will stay out of the way. Go back to torturing pencil thieves, or whatever it is your department does." He gave Hon a shrewd look. "I've got an Outside contractor on the case."

"A freelancer? But – " Hon stopped himself. He knew better than to ask questions. Besides, he had his own sources.

"Will that be all, sir?"

"For now," the Lower Down said, waving him toward the door.

Hon turned to leave.

"There is one thing you can do," the Lower Down added. "Send a team up on the roof to look search for a body. If it's not too scary, that is."

CHAPTER 5

Avery didn't take zip. Or slip, for that matter. But what with the previous night's excitement and the long Saturday ahead he figured he had no choice. Besides, zip would also make Kensington and Queenie's shower go by faster, which would probably be a good thing.

The day went better than expected. In the morning Avery had his monthly training session with the Weeds. Most associates were afraid of them, but not Avery. He found it hard to fear things that looked like four-foot-tall dandelions. They had arrived three years before in several interstellar craft, fleeing some disaster on their home world, and were given the abandoned lunar colony as a home. Naperville had acquired the hodgepodge of Quonset huts in some long-forgotten merger and certainly had no other use for it. Despite their strange appearance and advanced technologies, they seemed only to want what most immigrants wanted – to make a better life for themselves. And Naperville had given the Weeds what immigrant always got: overworked and underpaid.

They were excellent employees. Their manners were impeccable, their patience infinite and their voice synthesizers nearly flawless. The only way one could tell they were talking to a Weed and not a real person was the 9-second delay. And the superior customer service.

Avery enjoyed training them, and even thought he understood a few of their facial – make that *floral* – expressions. For instance, when they found something shocking or amusing their leaves would flutter and they would emit an odd rustling as if blown on by a stiff breeze. They did this a lot when Avery was speaking.

But the plant-like creatures could be dense as well. They clung to the simple notion that their main job was to assist the customer.

"We get many complaints about the Yike Tenderfoot Cross-trainer," one or all of them had noted (the odd timbre of their voices made it hard to tell which). "Perhaps SnappyCo could make them better."

Avery had shaken his head at this. "SnappyCo could spend a half a funbuck per pair to fix the problem, or a hundredth of that to have us deal with the complaints. Which would you do?"

After a moment of inscrutable rustling, the answer came back: "Fix the shoes."

The training had gone slowly. It was all he could do to get them to recite the primary rule of customer service: "If you can't make them happy, at least keep them busy." And when they pointed out that this sounded like bad customer service, he grew tired of arguing and simply said, "Maybe not, but it's the job."

At the end of the session, as he was collecting his materials, one of them approached him.

"Avery," it said in the peculiar omnidirectional voice of its kind. "Avery is … *spec-i-al?*"

"Sorry?" Avery replied. "Did you say *special?*"

"Special!" the creature repeated, and began that odd fluttering. The others joined in.

After a quick lunch, he went to his cubicle, only to find a large cardboard box taking up much of it. It was about five feet high and adorned with a large red bow. The box he had been using as a chair was sitting upright in its proper place.

"I have no idea what that is," Oink said, appearing out of nowhere (which was not difficult for someone shorter than the divider walls).

Avery said nothing.

"You going to open it?" she asked.

Avery stroked his pointy chin. The last thing he wanted to do was open a large package of unknown origin while his director looked on. It could contain anything from contraband to a pair of paint-gun-wielding Premium

Service associates sent by Kensington to take revenge. Unfortunately, Oink didn't seem to be going anywhere.

He carefully cut through the packaging tape with his scissors and opened the flaps. To his relief, he saw only foam packing material. Digging through it, he realized it was – his chair! Not his original, of course, which was literally toast, but the model Wize had intended to give him. So the Wizened Security Guard was real, was alive, and really did give presents!

It took a few moments to unpack, but soon the chair was resting on its casters, covered only with a loose, clear plastic bag. Oink's usually-squinty eyes widened with wonder.

"A chair," she breathed, as if seeing a leprechaun or a stack of one million funbucks. "With arms. Fully adjustable."

"I guess someone lower down likes me," Avery said absently. He too was filled with awe. He turned to Oink and saw her expression had changed to something like fear. It had just occurred to the director that the chair could indeed have only come from a Lower Down, which implied that Avery had some powerful friends.

Noticing her subordinate, she recovered herself. "You'd better log on. You should be answering calls." Then she scurried off.

Avery logged on. The call queue was full.

"Thank you calling Lagos International Bank, how may I brighten your day?"

"Who am I speaking with?" a curt female voice inquired. The woman's accent told Avery she was Indian.

"This is Rajeef," Avery said, affecting a Bangalore accent. "How may I help you today?"

There was short silence on the other end, punctuated by a sharp nasal exhalation. "You can connect me with someone in India," the woman said. "Or at least someone who speaks English."

"I understand your frustration, ma'am," Avery said. And he did. Assuming proper customer service procedures had been followed, she had been transferred at least twice before reaching him. "If you wish, I can transfer you to my supervisor."

The woman sighed. "Forget it," she said and hung up.

It was, by Naperville standards, another successful call.

Avery adjusted his chair. It felt great. A little lumpy perhaps, but he could live with that. The important thing was he finally had a chair!

Perhaps things really were turning around for him. And now he could ask Sauder to marry him. He thought about eh-mailing her the news. No, he decided, he'd surprise her at the shower.

He gave the fully-adjustable arm rests a pat, then took another call.

"Lagos International Bank. This is Rajeef."

The shower for Kensington and Queenie was a top-notch affair. One expected no less for a supervisor in Premium Services. It was held in one of the nicer residential lounges in that department, a vast room with high ceilings and real wood trim.

A visitor passing from Customer Service to Premium Services could not help but notice the difference. In Premium Services, the furniture was newer, the aisles wider, the dividers more colorful and the lights brighter yet somehow softer. The people themselves were, well – better. Handsome, well-groomed associates buzzed around like a hive of cheerful honeybees. Pride was more than a byword in Premium Services: it was the unit's heart and soul. Premium Services was the jewel in Naperville's otherwise dim crown.

Avery hated them for it, and also because two of their associates, Kensington and LePage, were the ones who had toasted his last office chair.

"Let's pay our respects," Sauder said, putting her arm through Avery's and yanking him across the room.

There were about a hundred associates in attendance, almost all from Premium Services. Avery, who had barely made it back from his adventure in time to change into a dress shirt and pants, felt sweaty and overdressed. Sauder, who was overdressed, looked as self-possessed as ever.

Kensington was sitting in a red loveseat that had been placed on a raised platform against the far wall. Queenie sat next to him, looking up at her betrothed with an expression of devotion and excitement.

"Congratulations," Sauder said as they approached. "I wish you two nothing but the best."

Kensington's smile weakened just a bit when he turned to Avery.

"How nice of you to make an appearance," he said.

"Ken," Avery replied. He knew that nickname annoyed him.

"We've brought you a shower gift," Sauder said, after an awkward pause. She handed Kensington a carefully-wrapped present about the size of a bread box.

Kensington turned it over in his hands. "Why, thank you, Sauder"

"It's from both of us," she noted.

"Really?" Kensington said dubiously.

"I signed the card for both of us. Avery's got horrible penmanship."

While Kensington carefully unwrapped the gift, Queenie jumped off the couch to greet Avery. He patted her head and she kissed his hand. Queenie was the only sole in Premium Services Avery didn't hate. But then how could he?

Seeing this exchange, Kensington opened his mouth in mock horror.

"Queenie, dear! We haven't even tied the knot and already you're fooling around on me!"

Avery shrugged. "She has good taste."

"Come!" Kensington demanded. "Come here now!"

Queenie happily complied. The future groom unwrapped the gift – a collection of bath oils and soaps.

"Oh, this is wonderful!" he cried. "Even the bubble bath is formulated for both dogs and humans. How thoughtful, Sauder."

Sauder nodded slightly in reply.

"We'll get a lot of use out of this, won't we Queenie?"

"Woof!" barked Queenie.

Avery moved his head in a noncommittal fashion. He didn't approve of interspecies partnerships and, quite frankly, found the idea repulsive. Also, he thought Queenie, a handsome weimereiner, could do a lot better.

"Oh! There's LePage," Sauder said. "He's got a book on the Roman Republic I want to borrow. Will you two excuse me?"

She was gone before either could reply.

"So, Avery," he continued, "would you like to sit down? I bet that would be a welcome change of pace."

Avery was still waiting for a witty retort to come to him when he was distracted by a buzz of conversation coming from the viewing area. Something on the floor-to-ceiling screen had the partygoers excited. Avery heard bits of conversation:

" . . . not far from here!"

"I'm locking my cube tonight, just to be on the safe side."

Kensington and Avery went over to get a better view. On the screen was a special bulletin from Corporate Communications.

" . . . of exposure," a serious newsreader was concluding. "Repeating: Internal Audit is confirming the death of a known terrorist following a high-speed chase by its agents in the sub-Morris area."

The broadcast cut to video showing the back view of a large, pear-shaped man in dark navy pants and a light blue shirt. A massive keychain jangled as he ran. He seemed to be carrying a jumbo bag of chips.

"The suspect, shown in this archival footage, calls himself the Wizened Security Guard. He was a known Outside agent whose mission, according to an IA spokesman, was to disrupt the orderly workflow of Naperville.

"In an attempt to outrun his pursuers, the suspect apparently drove a cart up an abandoned service exit and fled – "

She paused for effect.

"To the roof."

There were audible gasps in the room.

"No body has been recovered; however, it is assumed the suspect died of exposure. A fitting end for a ruthless criminal."

"I told you!" a young man wearing an orange beret and earth shoes. "IA always gets their man!"

"The Wizened Security Guard – he'd have to be two hundred years old." That was Kensington.

"The Wizened Security Guard isn't real," the beret replied. "Everybody knows that."

"Actually, the legend was probably based on an historical figure," Sauder said. "Or figures."

"He must have been deranged," LePage said, ignoring her. "Going out on the roof!"

"Probably eaten by mutants," another said.

It was assumed that no healthy human could survive on the Outside without inoculations, breathing apparatus and several heavily-armed bodyguards.

"Good riddance, I say," another associate repeated.

"Oh for crying out loud – he was just stealing cake!" Avery blurted.

"And how would you know that?" LePage asked. "Are you a secret IA operative?"

Everybody laughed, then quickly stopped, realizing it was a real possibility.

"What? No!" Avery said at last. "No, of course not. I'm just – I'm tired."

They remained suspicious until Kensington put his arm around Avery's shoulder and said, "Then maybe you should sit down."

The group got a big laugh out of that. But Avery, his mind on Wize, didn't seem to notice.

Avery wandered off and found a secluded sofa. It was odd that he would feel so sad about Wize's demise. He hardly knew the man. It was silly, but the crazy old man reminded Avery that there was a wider world. It was only gradually that he noticed Sauder next to him and realized she had been there for some time, talking history with LePage.

"Disney was a pioneer in corporate government, you know," Sauder was saying. "They basically took over the county government around their Florida park – "

"But that's hardly the same as subcontracting several states, as they've done today," LePage interrupted.

"So corporations rule the continent. Is that a bad thing?"

"It's better than living Outside," LePage laughed. He stood up. "I'm going to get some more of these dog biscuits. Have you tried them? They're much better than the cookies."

Sauder poked Avery.

"You're awful moody. Snap out of it."

Avery tried to smile.

"I was just thinking about the crazy guy on the news." And then he remembered. "Hey – I got a chair!"

Sauder punched him hard in the shoulder.

"Don't tease me."

"Seriously. It got delivered this afternoon. Do you know what this means?"

She practically leaped on him. "We can get partnered!"

She gave him a long kiss. Her lips tasted like grapefruit. Like success.

"Let's go tell everybody," she said.

Lying in bed that night, Sauder nestled in the crook of his arm, Avery felt at peace for the first time in years. He had a new chair. His job seemed secure. And he and Sauder could finally get married.

The next day his chair exploded.

CHAPTER 6

The sub-Dwight Chair Bombing, as it came to be called, was not only the largest explosion in Naperville history that didn't involve the sewer system, it was also very exciting. Associates now had something they hadn't had in years – a topic of conversation besides work. Although no one was injured (it being Sunday morning when most associates were clocking their mandatory motivational time), one would never have guessed it from the number of self-professed eye-witnesses.

"I had just stopped by my cubicle," Scribner was telling his friends at dinner in the local cafeteria, "to pick up my Amway songbook, when I hear this *boo-oosh!* The shockwave knocked me to the ground. When I came to, there was polyurethane and fabric everywhere – and my songbook was nowhere to be found."

He jabbed a barley tot for emphasis.

"Which is why I never made it to the service."

Others, like old Eberhard, suspected something more sinister.

"It's those SnappyCo folks from the Northwest, I say. They've never been happy since the Walt Syndicate won the contract for our food services." He wiped some soyberry from his mouth. "You'll see. This is just the beginning. It'll be the Branding Wars all over again."

Some shuddered at this. Others scoffed. Eberhard was a known conspiracy theorist.

Motivational leaders had their own peculiar takes on the event. The Schullerists blamed negative thinking, whereas the Ryndites chalked it up to moral laxity. The old-line religionists were more philosophical. "God works in mysterious ways," the priest at the Judeo-Catholic service said, to which the rabbi added a thoughtful, "Eh."

Avery, with good reason, suspected the Wizened Security Guard. Unfortunately, the Lower Downs suspected Avery. He was taken in for questioning by IA, thrown in a windowless office and left alone to sweat a little.

A less distracted or more intelligent man might have spent his time worrying about his fate. That was, in fact, the purpose of the exercise. Avery, however, was thinking only of Sauder. He pictured her in his mind: her long, braided hair, her short, gracefully fit body, her straight, confident stance. Was it possible his sex drive was finally returning? And was it normal to be turned on by someone's posture?

But Sauder had already been sent off to the Docks. A transfer was a transfer, incendiary furniture notwithstanding. It was at least a full day's walk to her new assignment, and he hoped she wouldn't fall in with any unsavory temps or floaters. Then again, considering her destination, those options might have been preferable.

Eventually, a man came to question him – a sharply-dressed executive with a striped shirt with a solid white collar. Despite the man's wardrobe, he looked tired. He had dark semicircles under his puffy eyes and a few days of stubble.

Avery sat on one of two plastic stacking chairs, with his elbows on a small cafeteria table. It was the only furniture in the room. The man paced slowly, then turned toward Avery. His haggard expression had hardened into a scowl.

"I'm just going to ask you this once," the man said slowly. "Where's your accomplice?"

"What? I don't have any accomplice."

"So you admit you acted alone."

"I didn't act – I didn't do anything."

"Then why is there a three-level hole where your cubicle used to be!?" The man slammed his fist on the table.

Avery sat up, startled.

"I – I didn't do anything. I don't know."

"Don't screw with me, son! We're Internal Audit. We know everything. We know you were targeting Director Oic – what we want to know is why."

The man leaned across the table, his face not six inches from Avery's. Avery found it very distracting, so he leaned back to consider the situation. He was a bad liar, but he had listened to enough angry customers to know a lie when he heard one. This guy didn't know anything. He couldn't prove anything. Of course, that didn't mean they wouldn't make him the scapegoat. The problem was he didn't know whether it would be better for him to say what he knew (which was nothing), make a false confession or just keep quiet.

He gazed down sullenly. The interrogator glared down at him for a long time, then seemed to give up.

"We've got you, Avery. We've got the goods on you. You just think about that for a while."

They left him alone for a few more hours. Avery spent the time filling in letters on an old print-out he found in the corner. His good fortune had barely lasted one day – less than that if he considered Sauder's transfer. Then he felt guilty for putting his own misfortune ahead of hers.

"Sorry to bother you, but we have a question," a reedy voice said.

Avery looked around. There was no one else in the room. But the voice, or voices, were familiar.

"Weeds?" he asked.

"Yes, Avery. We have been discussing yesterday's training session and–"

"How are you talking to me?"

He heard a hint of rustling, then, "Avery, we've mastered interstellar travel. Keeping track of you is not difficult."

"What do you want?"

"We need clarification. Some among us infer from yesterday's session that the job of customer service is to *not* help the customer."

"Bingo," Avery said. "Unless it's a change of address, you are to pretend to help but never actually provide help. You can sympathize, empathize – whatever. Just don't actually help. Help costs our clients money."

There was a pause. "Understood," the voice said.

"Great."

"Avery is special."

Avery jerked his head up.

"Hey, is there any way you guys could get me out of this mess?"

He heard more rustling. "We empathize with your problem. Would you like to speak to a supervisor?"

A few hours later the interrogator returned.

"Look, Avery," he said, pulling up a chair. "We're not out to get you. We basically have all the information we need. We just want you to fill in some of the gaps."

"I don't know anything," Avery said. He continued filling in letters.

"Look," the man said cheerfully, "we've even brought one of your co-workers. Maybe you'd feel more at ease talking to her."

The man crossed to the door and knocked. Someone unlocked it from the outside and in popped Oink. She was as sleepless and haggard as the interrogator. And frightened.

The man led the director to the chair and courteously pulled it out for her. She looked quickly back at him, as if expecting to be slapped. Instead, he smiled and pushed the chair back in as she sat down.

"I'll just leave you two alone," he said. "Take all the time you need."

As soon as the door closed, Oink fell apart.

"Please!" she whispered hoarsely, "tell them what you know!"

"I don't know anything."

"Oh, god – ! I'm so afraid. You must know something."

"Honestly, I was as shocked as everyone else."

Oink began wringing her chubby little hands. She was shaking.

"At least – at least can you tell them I had nothing to do with it? Because I *didn't!*" That last part she directed at the door. Then she turned back to Avery.

"Please – as a favor to me?"

Avery studied the director. Part of him felt sorry for her; after all, she had no more to do with the incident than he did. Probably less. But part of him remembered that this was the heartless weasel that had transferred Sauder.

He reached out a hand to steady hers.

"Of course you had nothing to do with it – *my dear friend.*"

At first, Oink was ecstatic. But then, as Avery continued to pat her hand affectionately, a look of panic crossed her face.

"No!" she cried. "I'm not your friend! Not your dear friend!" She addressed the door directly – "I'm *not* his dear friend. We're not friends!"

42

The interrogator hurried in and escorted Oink out the door. He put his arm around her shoulder, but she was not consoled.

Avery immediately regretted incriminating Oink, then immediately regretted his regret. After a while, he simply wondered what would become of him.

Sauder stopped to shift her knapsack, which was digging into her shoulders. It was loaded down with books. She could have stored them with the rest of her belongings, but decided they were too valuable to leave behind.

She had been walking for four hours or so, taking her time since she was in no hurry. Strange associates passed by: busy, purposeful and no doubt prosperous.

Just like I used to be, she thought.

She sat down at a nearby coffee shop, laid the knapsack on the table and pulled out the books with the idea of redistributing the weight. Looking at the topmost, she stroked the cover wistfully. *Botswana: The Last Democracy?* The books were all she had left of value, and they reminded her of the things she had lost: a career, a life – Avery. She had had worked so long and so diligently – and to have it all taken away in a single day seemed horribly unfair.

A tear welled up in her eye. She brushed it away.

"Plenty of time to cry in the Docks," she told herself.

As the name implied, the Docks were the shipping and receiving center for Naperville, although, since the corporation produced nothing but customer service, no shipping was involved. It was located toward the east end of Naperville. Beyond that, she knew nothing about the place, except for the rumors, which were not encouraging.

But Sauder was nothing if not practical. And she had decided that if she couldn't enjoy the destination she would at least enjoy the trip. And that meant delaying any crying over spilt milk and lost loves.

She counted out her meager cache of funbucks and cafeteria coupons and determined that the currency, combined with what snacks her friends had provided her on such short notice, would allow her three days of wandering.

She ordered an iced barley coffee, which, combined with an apple and some cheese doodles, made a fairly festive lunch.

In the afternoon, she headed north down a wide corridor. It was the wrong direction, but she was in no hurry. She stopped at each atrium to enjoy the open space and flower gardens, knowing it would be the last time she would see either. After a while, the crowds thinned out and the corridor became narrower and darker. She kept an eye out for a hallway leading east.

As she continued, she noticed a peculiar man following her. He was hurrying from post to plant in a self-defeating effort to remain hidden. She stopped a few times and looked back casually to get a better look at him. He was a short, emaciated man dressed in navy blue pants and a royal blue dress shirt. His face was impossibly thin, with almost no jaw to speak of. On his head was a dark blue baseball cap with what appeared to be a cartoon duck embroidered on the crown. Several large, electronic devices hung heavily from his belt.

Judging him odd but not dangerous, she sat down at a nearby bench and waited. Sure enough, the man approached with exaggerated stealth and sat down at the other end.

"Wonderful afternoon, isn't it," he said at last. To Sauder's surprise, he had a pleasant voice.

"Yep."

"Nice day for a walk to, er, where did you say you were headed?"

"I didn't. But if you must know, I'm going to the Docks."

The stranger shook his head sadly at this. Sauder noticed he wore a lapel pin bearing the image of the old American flag.

"The Docks, you say? Bad business, that. My regrets."

"Thanks."

"I assume you've been transferred. Where did you say you were transferred from?"

"Customer Service. Look," she said, turned to him for the first time, "are you a creep or something? Do I need to call Risk Management?"

"No, no!" the man objected. "Nothing of the kind. Just the curious type, you know."

"Why are you following me?"

The stranger looked hurt. "I can see that you want to be left alone. But just to show you that my intentions are honorable – here."

He stood up and handed her a business card. Sauder examined it. It was the right size for a business card, except that the stock was exceptionally thick. It was blank on both sides, except for two words printed in an ornate scroll: "Adams. President."

"That's me. Adams."

She tucked the card into her knapsack.

"Thanks, Adams. I'm Sauder."

"I know," he said, walking away.

"How do you know?" she called.

"Oh, no. I mean – you look like a Sauder. Good luck to you!"

He exited through a door and was gone. She considered following him, but what was the point? One odd little man, no matter how well-connected, was not going to get her out of her present jam. She hoisted her knapsack and continued north.

Adams, the odd little man in question, stopped as soon as he passed through the door into the maintenance corridor. He lifted the bulky walkie-talkie and pressed down the button. It squawked to life.

"U-S-Eight," he whispered, "Unit One to Unit Two."

"Yeppers!" came the deafening reply.

"The fawn has been tagged. Repeat – the fawn has been tagged and is headed for the pier."

"Never mind that," a crazed voice screamed back. "Have you seen any chips?"

CHAPTER 7

SNAPPYCO: Rethinking, Reshaping, Rejoicing
TRANSCONTINENTAL MERGER PROGRESS REPORT
CLASSIFIED – SENIOR SNAPPYCO PERSONNEL ONLY
March 2, 113 PNYP (Post Ten-Year Plan)
From: Kathie Wozniak, Special Assistant to Sen. V.P. of Tomorrow
To: Andrew Gates, Sen. V.P of Tomorrow

I. INTRODUCTION:
There is much reason for "rejoicing" as the Transcontinental Merger races toward the finishing line. Much progress has been made since last quarter – though much remains to be done, especially in the Midwest region. But the end result – one unified office park stretching from ocean to ocean – is more than worth the effort.

REPORT BY PARTNER
SNAPPY EAST. As expected, we are experiencing minimal challenges on our "home turf." Our corporate habitat now stretches to the Lincoln sector of Overland Park Industries, allowing a free flow of goods and services all the way back to the Sacramento Coast. I am happy to report that the Rocky Mountain dilemma has been resolved in a satisfactory manner. As you remember, cutting through the solid rock by conventional means was putting us behind schedule. Happily, our engineers "rethought" the

problem and came up with a solution – using our old stash of nuclear weapons to cut through the bulk of the range. By sealing both ends, most of the radiation was initially contained. Talk about "reshaping"! It is true that there was subsequent leakage during the massive cave-in at Gigacube 57; however the lost of human talent was minimal as most of the fatalities were from the Microsoft Division. Virtually all the radiation was subsequently vented to the Outside.

OVERLAND PARK INDUSTRIES. Satisfactory progress can also be reported for this segment of the Merger. As previously noted, the issues with Outside elements have been adequately resolved. The Osage Tribe has been provided with seven north-south throughways at ground level to allow it access to newly-annexed territories north of the transcontinental office park. Protests by neoNative elements were quelled with admirable zeal and should not affect us as we near our goal. On the east end, bordering Naperville Corp, the food riots I reported last quarter have also been dealt with. The solution was, if I must say so myself because it was my idea, a great example of "rethinking" a problem to bring about a "rejoicing." The workers, as you recall, were demanding more food and shorter hours. We compromised by giving them more food and allowed them to set their own hours. While this sounds counterproductive, wait until I tell you the twist – we placed the food at strategic locations along the path of the new office park. Now they simply have to keep building to get to their food and water. We call it the "Work to Eat" program. We already have a Creativity Team working on t-shirts and motivational media.

PENTAGON. As you know, our partners to the Far East have completed their part of the Merger. Since they have long had a self-contained complex running between New York, Old Washington and South Bend, it was not difficult for them to construct a 40-gigacube extension to the eastern wall of Naperville. There have been no reports of problems on their end – although their expense reports are consistently inflated.

NAPERVILLE. I have saved the biggest challenge for last, and it should be no surprise that it's this one. Despite having the smallest part of the project, they have been beset with problems from the start. Even at this late date, with the Connection Ceremony just two months away, this conglomerate still finds itself some twelve gigacubes short of the meet-up point in the Quad Cities. Part of the problem lies with the company itself.

As a world-wide supplier of customer service, Naperville has limited experience with construction projects. They did not construct their current facility, but took it over from WaltCorp after that company's mass retirement of 82. Naperville could have subcontracted their part of the project to Pentagon or Overland Park; however, given the delicate state of intercorporate affairs, they considered that option a security risk. Despite its shortcomings, Naperville would still be on track but for constant interference by Outsiders. In addition to bombings by neo-Natives, construction has been delayed by sabotage and outright attacks by Lucks, Democrats, Independents and others. I also suspect interference by 4M, WaltCorp and other competitors, as well as the Canadian Democracy.

CONCLUSION

Understanding the importance – symbolic and otherwise – that the Intercontinental Merger Project be completed on time, I believe we should focus our energies on Naperville. If they will not accept direct assistance – and it seems unlikely that they will even at this late date – I suggest we consider covert means. This would include: (a) using our existing agents to identify and terminate efforts by competitors to stop completion of the project, (b) providing the Naperville Senior Management (or Lower Downs, as they call themselves) with as much constructive advice and positive affirmation as they will allow, and finally, (c) consider sending a covert Reshaping Team to the area north of Naperville to deal with the Outside elements).

I will provide you a more personal and detailed report when I arrive in Las Vegas on Monday.

Sincerely,

Katie Gates

ps: I miss you, Lambiekins!

CHAPTER 8

On the wall of a penthouse office in the far Southeastern corner of Naperville hung a map of North America. It was a sad, sloppy thing; not at all like a map in a daycare classroom or information kiosk. For one thing, the middle of the continent was marred with irregular blotches of bright colors, as if someone had shot it at close range with a paint gun. There was not a right angle or regular curve to be seen south of Canada or north of Nuevo Nuevo/New Mexico. This haphazard effect was further enhanced by odd groupings of pushpins, flags and sticky notes.

Perhaps the strangest thing about this map, which took up the entire south wall of the large office, was that it was meticulously accurate. Acting President Clerihew Adams may not have been a man of action, but he was a person of precision. He was virtually powerless and all but forgotten, but the least he could do is stay on top of things; he owed the taxpayers that much.

Not that there were actually were any taxpayers, since the United States government no longer levied taxes. Most of his government's income came from the arbitration fees he charged for settling disputes between the corporations that now ruled over the country. The rest came from an annual bake sale. Even with only two people on the payroll it was a challenge to balance the budget.

At least the office space itself was free, although the Corporate Alliance had placed him in Naperville, the weakest of the conglomerates – and Naperville had made a point of giving him a dreaded window office.

He leaned back in his chair and carefully put his feet on the desk. The chair was like the man: ancient yet well-made. There was little in the room besides the desk, the chair, the map and the man. Adams liked it that way – space was the only luxury the position afforded him. Often, when considering a case, he would pace slowly back and forth across the room, from desk to map and back again. Today, though, he was tired.

He looked at the map and absently stroked his short-cropped beard. The pushpins told him all he needed to know – that the Transcontinental Corridor was nearing completion – an office complex sixteen stories high and up to one hundred miles wide stretching across the entire country. And if that happened, the United States, such as it was, would cease to exist altogether. Once the Pentagon merged with SnappyCo and the others, it would only be a matter of time until the other corporations would be annexed, voluntarily or not. WaltCorp was powerful, but basically alone. Its current ally, Halliburton, would switch to the winning side as soon as it was expedient. And those lunatics up at 4Em, well – Prosperity only knew what they were doing.

His chief of staff seemed much more optimistic about their chances of preserving the Union. But then he was relying on Outside elements, which Adams considered undercapitalized and untrustworthy, not to mention smelly. But the fat guy had a plan and he was welcome to pursue it.

His thoughts were interrupted by a flash of bright light outside. He looked out at the dark, greenish-gray sky. Seconds later a rumbling shook the room. No, he definitely didn't trust Outside elements.

He picked up the presidential seal – an ornate cylinder of carved metal on a gold chain – off the desk and examined it.

I'm the last acting President, he thought to himself. All the way from George Washington to Abraham Lincoln to Haley Osment to me. And now it's over. Unless the fat man can do something.

There was a loud clap of thunder. Adams dropped the seal and it rolled under the desk

"Prosperity help us," he said.

CHAPTER 9

Whatever doubts Avery had harbored about the malevolence of the Lower Downs were dispelled after his final performance review. Although the review board could not tie him to the bombing, they were intent on making him an example to other associates who might be thinking of getting involved in terrorism – even accidentally. They promoted him and gave him a pass for the bullet tram to the Quad Cities work site.

He sold off all his belongings (those few that weren't destroyed in the blast), stuffed the 400 funbucks he had made in his underwear and set off for the nearest tram station. He assumed the first leg of the journey – through Premium Services – would be uneventful. He was wrong.

Avery's first clue that something was amiss should have been the warm reception he got from that department. Associates he barely knew stopped him to express their sympathy. They offered him fresh coffee and cookies. But in his defense, he had other things on his mind.

He had almost traversed the department when a cherubic old woman insisted he sit down for a "rest." At first, Avery declined, but the woman was so hurt by his rejection that he relented. Soon they were sitting at a small conference table, drinking diet colas and chatting amiably.

Avery was just rising to go when he heard a familiar voice:

"Not leaving already, chum?"

When Avery saw who it was, he knew something was amiss. The jilted Kensington was addressing him – and to make matters worse, about ten random associate who had been milling about had now encircled the table. The nice old lady excused herself.

"What do you want, *Ken*? Revenge? I'm already going to Quad Cities."

"Not good enough," the other spat, his voice rising with emotion. "I won't get to see you suffer. I want to *see* you suffer!"

Avery laughed. "Well, it's too late for that, *Ken*, because I've got a transfer order to report Wednesd – "

But when he turned back to the table, his valise contained his transfer papers was gone. Taken by the old woman, no doubt. Now it was Kensington's turn to gloat.

"Whaaa? Lost your transfer, Avery? That's not good. Why don't you stay here until you find it – "

Kensington pushed Avery back into the chair. Before he could rise, three associates bound him with sealing tape. By now, LePage had joined the group.

"Why don't you wait in the conference room while we look for it," he teased. Then they wheeled Avery off to a glass-lined room and locked him in.

"Don't worry," Kensington said through the glass. "It should only take us a week or so to find your papers. Of course, by then you'll be seriously AWOL."

The group laughed and jeered for a while, but then it was break time so they went to buy coffee.

It took Avery several minutes to free himself with a pen he managed to grab off the marker board shelf. He tried the door, but it was locked. The glass was too thick to break. Still in all he wasn't too worried. Not reporting on time to the Quad Cities work site was probably a horrible thing, but then the work site itself was probably a horrible thing, so how much more upset could he be? And, after all, there was really nothing Premium Services could do to him.

Which is exactly what they did – nothing. The conference room was empty, save for a few obsolete paperweight premiums. They were blue plaster balls, flat on the bottom, with the phrase "Blue Chip Service 100!" etched on them. Since they didn't look edible, Avery left them alone. For the first two days, no one talked to him – even when they gave him crackers and water or escorted him to the bathroom. They left him alone the rest of the time, apparently an attempt at psychological torture. Sometimes he worried about Sauder, and other times he worried about himself. Mostly, though, he used the time to learn to juggle.

It took a while to master even simple juggling. The problem, he realized, is that there are three balls but only two hands, which means that one ball has to be in the air at any given time. He further deduced that before catching the ball currently in the air, the catching hand has to rid itself of the ball it currently holds. This ball then becomes the ball in the air.

Once this masterful piece of logic was completed, the rest was simply practice. Hours and hours of practice. But time was the one commodity he had and, after a few days, he became quite proficient.

On the third day, the old woman came to visit. She was very apologetic.

"They said they'd put me on vacation if I didn't go along with this," she explained. "With my meager savings, I can't afford to stop working." She was wringing her hands.

Avery was skeptical at first, but she was so persistent, and seemed so sincere, that eventually he forgave her. She was so grateful she took both his hands in hers and actually kissed them.

"Listen, dear," she whispered. "I can't do much for you – they watch me like a hawk – but if there's anything I can do – anything I can get you, let me know."

Avery thought for a moment.

"Well," he said at last, "if you could sneak me in some real food. I'm starved."

The woman looked out nervously, then nodded quickly.

"I'll try," she said.

"I've got some funbucks," Avery said, remembering his stash. Embarrassed, he asked her to turn her head for a moment.

"Clever," she clucked, her eyes closed. "Where did you stash it – your stockings?"

"My briefs!" he replied proudly.

Taking the money between two fingers (it had, after all, been in his underwear), she rose and crossed to the door.

"You stay here. I'll be right back."

"Where else would I go?"

She laughed, then closed the door behind her. It was odd, but Avery hadn't thought about eating until she had mentioned it. Now he couldn't stop thinking about how hungry he was. He wondered if she would bring back a sandwich from a machine, or maybe some kelp lasagna!

She returned sooner than he expected – with Kensington and six other associates.

"It's in his briefs," she told them matter-of-factly.

Minutes later, Avery lay on his back, angry, disheveled, underwear askew, funbucks gone, and not so much as a corn nut to show for his trouble.

After that, there was nothing to do but juggle. He juggled to keep his sanity, and to show he wasn't defeated. He had gotten fairly good at it, and could even do some advanced tricks like juggling four paperweights and juggling off the walls (the latter of which took a toll on both paperweight and drywall. Sometimes, the easily-distracted Premium Services reps would stop to watch him through the window – until Kensington shooed them away.

One day, he noticed a commotion in the office. It seemed to be about midday and associates were gathering and talking in that animated way that usually meant something fun was finally going to happen. Avery had no idea if it were a holiday, though he knew Codicil Day was approaching.

When he heard the blast of electric guitar, or at least felt the bass, he knew it could only be one thing – a Corporate Communications Caravan.

With the speed and precision of experienced nonunion professionals, a dozen or so brightly-dressed associates raced into the department and set up a stage in the empty space directly across from Avery's conference room prison. A similarly-attired team came in right behind them and set up rows of plastic stacking chairs. The stage was soon filled with speakers, stage lights and a five-piece band. They unfurled a banner and, when Avery saw the name on it, his heart literally skipped a beat. This was not just any Trip Cee (as associates called them), this was the jackpot, mother lode, granddaddy of them all – this was the Uncle Bobbie Show.

Trip Cees were always exciting. After all, anything was better than work. And most were entertaining shows, even if they were merely agitprop for the corporation. Uncle Bobbie, though, was a legend. Avery remembered watching his motivational show as a child, and even then it had been more entertainment than education. He was by far the most famous motivator in Naperville history (not that the average associate knew any Naperville history). At one time Uncle Bobbie had, concurrently, a motivational variety show, a children's show, a game show and a talk show. He was so popular, in fact, he no longer had to pay lip service to motivation: Uncle Bobbie was pure entertainment.

The man was past his prime now, but it was still a thrill to see him – and in person! Avery just hoped Kensington wouldn't block his view out of spite. He backed away from the window so as not to draw attention to himself.

Luckily, the associates were too busy jostling for the best seats to notice their captive. Soon, the house lights dimmed, the stage lights went up and the band started playing in earnest. The audience, immediately recognizing the Uncle Bobbie theme, burst into spontaneous applause. At the perfect moment, the great man himself bounded onto the stage.

Avery noticed that Uncle Bobbie had aged significantly. His lion's mane of hair was pure white and his face seemed bloated (the ample coating of base and rouge did not help matters). At the same time, his body looked skeletal even under the bright blue double-breasted suit. The overall appearance was that of an old Pez dispenser.

The twinkle was still in his eye, though. And he still had that toothy grin, which he flashed as he gestured to the adoring crowd.

"Thank you. Thank you!" he intoned as the band faded and the applause died down. "It is such a privilege to be with you here in Premium Services."

The associates cheered at the mention of their unit.

"What a great unit this is. You know, no matter how angry the customer is, no matter how tough the question, you Premium Service reps are always ready – to put the caller on hold!" *Laughter.* "But seriously, what would Naperville do without Premium Services? Probably about four percent better in year-end profits."

There were fewer laughs this time, mixed with grumbling.

"But of course I'm kidding!" said Uncle Bobbie, quickly gauging his audience. "I kid because I motivate. And you look like a motivated unit – am I right?"

Cheers and applause.

"We've got a great show for you today. The amazing Pencil Pushers are here, the inspiring hypnotist Blackball, all the usual sketches and nonsense. And don't forget the lovely and talented Naper Girls – "

On queue, a dozen cheerleaders ran in from the back of the room, doing leg kicks and shaking their pompons. As the crowd cheered, Uncle Bobbie exited the stage. Avery noticed the entertainer looked a little fragile as he stepped off the platform.

The band ripped into a current motivational hit, *What Can I Do for You?* and the audience clapped along. The show had the usual variety show stuff: animal acts, singers, comics. Avery's favorite, though, was a sketch in which Uncle Bobbie reprised a classic character called Sleepy Ted, the archetypal bad employee. As the scene opens, Ted is dozing at his workstation. When the boss wakes him, Ted, thinking it is quitting time, puts on his jacket and starts to leave. But the boss grabs him by the collar and pulls him back. It seems he has an important assignment for Ted – putting a large birthday card for the Lowest Down into a small interoffice envelope. Avery found it quite amusing.

He was enjoying the show immensely, even the hypnotist, Blackball. He made the old woman act like a young ingénue, he convinced a young associate that he hated the taste of his caffeine cigarettes – he even made a middle-aged man cluck like a chicken – all through hypnotic suggestion.

But Blackball wasn't done there.

"We've had some fun here, but now I want to attempt something," he paused dramatically, "very serious." He was a short, balding man with a lumpy, asymmetrical face – but he had such a voice. Soothing and sonorous it was, with a rhythmic pace like gently breaking waves.

"I want to hypnotize you all – don't be afraid!" he added quickly. "I'm simply going to make you better at whatever it is you do for Naperville."

Blackball began to wander through the crowd, putting people at ease. Avery could make out some of the words:

"There – just uncross your legs. Yes, yes. Relax your arms. No, you can keep your eyes open – whatever makes you comfortable."

When the little man returned to the stage, the room was still.

"Now, I will count backwards from three, and when I reach one you will be asleep, you will be at peace, and you will hear only me."

Seeing that the act was reverting to typical hypnotist shtick, Avery lost interest. He picked up his paperweights and began juggling absently.

"Now – what is it you do?" Blackball asked the associates after he had put them under. Answer calls? Reply to eh-mails? Generate reports? Manage associates? Whatever it is you do right now, when you wake up you will do it better than anyone."

Avery frowned as he tossed one of the plastic orbs behind his back. The act had turned into a trite motivational lecture.

"When I count to three you will all wake up. You will be happy, you will be refreshed and you will be the best!"

Avery yawned.

"One!"

Avery picked up a fourth paperweight.

"Two!"

He juggled faster.

"Three!"

At the sound of the word, the associates' heads popped up like prairie dogs. They looked around, smiling and laughing, then burst into applause.

Avery shook his head in a condescending manner. At the same time, he began juggled at a furious pace. Orbs flew in seemingly random arcs, his hands and forearms pumped crazily. Yet he was perfectly calm. Happy even. And refreshed.

Uncle Bobbie returned to the stage as the applause died down. He was attempting to introduce the next act – a dance routine by the Naper Girls – when he noticed a rhythmic, mechanical thumping, like a washing machine with an unbalance load. He looked around for the source of the distraction, finally pinpointing it. The thumping was coming from the back of the room. With barely a pause, he gestured to the wings, then continued his introduction.

The source of the noise was Avery. He was now bouncing five paperweights off the window of the conference room. The orbs caromed crazily, crossing each others' arcs but never colliding.

The band began its accompaniment, pretty much drowning out the noise. As the girls took the stage, two serious-looking crew members walked quickly back to the conference room. They tried the door, but it was locked. One of them went to the window and gestured angrily at Avery, who smiled warmly and continued juggling.

Uncle Bobbie himself slipped back and, grabbing a supervisor at random, whispered a few friendly words in her ear. Immediately, she raced back and unlocked the door.

The crew members quietly entered the room, closing the door behind them. One of them told Avery to stop, but he found he could not. He simply couldn't stop juggling. One of them lunged at him, but he stepped aside and continued to juggle. Even as they wrestled him to the ground he still managed to keep three orbs in the air with his free hand.

By now, Uncle Bobbie had entered the room, followed closely by an alarmed Kensington.

"I'm so sorry, Uncle Bobbie," the latter said. "He's an, er, disturbed employee. We were keeping him in here until Employee Assistance can pick him up. We'll move him immediately."

Uncle Bobbie smiled at Kensington and slapped him loudly on the shoulder. "Are you kidding? This kid's part of the show now!"

The crew members, who were now sitting on Avery (he was still juggling two balls with his foot), looked up in surprise.

"Let him up, boys! Don't want to wrinkle the talent."

"But he's due at the Qua – I mean, at Employee Assistance," Kensington stammered.

"I'll handle those mindfreaks. Nobody says no to Uncle Bobbie." He spread his arms out as he said this. It was a gesture of such benevolence and power that it ended all debate.

The legendary entertainer helped Avery to his feet.

"The dance number's almost over," he told Avery. "You're on next. Think you can handle that, son?"

"I'm the best!" Avery beamed.

So it was that Avery escaped Premium Services to become a temporary motivational juggler.

CHAPTER 10

The Wizened Security Guard looked to the west and squinted. It was still early spring in the Midwest and the late afternoon sun was low in the sky. He had just finished a late lunch (an entire box of toaster pastries and a lukewarm can of diet soda), and had decided to rest his legs a few more minutes before moving on. He had come what he considered a long way since his narrow escape from Naperville, although in fact it was only about ten miles. He was still on the roof of the massive corporate office building. It was a good way for him to travel, since few Outsiders came near the building; plus, he had hidden several caches of food and supplies around the roof for just such a contingency.

He examined his torn blue dress shirt and frowned. It was beyond repair, and it would be a while until he could steal another one. He had also lost his walkie-talkie and his mace while squeezing through the roof access doors, but his unwieldy ring of keys and cards had miraculously remained attached to his belt.

He rose stiffly, carried his trash to the north edge of the roof and dropped it off. It was too late to worry about the environment, especially anywhere near a corporation. To the northeast he could make out a few fires from Luckport. Directly east were the pulsing lights of the Joliet casinos. Wize would eventually have to choose between one of those two destinations, but he currently had no clear goal in mind.

The rotund guard was actually worried, or as worried as his carefree soul ever got. He glanced west again. He couldn't shake the feeling that someone was following him – probably because he could see the person. They were still about a hundred cubes behind him, but with the lengthening shadows it was not hard to chart their progress. Even now Wize could see the person darting from an air duct to a satellite transmitter.

Yes, he had certainly screwed up by giving one of the exploding chairs to that young customer service rep. Now the Lower Downs were on alert. Plus, it was a waste of C4. He certainly hadn't wanted to get the Avery kid in trouble, as he no doubt was.

Still, what's done is done, he thought, wiping his hands on his pants. The old guard, possessed of the undying optimism that lies at the heart of every true cynic, somehow knew that things would work out. He believed strongly in Fate, whose job it was to take all the mistakes made by fallen humans and turn them into something good, like a great chef whipping up a five-star meal out of week-old leftovers.

He turned east and trudged off along the edge of the roof. There should be another cache of supplies in a mile or so, and he was certain he would find something there to deal with his follower. Like a nine iron. Or a nice tin of beef.

His mouth watered.

Chief Illiniwek was not a chief. He wasn't even a very good Indian. But he was ambitious.

His father didn't think much of him. But then his father was a sellout. As Illini chief, his father ran the Shabbona casino and several other businesses on the Jefferson Street Strip in Joliet. He was powerful, but he knew nothing of what it meant to be a true Native American.

Actually, neither did Illiniwek. He didn't know a garter snake from a water moccasin, or an oak from an elm. But he wanted to. And that's what mattered.

Illiniwek was what Naperville associates called a neoNative, an Indian gone back to his roots: living off the land, shunning modern conveniences, making funny bird calls. Many neoNatives were, in fact, quite good at these things. In some areas of the continent they were guerilla fighters feared by nearby corporations and traditional tribes alike. But in the case of Illiniwek and his followers, their outdoor skills consisted of two weeks at a rundown

YMCA camp in Wisconsin and a book on edible herbs he had purchased at a used book store in Luckport.

It was not uncommon for neoNatives to contract out for covert operations, and in this Illiniwek was in the norm. Currently he was in the employ of the Lowest Down. He had met the man one day while snooping around Naperville. To be precise, he had fallen through an atrium skylight and been apprehended by Risk Management. Upon discovering he was a true neoNative, his captors had sent him to the Lowest Down. There, he was hired to track a person of interest. In exchange for this task, Illiniwek was given his freedom and a *boomstick* (as the odd, orange man had condescendingly referred to the WaltCorp bb gun). Illiniwek had shrewdly accepted both.

And so it was the neophyte neoNative found himself crawling around the roof of Naperville, getting soot all over his new buckskin pullover. His prey was easy to track. How could he not be – he was big and fat and shuffled his feet, leaving large footprints as he walked. He wasn't even aware he was being followed; he had taken a three-hour lunch, for heaven's sake!

The light was fading when Illiniwek lost sight of the security guard. He was nowhere to be seen. The young man stood up, forgetting to be stealthy, and looked about anxiously. How could he have lost the man? It was like losing the sun.

As he hurried forward, he saw a brightly-colored object about 70 yards in front of him. Coming closer, he realized it was a large plastic cooler nestled up against an air intake duct. He looked about warily; there was nothing in sight, save an old tarp held down with bricks. He knelt down and looked inside the container. There was a box of rye crackers and a squeeze tube of cheese product.

Suddenly, he heard a scraping sound. Before he could turn around, a voice said:

"Get up easy, boy. No sudden movements."

He turned without getting up and saw the man he had been tracking. In his right hand, he held three small cans; in his left, another tube of cheese spread which was aimed at Illiniwek.

You think this is ordinary cheese?" the man asked. "It's napalm, made to look like cheese. So just keep your distance."

As noted, Illiniwek was not a skilled woodsman. But he was young and fast, and an expert shot at the Joliet arcades. He swung his bb gun off his shoulder and fired a shot from the hip. The large man yelped and grabbed his forearm, dropping his cheese spread in the process.

"You little punk!" the man cried. And before Illiniwek could get off another shot, his adversary lined one of the cans off his forehead. Now it was Illiniwek's turn to yelp. He collapsed, holding his face.

"I think you broke my eye socket," he said in a voice that was suddenly prepubescent.

"You nitwit," Wize said, grabbing the rifle. "That stung like crazy!" He pulled back his sleeve to reveal a small but distinct red welt. "I'll probably get a blood clot!"

"I could be blind!" Illiniwek retorted.

Wize softened at this. After putting the rifle out the other's reach, he examined the wound. There was a fairly deep cut along the right eyebrow.

"Ye-ow!" the guard said. Then, recovering his bedside manner, added, "I mean – it's not too bad, but you might need stitches." He hesitated. "I have a sewing kit, I could probably – "

Illiniwek jerked his head back. "You stay away!" he said, frightened and angry.

"Okay, okay." Wize backed up a step. "I really wasn't looking forward to it, anyway. Blood makes me queasy."

Illiniwek sat down, his back against the cooler, and hugged his knees.

"Why did you have to sneak up on me," he said petulantly. "I wasn't doing anything to you."

Wize sighed heavily. He didn't want to argue with the kid.

"Look, I'm sorry I clocked you, er, what's your name?"

"Illiniwek – chief of the Fighting Illini!"

"Oh. The neoNative kid." Wize picked up the rifle. "I'll tell you what, Illiniwek – let's just go our separate ways and forget we ever met."

"I can't. I'm tracking you," the other mumbled.

"Well, duh! Not any more, you're not," Wize said harshly. "Now – get down."

"What? On the roof?"

"No – *off* the roof."

Wize didn't need to ask Illiniwek any more questions. He knew who he was, and more importantly, who his father was. He knew someone in

Naperville had wanted to keep tabs on him, and it didn't really matter who. Interrogating the kid would give him no useful information and would only serve to further humiliate Illiniwek. And that wouldn't be nice. Wize vaguely remembered a time when he was not so nice, but that must have been before he had become the Wizened Security Guard. Or after. His long-term memory was rather fuzzy.

Wize helped Illiniwek to his feet. He cleaned and bandaged his forehead, gave him a box a crackers and led him to the edge. There was a maintenance ladder built into the side of the building.

The neoNative looked over the lip of the roof and gulped; but he quickly straightened up. He was afraid of heights, but he wouldn't let this man see his fear.

"What about my rifle?" he asked.

"You have any rope?"

Illiniwek did – in his knapsack. About a hundred feet.

"I'll lower it down on the rope after you reach the ground," Wize said. "Then I'll drop it the rest of the way."

"How do I know you won't keep it?"

"Are you kidding? This is WaltMart junk. You're welcome to it."

When Illiniwek was about three stories down, Wize called after him: "Hey kid – I let you go. You remember that!"

The young man continued his descent. He would remember, all right: remember that he was a neoNative and Chief of the Fighting Illini, that he had no friends and wanted none save the small group of recruits that made up his tribe. He would remember that the fat man in the blue shirt had humiliated him and therefore was his sworn enemy.

By the time he reached the ground, his confidence had returned. He was a man – his own man.

Now all he had to do was make his way back to Joliet and get an advance on his trust fund.

Avery's short time with the Corporate Communications Cavalcade was, unlike most childhood career aspirations, everything he had hoped for all those years ago in daycare. He was well-fed, he stayed in the finest hotel rooms (actual rooms, not cubicles), and there was little work to be done. The best thing was the lack of competitiveness. There was cattiness, to be sure, among the dancers. And one act always thought it was getting short shrift. But there wasn't the desperation to get ahead common to most of Naperville. After all, these people already had fun, rewarding jobs.

Avery was actually only a small part of the show: the finale of Blackball's act. The hypnotist would go through his routine of motivating the audience through hypnosis. Then, as a living example, he would bring out Avery, the Amazing Juggling Associate. Blackball himself was very grateful. Uncle Bobbie had been thinking of replacing him with a trained cat act before Avery turned up.

But Uncle Bobbie also had a feeling about Avery. He told him as much one night as they dined in his suite overlooking the atrium in Peoria Center.

"I figured you were in some kind of trouble," he told Avery as he carefully sipped seltzer water. "I was in a lot of scrapes as a youth myself. How do you think I ended up in this disreputable trade?"

Avery laughed. That disreputable trade had made Uncle Bobbie a rich, famous man. More importantly, it made him indispensable to the Lower Downs, an achievement most Lower Downs couldn't claim.

But the more they traveled around Naperville, the more disillusioned Avery became. The troupe did shows as far south as the Springfield Fulfillment Hub, as far east as the Danville IT Center and as far west as the massive Institutional Markets Department near Galesburg. Avery arrived at each location with anticipation; he had heard so many great things about those faraway units. Yet without fail each place turned out to be disturbingly identical to his home unit of Customer Service: he found the same EssBee's Restaurants with their barley cappuccinos, the same limited selection of merchandise in the WaltMart stores and the same gray rows of work and domestic cubicles. But there was something worse.

He began to use his long stretches of time offstage to watch the audience. And it eventually dawned on him that something was wrong with his fellow Naperville associates. They loved the show, of course. They loved it too much. They laughed too hard, and they applauded too quickly and emphatically.

One night in LaSalle he put it together, when he received a standing ovation for his juggling bit. As he took a brief bow he noticed an elderly associate in the third row. She had tears in her eyes. Tears. For a juggler.

In came to him then: these people are desperate. Desperate for anything that isn't the endless monotony of work or the desperate hours between work and sleep. Virtually every associate longed for something that Naperville couldn't provide.

He knew that afternoon as he exited the stage that his days as with the Uncle Billy show were numbered. And thereafter the audiences depressed him.

But where would he go? To his assignment at the Quad Cities work site? If they were sending him there it had to be a punishment. Become a freelancer, then? A nameless floater making photocopies for scraps of food?

No, there was only one thing Avery really wanted to do: find Sauder. And that meant going east to the Docks. He found himself missing Sauder's dark skin, her compact body and the way she glared at him when he said something stupid. But he also felt guilty that she had been sent to the Docks in his place. Maybe, he thought, love was that precise combination of lust, guilt and friendship.

When he told Uncle Bobbie of his decision, the bouncy old man frowned. It was an hour before show time, and Bobbie was sitting on a chair in his hotel bathroom, wearing a red terrycloth robe and little else. His bald head shined like polished oak (his wig was out being fluffed) and his spindly legs stuck out of his striped boxers. He looked more like a geriatric boxer than a famous motivator.

"The Docks, eh?" he said. "I've heard bad things about that place, but love conquers all, as they used to say."

He rose slowly, letting out a theatrical groan as he did so.

"Here, I want you to have something."

He reached into a nearby valise and pulled out a few business cards. "They have my picture and autograph. They might be good for barter."

Avery examined the glossy cards. A young Uncle Billy looked back up at him.

"Why two cards?" he asked.

"One to get you in, maybe two will get you back out. I'm an icon, you know," Uncle Billy said. Then he laughed.

Avery pocketed the cards. "Do you know anything about the Docks?" he asked.

"Nothing you want to know right now – just keep your head down."

This time Uncle Billy didn't laugh.

CHAPTER 11

The Lowest Down was in a mood.

"Does anybody at this table have a clue?" he asked.

Hon, Lower Down of Internal Audit, bit his tongue. It was a rhetorical question. There was a long, uncomfortable silence. Hon could hear the muted sound of the waterfall in the atrium. He looked around at the other Lowest Downs; they were all staring deliberately down at the conference table.

"Seriously – does anybody know what's happening two months from today?"

"The, er, Completion Ceremony for the Transcontinental Merger." That was Wilson-Jones from IT.

"Very good. You get a gold star."

A smartly-dressed woman with fashionable blonde highlights began to laugh.

"Something funny, Hewitt?" the Lowest Down asked, without turning his gaze from Wilson-Jones.

The laugh caught in Hewitt's throat. "Nothing, Lowest."

Hon, who had worked with the current Lowest Down since they were both Risk Management cadets, knew this mood. The big guy was cajoling, teasing, ridiculing – waiting for a target to present itself onto which he could vent his anger. Hon waited patiently; he was not going to be that target today.

"Because," the Lowest continued, "I find nothing humorous about the fact that we're in danger of screwing up the most important project in Naperville history." He looked around the table slowly.

"Hon – report!" he barked suddenly.

Hon, who was expecting just such a sneak attack, immediately launched into his list of bullet points.

"Subsequent to the sub-Dwight Chair Bombing, Internal Audit has redoubled security and surveillance. Random interrogations and cubicle searches have been implemented. We are currently compiling a white paper of useful intelligence gathered as a result. We are also working with IT to compile a related database. We've asked Security and Risk Management to increase perimeter security."

"Has any thought been given to electrifying the campus exterior?" Wilson-Jones asked.

"Uh – that would be impractical due to the drain on the power grid by the Merger project," said the Lowest Down of Facilities, a beefy man named Adler.

"I'm afraid that's true," Hon admitted. "However, we feel our monitoring and security resources are adequate – "

"Then why did we have a bearded terrorist running around, stealing supplies and blowing up departments?" The Lowest Down asked.

Hon shrugged. "We believe we have plugged the gaps in our perimeter."

The Lowest Down actually harrumphed. "And what of your efforts to apprehend this intruder? I believe he still lives, does he not?"

Hon hesitated. "Didn't the Lowest Down instruct me to – ?"

His superior's raised eyebrow signaled that their previous meeting was off limits.

"I mean, we seem to have lost him somewhere over the Minooka Docks."

"I see," the Lower Down said.

So – he's putting the blame on me, Hon thought.

"We could send out a team – "

"No," the Lowest Down cut him off. "Leave it be. You obviously have too much on your plate already."

"Yes sir," Hon said. There was no point in arguing.

"Jones – what have you got?"

Wilson-Jones looked toward the ceiling. It was the position she took when accessing her internal processor. Hon found retinal computer screens annoying affectation. Still, when you were head of IT you had to have the lately upgrades.

"The Information Technologies Department has increased its electronic surveillance of the associates." Her eyes and right index finger zigzagged as she called up information. "We are red-flagging eh-mail with certain criteria that indicate potential malcontents."

"What criteria?" asked Hon. He had a professional interest.

"Key words, expletives, excessive capitalization and bolding, repetitive, lengthy missives" she replied.

The Lowest Down frowned. "Any candidates?"

"Um, thousands actually," she admitted.

"Not very good criteria, is it?" the Lower Down noted.

Wunderlic of EAP was next. He was a balding, middle-aged man, dressed in immaculate business casual.

"Issue One – optimizing productivity of Transcontinental Merger Project associates. I visited the Quad Cities work site earlier this week and am happy to report that the stimulants we introduced have significantly increased the pace of the manual laborers – er, I mean temporary transfers."

"And the downside?" asked the Lowest.

"None to speak of, sir," Wunderlic continued. Hon wondered if he over-articulated for effect or out of nervousness. "I readily admit the average work-life per capita has declined from about forty days to thirty-two; however, the extra work done in that shorter period more than compensates for that loss."

The Lowest Down grunted. He had nothing to say about good news.

"Issue Two – Increased Food Rations. I cannot report the same positive results from our Lunch Buffet experiment. Despite early indications, providing the workers all the food they wanted did not help the project move any faster. In fact, many of the subjects merely overate, worked less and died – or *retired early*, as it were. Excuse me, I'm not very good with euphemisms."

"Lunch buffet!?" The Lowest sat back in astonishment. "Whose genius idea was that?"

"Young Sandler, sir. He's already been transferred to the front of the Project. I must say the stimulants seem to be having the desired effect on him. He's shoveling dirt like a frightened mole." Wonderlic gave a little, unnatural smile. "That's a burrowing animal."

"The obvious conclusion, Wonderlic – as I've told you many times – is to use less carrot and more stick."

"You are correct, as usual, Lowest," the Wonderlic said.

The Lowest Down leaned forward for emphasis. "And that goes for your little Premium Services pets as well."

Wonderlic showed surprise, then sadness at this implied order. Officially, the Premium Services experiment was an exercise in what the old-time psychologists called unconditional positive regard – the theory that if you treated a group like it was exceptional it would eventually live up to that expectation. Consequently, everything that unit did, good or bad, was rewarded.

It was a failure, of course, as Wonderlic suspected it would be. Instead of working harder, the reps in Premium Services had turned into incompetent, demanding, vain loafers. They had foisted most of their work off on Customer Service and still complained about their workload.

But Wonderlic had enjoyed the experiment, Hon knew, not because he liked Premium Services, but because the crazy mindbender enjoyed studying the suffering it caused other departments..

"Certainly, Lowest Down," Wonderlic was saying. "A failed experiment."

"I'm sure Hewitt can help you reallocate those resources," the Lowest said shrewdly. "Can't you, Hewitt?"

"Certainly we can. Always looking for qualified personnel for the Quad Cities Project," said the young Human Resources Lower Down. "If EAP can provide me with the names – er, Wonderlic, you've got a something on your shirt."

Wonderlic looked down. Sure enough, there was a red blotch on his bleached white dress shirt.

"Oh," he said, brushing at it. "It's nothing – just someone's blood." Then he went into a giggling fit.

"Please continue," the Lowest said quickly to Hewitt. Apparently, Wonderlic bothered even him.

"Our internal recruiting efforts for the Transcontinental Merger project are in full swing," she said, rifling through her papers. "We're transferring about 540 associates a week, which is just excellent. Of course, as Wonderlic points out, the high retirement rate means we always have a need for qualified personnel. So please remind your AVPs and directors to forward the names of any candidates they deem, uh, qualified."

"What's the word on freelancers?" Adler, the big-featured Facilities Chief asked.

"Not good, I'm afraid. Our teams are having trouble recruiting. The Outsiders seem to be better armed than in previous years, which is troublesome. And those we have recruited – Lucks, mostly – are doing more damage than actual work."

"I suspect that's intentional," Wonderlic said. "Perhaps I can help you develop a strategy – "

"In short, we're losing more laborers than we're recruiting, the Lowest Down moaned. "Adler – what can you add?"

The beefy man hunched his shoulders a few times.

"Despite all the setbacks mentioned by the others here, the project turnaround is," he coughed dryly, "ahead of schedule."

"Project turnaround?" the Lowest repeated skeptically.

"Yes. We're, uh, falling behind schedule at a slower pace."

The Lowest Down rose slowly. He crossed his arms and exhaled slowly and loudly. It was for effect, Hon knew.

"Gentlemen," he began, "and Ladies," he added, as if the very words were a waste of his valuable time, "I cannot emphasize enough just how *screwed* we are! We are at the nexus of the greatest project in capitalist history – the uniting of four corporations into one glorious campus – stretching from Atlantic to Pacific, from Washington to Sacramento. It is not only a marvel of engineering, but of cooperation as well. And all you give me are excuses!

"SnappyCo and the Pentagon have virtually completed their pieces of the project – hundreds of gigacubes in length, dozens in width. Even Overland Park is on schedule. And we can't even complete a simple 100-gigacube stretch.

"Now I want this project done – done right and done on schedule. Because if we can't do it, the other corporations will move in and do it for us."

He looked around the room again.

"And if that happens, gentlemen and ladies, this changes from a merger to a hostile takeover."

An hour later, Hon was back in the Internal Audit control room. He poured himself a big cup of barley coffee, dropping in a few caffeine pills just to be on the safe side.

After the other Lower Downs had left the meeting, the boss gave him a more specific overview of the situation. The partner corporations were having serious doubts about Naperville's ability to complete the project. To its credit, Naperville had overcome many challenges, but one major obstacle remained – Outside opposition.

Somehow, the Democrats and others had acquired some advanced weaponry – and they had planted at least one bomb inside the campus. The Lower Down strongly suspected they were getting aid from one or more of the non-participating corporations. Maybe WaltCorp, maybe even Canada or a Eurafrican government. The Outsiders needed to be crushed – and the Lowest Down expected Hon's people to do it.

"I've got to go meet with our partners," he had explained. "Assure them things are under control. I want you to make sure they are. I don't have to tell you what's at stake."

Hon took a sip of his coffee. It was hot and stale. He knew all of what the Lowest Down had told him, of course, and the Lowest Down knew he knew it. It was just his boss's way of putting the fear of Prosperity into his direct report.

"Snoop," he called. "Where is our tracker?"

Hon had no way to track the fat security guard once he had escaped the building, but his people had placed a transmitter on the bb gun the Lowest Down had given Illiniwek. So they could track the tracker, which was the next best thing.

"The tracker?" Snoop asked meekly. He seemed unusually nervous, even for him.

"Yes. The neoNative! What's his location?"

Snoop gulped. "He's, um, off the roof, sir."

"So our target has left the roof as well?" Now they were getting somewhere; he was sure the guard would lead him to a weapons cache of some sort.

"Not really, sir. It seems they've parted company."

Hon did a spit take.

"What are you saying?" he demanded. He grabbed a napkin and dabbed it at the coffee on his power tie.

"We had a visual of the tracker climbing down the building, but the big guy didn't go with him. Sir."

"How did that happen?" Hon asked. This was not good at all.

"I . . . I really can't say," Snoop replied weakly.

The Lower Down rubbed his hand thoughtfully up and down one of his braces.

"What about that kid from Customer Service?" he asked. "The exploding chair guy?"

Word is he got drafted by a Trip Cee show that's touring somewhere near the Peotone Wing – "

"*Somewhere?*" Hon was aghast. "You don't have a tracking signal?"

"IT removed the tracking implant when he was transferred to the Quad Cities," Snoop said. "Reusable equipment and all that."

"So all we know is he might be with a Corporate Communications Caravan that might be somewhere near Peotone?"

"The Uncle Bobbie Show!" added Bush, the other monitor.

"Damn!" Hon burst, slamming his cup on the console. "Damn and blast!"

"That's 50 cents, sir!"

Hon coolly eyed the swear jar, then took out a ten-funbuck bill and stuffed it in.

"Come into my office, Snoop," he said. "I want to have a word with you."

CHAPTER 12

Avery stood at the entrance to the Docks. It was a long, wide hall that curved gradually to the left so it was impossible to see the other end. The walls were a beige cinderblock and the floor was gray concrete. Delivery carts lined one wall.

He had already said his goodbyes to Uncle Bobbie and the rest of the crew. A few of the Naper Girls teared up, which was not encouraging. Only Blackball the hypnotist had walked him this far.

"I wish I could give you some advice but," The older man shrugged.

Avery extended his hand. "Thanks for everything – it was really fun."

"I'll keep your money safe. For when you come back."

Avery thanked him again, but they both knew that was unlikely.

"You'll be okay, without me, won't you?" the young man asked. "I mean, with the act and all."

"Don't worry about me," Blackball said. "I've got lots of things going."

As Avery turned to go, the older man slapped him on the back. It was a surprisingly strong slap, and stung Avery's back. Like a bee.

Blackball waved as Avery trudged away down the corridor. As soon as he was out of sight, the hypnotist tapped his temple to get a dial tone.

"Yeah, Esselte?" he asked. "Tell your boss I've tagged his boy. What? No, I *can't* get you Uncle Bobbie's autograph!"

Avery wandered down the curving hallway. He had nothing but the jeans and T-shirt he was wearing, a sweater and raincoat stuffed in a shoulder bag and some work boots someone in Props had scrounged for him. The only other belongings – Uncle Bobbie's cards – were tucked away in his underwear. He hoped they wouldn't frisk him.

He saw no one as he walked, but after a few minutes he began to hear vague noises. Some were voices yelling, others were mechanical. The hall got darker as he progressed, lit only by an occasional overhead bulb. About a hundred yards after that, the hallway abruptly ended at a massive corrugated steel door. Avery was wondering if he should knock, when an alarm went off and green lights began flashing around him. He was holding his ears to mute the *aihnk-aihnk* of the sirens, when the door began to rise and a battalion of freight carts raced out at him. He had to flatten himself against the wall to avoid being run over.

Avery watched as hundreds carts drove by, each laden with boxes and crates. None of the drivers gave him so much as a sideways glance. When the last one had passed, the siren and lights stopped and the door began to close. Avery slipped through.

The door thudded shut behind him. There was a glare to the left and it took Avery's eyes several seconds to adjust. When they did, he was amazed. He was in a massive room, larger than any atrium he had every seen. To his right were several unwalled levels, each filled with crates and pallets. These went on for at least 500 cubes – he couldn't see the end.

On the concrete floor in front of him a few carts drove by. There were more stacks of crates and, near them, men busily jotting things on electronic clipboards. None of them seemed to notice Avery.

But Avery's attention was drawn to the left. Through endless rows of loading dock doors streamed a light that was bright but not at all harsh. He walked toward it, shielding his eyes until his eyes adjusted. There was a massive space beyond the doors, larger than any atrium he knew of. Twenty feet from doors the realization stopped him.

He was looking at the Outside.

"Hey dumbass – you're blocking my light."

Avery pointed stupidly. "That's the Outside," he said.

The woman looked up from the shipping label she had been trying to read and looked hard at Avery.

"Oh, you're a genius, ain't ya? What are you, Bill freaking Gates or something?"

Avery looked back Outside. There was an irregular line of gray posts in the distance. He wondered if they were trees. The air itself was active, pushing him backwards then sideways, then suddenly stilling. It had a scent that was at once organic and fresh. He started to take a deep breath, then stopped himself.

"How do you breathe without getting infected?" he asked the woman.

"Do I look like a tour guide?" the woman asked. She pulled a gun out her belt and started labeling a long row of boxes.

Avery looked about the floor. It was hard to make out any details now that his eyes had adjusted to the Outside light, but he could make out several human shapes moving about. None of them seemed concerned about breathing Outside air, which was supposed to be toxic.

He approached the nearest opening. Perhaps, he thought, there was some kind of ionizer or invisible barrier. Tentatively, he reached his arm through the doorway. There was no resistance. A fly buzzed over his head and into the Docks.

He took a deep breath, a full one this time. The air was cold, like a walk-in cooler, but seemed wholesome.

He looked North at the line of trees. They were larger than the ones in Naperville's atria, and devoid of leaves, but they were certainly trees. He looked beyond them at the brown lands. They were slightly uneven, like a hastily tossed rug. He had a sudden urge to jump down and run toward them.

"Hey!" it called. "Get back to work!"

Avery turned and saw a very large woman approaching. She did not look friendly.

"What unit are you with, maggot?" she demanded. When she got within a couple of cubes, she actually did a double take. "What the hell are you?"

"Oh! I'm sorry," Avery said, waiting for his eyes to readjust. "I'm Avery, a transfer from Customer Service."

"A transfer!?" the woman cried. "It's Monday-freaking-morning! Transfers report on Wednesday."

"I was, um, I was delayed."

"Oh for – " the woman started. She grabbed a walkie-talkie from her belt and called into it: "Commodore!"

A voice crackled back.

"We've got a stray, sir. Should I send him up?"

The voice crackled a reply.

It was then that it hit Avery – this woman was wearing the same uniform as the Wizened Security Guard. She had a blue shirt, dark blue pants, and all manner of implements hanging from her belt. The only difference (aside from the better fit) was that her cap bore the Naperille N on its crown instead of a cartoon animal.

"This way, maggot," she said, signaling with her walkie-talkie.

They walked briskly toward the storage levels. The woman was leading, but looked back at Avery periodically.

"May I ask your name?" Avery said at last.

"You won't need it, maggot," she said coldly.

"What's a maggot?"

"You are, maggot."

They reached a freight elevator and stepped in. Avery noticed there were sixteen levels, the same as the rest of Naperville. The woman pushed the button for 8 and the elevator began to rise.

As they rode, Avery could see associates hard at work on the levels. Some were loading freight onto carts, while others drove forklifts. All wore the same faded brown jumpsuits.

The elevator stopped.

"Let's go. To your right," the woman said as the door opened.

Not far ahead, a square-jawed man sat behind a large gray metal desk. He was also dressed as a security guard, except that he wore an officer's hat. He looked up from his paperwork as they approached. Avery noticed the walkie-talkie on his desk.

"Another truant?" he asked the woman. She grunted in the affirmative.

"We can't process him until Wednesday," the man continued. "Shoot him and throw him in the Factory." He went back to his paperwork.

"But – " the woman began to object.

"Unless you want to watch him for the next two days."

"No, commodore!"

"Dismissed," the man said.

The woman led Avery back toward the elevator. She walked over to a nearby storage cabinet, opened it, and pulled a gun-like object off a shelf. Avery, thinking of the *shooting* remark, backed away.

"Relax, maggot," she said. "It's an inoculation. Against the Outside. Roll up your sleeve."

So that answered one question. There was a vaccination against the Outside. Avery rolled up his T-shirt sleeve and closed his eyes. Suddenly, he felt a sharp pain in his left butt cheek. He opened his eyes and saw the woman was actually smiling.

"That never gets old," she chuckled.

She headed past the elevator. Avery followed, rubbing his butt. They turned a corner and headed toward the back of the storage level, away from the loading docks. In a minute or so, they came to a large, reinforced metal door. The woman started sorting through the key ring on her belt.

"You're lucky," she said. "You get to live a few more days."

She unlocked the door and opened it.

"Enjoy your break," she added and gestured him inside.

Avery paused for a moment. It seemed like he should ask a question, but nothing came to him. He sighed and went through the door, which immediately slammed behind him.

Avery paused to get his bearings. It was another large room, though far smaller than the Docks themselves. He was on a catwalk near the ceiling, looking down on the floor two stories below. A U-shaped conveyor belt system ran out from an opening in the far wall, continued parallel to the wall for about twenty feet, then turned and exited into a second opening. Small cardboard boxes moved along the belt.

Behind the belt two men sat on incredibly tall stools. Both wore safety goggles. Both pairs of eyes stared intently at the two feet of the belt directly in front of them. The man on the left was very short, and the other even shorter.

Avery was about to call out to them when the conveyor belt slowed to a stop.

The two workers sat motionless for a moment, then simultaneously let out a troubled, "*Oooooo.*" They looked around carefully and, upon seeing each other, emitted fearful cries and ran off in opposite directions.

Avery watched, fascinated.

"I've, I've never seen you here before," said the man Avery would soon nickname *Short*. He returned cautiously to his stool.

"I've never seen you here before either," replied *Shorter*, doing the same.

"How long have you worked here?" asked Short.

"Twenty-three years," said Shorter.

"Oh – you're new!"

Both had climbed back on their stools and studied the conveyor belt, bent over it like dejected vultures. Neither seemed used to conversation.

"But, um – it's a great job!" Short said awkwardly.

"Oh, yeah – great job!" his companion hastily agreed. "Great benefits– "

"Great facilities – "

"Great big girders – "

"Big tall walls – "

"Great job – "

"Great job."

Another pause followed.

"I've never seen the conveyor belt break down before," Shorter observed.

"Me neither. Never, ever."

They resumed their quiet vigil.

"Uh, well, it's, uh, nice to meet you." Short reached out his hand to the other.

They barely touched hands, and retracted them immediately. There followed a more awkward pause than usual.

"Great benefits!" Shorter said

"Oooh! Great benefits!" Short said.

"Good bathrooms!"

"Free water!"

"Great lunchroom!"

"Great lunchroom!" Shorter concurred. "Hey – what about that snack machine?"

"Great snack machine!" Shorter beamed. "They've got cookies . . ."

"Hot chocolate!"

". . . potato chips . . ."

"Hot chocolate!"

". . . candy bars . . ."

"Hot chocolate!"

". . . mints . . ."

"Hot chocolate!"

". . . hot chocolate . . ."

"Hot chocolate!"

Shorter thought for a moment.

"Of course, I guess not many people use it, because when I'm there at 11 a.m. I'm the only one in the lunchroom," he noted.

"And I'm the only one in the lunchroom at noon," Short said, "but I can tell lots of people use it because there's always lots of food and napkins and newspapers scattered all over the place."

"That's, uh, me," Shorter confessed.

"Oh."

They both resumed their sad, slumping postures, pondering their last exchange. Avery, having heard as much as he needed to, found a flight of stairs and began his quiet descent.

"So, what is it you do here, if you don't mind my asking," Shorter said.

"Well, it's rather technical."

"I see."

"When the boxes come down the conveyor belt I take the little one and insert it into the big one."

"Oh."

"And what do you do?"

"Well, uh," Shorter looked away and cleared his throat. "When the big box comes down the conveyor belt I remove the little one."

Both men were silent for a moment.

"But it's a great job," Short said at last, albeit with less conviction than before.

"Oh yeah," Shorter agreed weakly.

After yet another pause, Short spoke:

"You know, one thing I've always wondered about this great job – "

"Great job!"

"Oh yeah. Great job," Short continued, "is what happens to the boxes when they go around the corner.

"Yeah," Shorter said. "What happens to the raw materials when they leave our area?"

"I wouldn't mind taking a look – if it's okay with you."

"Well, you're the supervisor," Shorter conceded.

Short's mouth dropped open. "I thought you were the supervisor!"

Both men looked down. Suddenly, Short jumped down off his stool.

"Well – here goes!" he said.

He crossed to the opening where the conveyor disappeared.

"Oh, I see. The boxes are weighed. They're measured."

He disappeared behind the wall.

"They're stacked. They're separated."

Then Short appeared at the conveyor entrance.

"And then they come back out here."

The two men stared at each other.

"Well, then that means – " Shorter started.

"Excuse me," Avery said, arriving at just that moment. "I'm new here."

"Oh!" Short said, happy for the distraction. "You'll like it here – it's a great job!"

"Yes!" Shorter chimed in. "A great job!"

The duo, presented with what they assumed was their new supervisor, immediately forgot the peculiarities of their task in their hurried attempt to accommodate him. They made room for him at the conveyor belt (he had to stand – once again he had no chair), but they could never work out a proper work flow; the system (or non-system) worked only with an even number of operators. Avery finally left them to their task. He spent the morning resting on boxes and trying to ask questions.

The Short Brothers, as he called them in his head, were not good at multitasking. This made it impossible to get much out of them while the belt was running. It also seemed that both had memory problems, because every time the belt stopped they had basically the same odd conversation Avery had heard when he arrived.

It was not until lunchtime that he got any information out of the two. Shorter, who went to lunch first, was really no help. He was as focused an eater as he was a worker. By the time he had finished his lunch and read his newspaper (some kind of company newsletter with the banner headline – *It's a Great Job!*) he was fast asleep for the duration of the hour.

Avery had better luck with Short. It was less nauseating to watch him eat, for one thing. But although Short was talkative, he really didn't know much. He knew he was in part of the Docks, but couldn't remember how he had ended up there. He lived and worked in a series of rooms that were all connected by a main hallway. He didn't know where Shorter lived, but Avery assumed it was a similar arrangement.

Short did tell Avery that the factory job was much better than Dock work.

"No shooting," he noted, sipping a cup of hot chocolate. Avery assumed he meant they hadn't been inoculated.

Switching subjects, Avery asked if they had seen Sauder. He described her to him, but nothing rang a bell. He was about to give up, when he mentioned her history books.

Short brightened. "Book girl! She was nice. Gave me an apple!"

"Do you remember what happened to her?"

Short thought about it for a moment, then shrugged and said, "Ask him."

Avery took this to mean Shorter. He asked him at the next work stoppage. It was not easy, since he had to interrupt the Short Brothers' now-familiar comedy routine.

"The book girl?" Shorter mused. "Yes. I remember – apples!" He shrugged. "Santa told me to give her the boat."

Short looked hurt. "You gave away the boat?"

"We have a boat!?" Shorter replied.

Avery wanted to know where the boat (or whatever vehicle it really was) had been parked, but the belt started up again and they were back to their boxing and unboxing. Avery looked around the room and soon found a large lever marked Conveyor Belt Emergency Off. He flipped it down, then rushed back to the duo before they had a chance to begin another conversation.

At his command – he was, after all, the supervisor – they led him to a door in the hallway. It opened on a stairway that led down several floors. It was humid and musty inside. At the bottom was what appeared to be another loading dock, only instead of leading out to the Outside, this one was surrounded by a huge pool of water. It was bigger than any Avery had ever seen: at least a hundred cubes across and leading off in both directions like a large ribbon. It was completely covered by an arched roof with a latticework frame about 150 cubes at its zenith. The place was dimly lit. Avery assumed it was either off-hours or rarely used.

There was not a boat in sight.

"She left from here?" he asked them.

"Who?" Short replied, taking in the place as if seeing it for the first time.

"Sauder – the book girl!" Avery shouted. "You said you gave her a boat."

"We have a boat?" Shorter said, equally flummoxed.

Avery took a breath and tried again. "You said Santa told you to give the book girl your boat."

"Yes!" Shorter answered. "Santa told me to give her our boat. It's right here – "

He pointed to a rope tied to the dock, then stopped abruptly.

"Where's our boat?" he asked.

"We have a boat?" Short added.

When he was sure he would get no more information out of them, he led them back upstairs. They were all huffing and puffing when they reached the Factory, so Avery gave them a few minutes to catch their breath.

"By the way," he asked between gulps of air, "who is Santa?"

Short looked at him as if it were obvious. "Fat man with a beard," he said.

Avery spent the next two days exploring the Factory compound. There was not much to it: the main room, the lunch room, a communal bathroom and two sets of living quarters at opposite ends of the hallway. He assumed the place must get serviced periodically, but saw no one besides the Short Brothers.

He wandered back down to the water a few times, trying to determine if there were any means of escaping. Nothing came to him. He had no boat and he didn't know which way Sauder had gone. Plus, the dark water might contain fish or lobsters, and that frightened him.

That night Avery slept on a pile of musty storage blankets. It was a few steps down from his accommodations with the Trip Cee; on the other hand, it was better than sleeping on the floor, as he had in the Premium Services conference room.

It had been an eventful day, and, although he was tired he tried to make some sense of it. He had made it to the Docks, but Sauder was gone. Gone on a boat to Providence knew where. And he had no idea how to find her.

Or get out of the Docks, for that matter.

The next day dragged by at a snail's pace. For breakfast, he jimmied the vending machine and got out two oatmeal bars and a soda. Then he wrangled three packs of mints from the lowest level and spent an hour or so juggling. Before lunch, he wandered the hallways, but there was not much see. The walls of Short's living quarters were covered with dubious corporate awards, including "Recycler of the Year", "Perfect Attendance" and "Conflict Resolution Workshop – Certificate of Completion." There was a framed photo of a much younger, sharper Short with the caption, "Lance Boyle/Director of the Year 82/Honorable Mention."

Shorter's room was cluttered beyond belief. The man didn't have much, but he apparently never threw anything out. The furniture was covered with wadded-up brown jumpsuits, dirty socks, and underwear that had once been white. Against the walls were stacks of back issues of the company newsletter. A year was written on the wall above each stack. There were no certificates or awards in sight.

Avery was about to leave, when he noticed a single, unframed photo hanging by the door. It showed Shorter in his work clothes and another man next to him – the Wizened Security Guard! The fat man with the dirty white beard was smiling and giving the camera the thumbs up. Avery leaned closer to read the message scribbled across the bottom. It took him a moment to decipher the chicken scratch. It read, "Fester, Merry Christmas and thanks for the boat! Wize."

Avery rushed back to the cafeteria, where Shorter was already in the process of destroying his lunch. Avery literally had to shake the man to get his attention.

"The big man with the beard – Santa – when was he here?" he demanded of the man.

Shorter looked back at him in confusion. Then a look of recognition came to him.

"Santa! He told me to give her the boat," he stated.

"Yes, yes!" Avery said. "When was that? Think. When did Santa come?"

"Yesterday," Shorter said with conviction, then knitted his brow. "Or was it last month?" Then with even more conviction: "Yes. Yes – definitely last week." Then after a pause: "Tuesday!"

Avery let him be. At least he knew Wize was still alive, and Sauder had escaped. That gave him some comfort.

He went down to the dock after lunch, but things didn't look any more hopeful. There were no boats, and no clues as to what had happened to Sauder. He pictured her canoeing down the dark channel like an Indian princess in a cartoon he once saw: confident, erect, unafraid. He wished he could swim.

He went back upstairs and whiled away the afternoon fantasizing about Sauder. He imagined her being taken in by neoNatives and being made their president or chieftain or whatever kind of leader they had. Then he went to bed early.

The next morning they came for him.

CHAPTER 13

Sauder was dreaming. She was an infantryman in the Texas War, fighting for the United States against Islamista invaders. Her unit's mortar had just taken out a nest of snipers in an office building in Las Cruces and she was charging across a parking lot to secure the structure. Her comrades thought it was a victory, but Sauder knew it was a trap. This was the famous Hatch Offensive in which the North Americans were pushed back and would have to call on the corporations for assistance, a move that would win the war but lose the country.

She heard the whistle of an incoming shell and dove for the ground. The shell exploded and she felt the sudden concussion. Which is what woke her up.

Sauder opened her eyes. She was in a sidecar, riding down a crumbling expressway. A large bearded man was driving the attached motorcycle.

"Sorry," he shouted. "Hit a pothole!"

She yawned and stretched and tried to remember the past few days. Deep sleep had given her a case of amnesia. *Was this strange man her father? Her husband?* She had to struggle to remember her name, her age, and even her marital status.

When the fog of sleep lifted she realized that those three pieces of personal data were the only certainties she had left.

She had made it to the Docks, and on time after all. She was processed with about eighty other transfers. Her books were boxed and stored away.

The group was inoculated. They were given one-size-fits-all brown jumpsuits and cheap WaltMart work boots. Each jumpsuit bore a series of numbers above the breast pocket. The number was simply that day's date with a few extra digits. Sauder's was *032316-72*.

About half of the group – men mostly – were assigned to moving and stacking. Most of the people of smaller build were made pickers and packers. For whatever reason, Sauder was assigned to shovel duty.

Despite her innate curiosity, Sauder had never before thought about where Naperville's food and supplies came from. As a customer service provider, the corporation obviously didn't produce anything of a physical nature. It all had to be imported, and the Docks were where it arrived.

During the day, a constant stream of semi trucks backed up to the loading docks. Most contained pallets of boxes, which were quickly unloaded and moved to the multi-tiered storage structure against the back wall. Some of this was done by forklift, but an alarming amount was moved by hand. Many of the workers, who were unused to physical labor, would collapse at some point. When this happened, one of the blue-clad guards would give them ten minutes to return to work; if they didn't comply, they were dragged away.

Sauder asked a veteran shoveler about this (a fellow named Hobart who had been at the Docks two months). He said those people never returned and that it was rumored that they were transferred to Employee Assistance and forced to take part in voluntary medical studies.

Some of the pallets went to the pickers and packers, who sorted the individual items for shipping throughout Naperville. This was the best job one could hope for in the Docks.

But Sauder was a shoveler, which was almost as bad as being a mover and stacker. She was stationed at the far end of the docks, where several different types of shovels hung on the wall. Some were large and flat, some were small and almost like scoops. Most were plastic. When a truck full of food stuffs arrived, it was the shovelers' job to transfer the material from the original packaging to the Naperville packaging. It could be anything from rice to candy, but the process was the same: load the appropriate Naperville bags into the automatic bagger and shovel the material from the open-bed truck into the feeder.

Sauder was in good shape and bore up better than most. The hardest thing for her was the blistering on her hands. That and the hopelessness.

They worked twelve hours a day, seven days a week. Most workers spent what free time they had drinking, gambling, fighting, complaining, having sex and crying – often all in the same evening. Sauder asked about her books, but the guards only laughed and called her *maggot*. Eventually, she began to explore.

The workers, both men and women, lived in a communal barracks that was located behind the storage structure. Guards were posted at the three exits, but there was little need for them after 10 p.m., by which time virtually all the workers had passed out. As a result, the guards often slept through the night themselves.

Sauder started taking naps right after work, then waking up in the middle of the night. After a few weeks, she was familiar with all the hallways in the Docks (although none of them led to an exit). It was in this way that she met Lance and Fester.

She was wandering on one of the middle tiers and came upon a room in which there was a conveyor belt. Noticing a door on the opposite wall, she descended the stairs to try it. She soon found a lunchroom in which there was a little man sitting with his back to the door, wearing a ratty terrycloth robe and sipping from a cup.

When Sauder called out to him, the man jumped straight out of his chair. Seeing that the newcomer blocked the door, he fled behind a vending machine. Sauder was able to coax him out with an apple. His name was Lance, and he was not much of a conversationalist. But at least he wasn't drunk or crying, which was more than she could say for her co-workers.

When she visited the next night she met Fester. Aside from being slightly shorter than Lance, he was much the same. He didn't have much to say, and didn't seem to know (or remember) anything. But he was friendly enough, though an incredibly messy eater.

A few nights later when she was visiting Fester, he said, "We should go fishing!"

Sauder laughed. "Where would we do that?"

"Downstairs. I've got a boat."

"You've got a boat?" she repeated, as if encouraging a child's wild story. But Fester only replied, "I do?" and the spell was broken.

Later that night, while heading back through the conveyor belt room, she found her box of books. She found her favorite one and took it to bed.

Her cot was next to the door, and a triangle of light from the hallway fell on the pillow. Most of the workers shunned it, but Sauder found it perfect for reading. And tonight, though it was late and she was weary, she felt the need to escape.

A Picturesque Tale of Progress, Vol. I. It was an ancient children's book, possibly two hundred years old, richly and accurately illustrated. She had only read it once, for fear of breaking the spine. She opened it now and read about the Egyptians. They had built a great civilization through agriculture and trade over the inland sea of that was the Mediterranian. They had built towering monuments to their own greatness. Now they were gone. As she drifted to sleep she thought about Chicago.

A week of sleeping in shifts finally caught up with Sauder and she slept straight through the next few nights. The day after that, she went to war.

It was around 6 a.m. and work had just started when she heard shouting and some kind of popping noises Outside. As she turned to look, an alarm sounded. Then the alarm lessened in volume and a woman's voice came over the PA system:

"This is an emergency," it said. "Naperville is under attack. Repeat: Naperville is under attack by Outsiders. Man your stations!"

A group of armed security guards racing toward Sauder's workstation. One of them addressed the workers.

"Grab a stick and defend the Docks!" he ordered.

The workers stood open-mouthed. No one moved.

"Now, you toads!" the guard ordered, raising his rifle.

The threat, combined with renewed shouting from Outside, brought Sauder around. She leaped off the bed of the truck, where she had been unloading puffed rice. A second guard dragged up a tall box containing what looked like axe handles.

"Grab a stick and follow me," the second guard said.

Sauder was confused. "But don't I need a gun?" she asked.

"Survive the day and you'll get a gun," the first guard said. "Grab a stick!"

Sauder correctly guessed she didn't have a choice. The guards had guns and were just as likely to use them on the workers as the attackers. She took a stick and her fellow workers followed suit. When they were all armed, the second guard led them out to the loading dock. There, they assembled in groups of twenty. Then they were led north.

What she remembered most about the battle were the trees, which were unlike any she had seen in books or e-media. There were no leaves – only thin branches reaching up like a dying man's fingers. Some had been decimated from the constant fighting, making the image even more macabre. And there was none of the color she had assumed would be on the Outside. She knew spring only as a concept, and it was disappointing to experience it in person. The sky, the rain, the mud, the trees – all were a uniform gray.

As soon as her unit reached the top of the concrete apron the bullets came at them. As first they were no more than sounds – *phlitt!* – like large flies whizzing by. It took Sauder's mind a few minutes to connect the sound with the cries and stumbling of her comrades, and by that time she was too busy running for the ridge ahead to change direction.

She reached the low berm, crawled to the top and peered over. She barely noticed the shouts of a nearby security guard; her attention was on the approaching enemy. There was only a handful – about twenty or so – charging over a rise some fifty yards away. It was an odd assortment: some were shirtless with brightly-painted faces, while others wore mottled green and beige uniforms. One, obviously the leader, was on horseback and urged his troops on with the wave of a sword. Many had rifles.

There was another *phlitt* near Sauder's face, and a spray of mud blinded her. Terror overtook her and she flattened herself against the ridge, covering her head with her arms. She heard the strange whoops and cries of the enemy as they overran her position and she prayed to no one in particular that it would all simply stop. Time slowed to a crawl. She heard, as if from a distance, grunts and cries and thuds and more horrible *phlitts*. Then she heard a noise that brought her back to her senses. It was a sharp, piercing cry of pain from the man beside her. She opened her eyes and saw one of the painted men standing above her. He was holding his rifle like a shovel, the bayonet fixed to its barrel buried deep in a man's back. The victim let out weak cries and squirmed like a bug on a pin. But it was not the violence and needless pain that roused Sauder – it was the smile on the attacker's face.

Sauder was up before she knew it, stick in hand. She swung hard, hitting the enemy square in the mouth. Before he could react, she hit him again and again until he reeled and fell back down the ridge.

Without thinking, she attacked a uniformed man who had just scaled the ridge, striking him hard on his trigger hand. Another two hits to the side of his knee brought him down. Several more to the head stopped his movement.

"*Sic semper tyrannis!*" she cried, flush with victory and adrenaline. She couldn't remember what the phrase meant or what war it was from, but it sounded appropriate. She called it out to her comrades, who were either cowering or retreating:

"*Sic semper tyrannis!*" she repeated. "For Naperville!"

The remains of her unit – about ten workers – rose up and ran forward, brandishing sticks and metal pipes. The enemy soldiers, who were charging up the ridge, halted uncertainly when they saw the determined resistance. Sauder and her unit bore down on them. The first two workers were shot, but that didn't stop the rest. They attacked the enemy, swinging violently. Two more picked up rifles from the ground and started firing wildly. The leader, who had been urging his soldiers on, suddenly turned his horse around and galloped off. The rest of the attackers followed.

The Dock workers cheered wildly. They laughed and shouted and hooted.

All except Sauder, who fell to her knees and vomited.

Sauder was made a trustee after that, which basically meant she got better food, semi-private quarters and combat training. She was also offered, but declined, a transfer to picking and packing.

She actually enjoyed combat training, although she had no desire to fight again. She enjoyed the physical challenge and, even more so, learning about the enemy. It seemed the attackers were more raiders than invaders. This made sense, considering the relatively small numbers involved. The shirtless men, it turned out, were neoNatives, while the men in camouflage (as it was called) were probably Lucks, a predominantly Polish community that held the locks on the river leading to Lake Michigan. Actually, many groups fought in fatigues, but the fact that the leader was on horseback and waving a sword indicated they were Lucks. They were known to be good fighters, but also practical. Faced with stiff resistance from the Dock workers, they had cut their losses and retreated.

Yet despite the training and the improved conditions, Sauder did not like her chances. She realized that all Dock workers, including herself, were expendable. She did not want to fight, nor did she want to collapse and end up an Employee Assistance lab rat. More than that, the injustice of the situation rankled her. None of these people had done anything wrong; they had simply been deemed troublesome or expendable by some middle manager (as Oink had deemed Sauder).

With all the excitement, it was not surprising that Sauder forgot about Lance and Fester. However, a few nights later, she awoke in the middle of the night, haunted by memories of the fight. She got dressed and wandered the halls until her feet took her to the Factory. She found Fester sitting in the lunchroom, fast asleep. He was happy to see her. Relieved, in fact.

"Santa came!" he said. "He left you a present!"

Sauder smiled. Most of what Lance and Fester said was nonsense.

"Come, I'll show it to you," he said. He grabbed her by the wrist and pulled her toward the door. She resisted.

"Where are we going?" she asked.

"To the boat."

She let the comment stand. Both Fester and Lance had a limited capacity for concentration, and unnecessary conversation seemed to throw them off track. She followed him to a door that opened on a stairway. They followed it down to a lonely dock on a wide, dark body of water. Tied to the dock was a fiberglass canoe loaded with supplies.

"You've got a boat," Sauder said.

"We do?" Fester replied. Then, seeing the canoe, he added, "Santa said to give you the boat."

"Who's Santa?" she asked, examining the contents of the canoe.

"Santa comes. He brings presents. Oranges sometimes. He wants you to take the boat."

"What am I supposed to do with it?" she asked.

"Go see Santa."

"Where?"

"Upstream," Fester replied.

"We put your books in it," Lance added.

By the time the two had reached the top of the stairs, Fester had forgotten about Santa and the boat. He was busy recounting all the great snacks in the vending machine.

Sauder returned to her cot and lay down, but she didn't sleep. She had a lot to think about. Who was this Santa, and why did he want her to follow him? Where was the end? Probably Lake Michigan, she realized, which meant he was from Chicago. This piqued her interest. Chicago wasn't exactly a democracy, but it was the last bastion of Democrats. It was said that a Daley still ruled there.

But she had never been Outside, never ridden in a canoe, so the trip would be dangerous. On the other hand, what did she have to lose? She would never see Avery again and she had no career. As she considered these things, she drifted off to sleep.

The next day, she was hard at work shoveling bran flakes and mulling her options when the alarm sounded. A security guard ran up and tossed her an old rifle.

"It's a big raiding party this time," he said. "Looks like fifty to sixty."

Then he ran off to round up workers and dispense sticks. There was confusion as workers and guards ran back and forth.

Seeing her chance, Sauder slipped away and headed to the Factory.

"But how did you know where I was?" Sauder asked Wize as they motored down the decaying interstate. "Or who I was?"

The old man smiled broadly, just before grimacing and spitting.

"Sorry – bug," he explained. "You still got that card from President Adams?"

Sauder felt for the card in her pocket. It was crumpled and bent but she had held on to it for good luck if nothing else.

"Feel it," Wize commanded.

She ran her fingers over it and noticed, right in the center, a small lump.

"GPS transmitter," he noted before spitting again. "Damn bugs!"

Senior Lieutenant Grumman gazed into the haze that had settled over Lake Michigan. Despite the cool weather and the fact that he was shirtless, he was sweating from the day's march. He removed his neoNative headband to wipe his brow.

"That's it!" he called wearily to his men. "We'll bivouac here for the night."

He watched as his brigade dropped their faux-deerskin bags and collapsed to the ground. They were too tired to unroll their blankets. Some had taken off their shoes and run into the shallow water, only to beat a hasty retreat – the greenish-blue lake was too cold even for wading.

Spotting something amiss, he barked:

"Northrup! Take off that jacket now!"

"Aw sarge, I'm freezing my nipples off!" the man said even as he complied with the command.

"We're supposed to be Neos," Grumman grumbled. "That means no backpacks, no sleeping bags, no mess kits and definitely no fatigues!" He glared at the rest of the nearby soldiers to make his point. "I don't care if you're General-freaking-Electric hisself – no fatigues. Got it?"

"Yes, sir," they replied almost in unison.

"And that includes mittens!" he called, spotting another rule-breaker.

Grumman plopped down atop a sand dune to chew his wad of bubble gum and ruminate on the mission. He was leading a group of 400 men to wipe out the troublesome Outsiders north of Naperville. He thought the disguise unnecessary, but the big boys didn't want anything traced back to the Pentagon. Unfortunately, this also meant they had to disembark from their transport vehicles several miles from their destination. But he was a soldier and he followed orders.

He felt something pinch his neck and smacked it; it was a flying insect of some sort. He examined the remains of the tiny thing with distain. Several months of outdoor conditioning training he prepared him for such things – but that didn't mean he had to like it. Even this early in the year, it seemed, there were crawly things.

He checked his GPS implant. It told him what he already knew – they were on the south end of the lake, in what once was Indiana. The dunes were a little surprising, but then one never knew what one would come across on the Outside. He estimated they were one or two days' march from their initial target of Joliet.

"Sgt. Douglas," he said.

The young officer reported immediately. He was never far away.

"Tell the men to keep their M-24s tightly wrapped. We don't want to be cleaning sand out of them."

"Yes, sir!" Douglas said and ran off to spread the word.

Grumman lay back and rested his head on a tuft of tall grass, but not before poking at it with his knife just to be safe. Training had not prepared him for the immensity of this body of water. It stretched north into what looked like a wall of water a few miles away. An illusion, he knew; what he was seeing was something called the horizon line. The shoreline disappeared to the east, and to his left he could make out in the fading light the lumpy outlines of old Chicago.

The sky, of course, took the most getting used to. The first few days out there had been a uniform gray ceiling of clouds, solid-looking enough to simulate a normal, indoor environment. But today the unit had awakened to clear blue – distant – skies. Seeing his soldier's uneasiness and frequent glances skyward, he opted to run them hard to keep their minds off the miles of nothingness above them. It had worked; by the time they reached the dunes, most were too tired to be nervous.

Something grazed his ear. He sat up and whirled toward the tuft of grass, knife at the ready. *Easy soldier: not a crawly, just a blade of grass,* he told himself. He took a few long breaths, as they had trained to do in such cases, before, as they also taught him to do, concentrating on the positives of the situations.

At least we won't have rain tonight, he thought and forced himself to smile.

CHAPTER 14

A week after Sauder's escape, Avery began his life on the Docks. He was given a new name – 032306-01, or *Oh-One* for short – a set of cheap overalls and assigned to move pallets. It was grueling work, especially for someone not used to manual labor, and the young man soon had a laundry list of minor ailments: sore back, bruised toes, tendonitis of the elbow and scores of paper cuts and slivers in both hands. He was fairly bad at the job, and his only asset was his height, which allowed him to reach boxes without a ladder.

Like Sauder, he was sent out to battle with nothing but a stick, and when the bullets flew he also dropped to the ground in fear. But Avery, unlike his long-lost companion, never got back up. He stayed down despite the beating and prodding of the guards. He stayed down when the raiders overran his position, and he stayed down when they were repelled by Naperville forces minutes later.

It was not that Avery was a coward. He never really got that far in his thinking – he simply saw no reason to fight for the company that had so recently abandoned him and his friends. If he had thought it was his duty to fight and lost his nerve that would have been different; in this case he was more or less a conscientious objector.

It was for this reason that he felt no shame when he was threatened with a court marshal for cowardice. He simply viewed it as the latest piece of a whole stack of abuse dumped on him by Naperville. He was not surprised when the imposing Commodore, acting as judge, sentenced him to death – though it did fill him with panic. This was obviously the intent, because they subsequently offered him a chance to redeem himself. They told him if he led the next counteroffensive, he would be granted a full pardon. He quickly agreed.

Avery knew he couldn't lie down during the next battle. He would have to keep moving forward or die. The predicament filled him with a grim determination and a queasy stomach. The only thing keeping him going was the slim chance that he could find Sauder again, and to do that he would need to survive the next battle. After some thought, he developed a plan. It wasn't a great plan, but it was all he had.

Since he didn't know when the next raid would occur, he started preparations immediately. He was allowed to take the best stick in the box – a sturdy, tapered axe handle that felt comfortable in his hand. This task was slightly easier because Oink was now in charge of handing out the sticks. She had been sent to the Docks soon after Avery had implicated her; her rank, however, kept her from having to do manual labor.

"Those aren't your size," a small voice said to him when he was pawing through a barrel of broken mop handles in the supply room.

Avery hardly recognized Oink at first; she seemed even tinier than before – a mere speck behind her large metal desk.

"I'm trying to keep these sticks organized, but every time I turn my back somebody is rifling through them," she complained.

Avery apologized.

"You look to be a size seven or eight, stick-wise," she said. She was much nicer than he remembered and he wondered if Internal Audit had done something to her. "I think I've got just what you need."

She spun her chair around and opened the drawer of a decrepit credenza that was held together with bungee cords. She removed a wooden object, closed the drawer and drummed on the fragile piece of furniture with her fingers before turning back to Avery.

"This looks like it's just your size," she said, handing him an axe handle.

Avery hefted it in his hand. It was smooth and heavy and easy to grip.

Oink winked and said, "I remember you, you know. Take care of yourself." It had only been weeks since their last meeting, but she made it sound like years. Perhaps for her it had been.

"Thanks," he said, caressing the axe handle. "I will."

The little woman gestured for Avery to lean in close, her face taking on a sudden look of despair.

"I hate it here," she whispered.

He nodded.

Oink then straightened up and said, "You make sure I get the proper request form for that by the end of the day."

Now that he had a good stick, Avery set about gathering the other items he would need. It wasn't hard, due to the multitude of products he handled each day. He then hid them in a corner of the ground floor, high on a stack of boxes that only he could reach. The stash also included the jeans containing the Uncle Bobbie cards, though he wasn't sure if they'd ever be of any use.

Within a few days he had most of what he thought he needed. The only item he lacked was in the Factory, and it was quite a trick getting in there. During the day, he would sneak away once or twice to prop open the door with a short length of pipe. But when he would return that night, the door would shut tight. On the third day, he got the idea to put a piece of duct tape over the bolt.

Sure enough, when he returned that night, the door opened easily. It was quiet inside as he crept down the stairway and into the hall. He snuck into Fester's bedroom, where the little man was sleeping fitfully, and searched in the dark for what he needed. He knocked over a lamp in the process, but Fester seemed to remain asleep. However, just as Avery turned to leave, he heard Fester's clear, high voice call to him:

"Why are you taking that?" he asked. He seemed wide awake.

"Santa needs it," Avery explained.

"Santa!" Fester cried happily. "Yea!"

After hitting the vending machine (literally) for some trail mix, Avery went back to his own barracks. There was nothing to do now but wait.

He didn't have long to wait, either. Two days later, there was an attack by a large contingent of Lucks. A large shipment of grain had arrived and that seemed to attract raiders like accountants to spreadsheets.

Avery, who was on the seventh floor when the alarm sounded, had to grab his stash before reporting for battle.

"Thought you were going to chicken out again, Oh-One" a guard said when he arrived. "I was looking forward to killing you myself."

"No, sir. I'm ready, sir," said Avery, who felt anything but.

"Good, because you're leading a unit," the guard said, waving to a group of ten frightened and confused newcomers. "They're all yours, Oh-One."

Avery took a deep breath, as if the air would stiffen his resolve, before addressing his unit.

"Men," he said, then paused, "and ladies, of course. "Be brave. Run hard. Don't be afraid. Everything will be all right." He looked slowly around at them; it wasn't much of a speech and they didn't seem reassured. "Hey!" he cried. "The Commodore has told me that after this victory we can have the rest of the day off!" The promise came as a surprise to the guards, but it perked up the Dock workers. "Now grab your sticks and follow me!"

Avery raised his axe handle and let loose with a yell that was powered as much by fear as determination. The workers in his unit looked around uncertainly. However, others nearby started hooting and yelling and waving sticks and rifles.

"I'm following Oh-One!" a large man shouted.

"Oh-One!" a larger woman concurred.

Soon all the workers on the Dock were chanting Avery's number:

Oh-One! Oh-One! Oh-One!

Even the guards got caught up in the excitement, and a few joined in the chant. Avery suddenly realized he was not leading ten defenders, but one hundred. He turned toward the loading dock doors, raised his axe handle and cried at the top of his voice:

"Run like hell, you maggots!"

With that, the unlikely commander leaped out of the Docks and raced across the lumpy field toward the attackers. Bullets whizzed past him; he ignored them as best he could. He was scared beyond belief, but managed to run all the faster because of it. His army of workers was close behind him, though some fell: shot or scared or just clumsy. Avery ran on, gulping air like it was pop corn. They reached a twenty-foot berm and collapsed behind it to await the onslaught of the raiders.

All except Avery. He ran straight up the ridge and down the other side. He no longer heard nor saw his comrades, having left them twenty yards behind. The Luck raiders were still advancing, not thirty yards away. He fixed his eyes on a blonde woman in the rear of the raiding party. The woman paused for a moment, impressed with Avery's bravery or stupidity, before raising her rifle.

Just a few more steps, Avery thought. Just one more step.

He had to make it look good, but he didn't want to make it look too good.

Avery fell just as the woman fired. He fell face first into a puddle. He heard the axe handle clatter on some old concrete as it left his hand. Then he heard the Lucks advance and run him over. He waited a few minutes before pulling himself up, muddy and sore and dizzy.

Avery looked up. The woman was directly in front of him, not ten yards away, aiming the rifle at his head.

"I surrender," he said happily.

CHAPTER 15

The room was as dark as Hon's mood when Snoop knocked on the door. He waited a few moments before grunting permission to enter.

"Um, sir?" the junior executive said quietly.

"Come on in, Snoop," Hon said with mock cheerfulness. "Tell me the bad news."

The Lower Down of Internal Audit was stretched out on his black leather couch, holding a throw pillow over his head. It was a souvenir from Huck Finn Rock. He had turned off the lights and monitors in his office, as well as his internal intercom. It had been a bad morning and he needed some alone time.

"Avery. The exploding chair suspect – he's no longer in the Docks."

Snoop braced himself for shouting, or at least an acerbic remark. Instead, his boss merely let out a weak laugh.

"He went out to battle and never came back. He is presumed dead."

"Did we not tell the security guards to keep him off battle duty?" Hon said slowly.

"Apparently there was a mix-up with the DANs – uh, Docks Associate Numbers. Avery, as you recall, was a surprise transfer. They've been, um, protecting the wrong man."

Hon sighed, only half listening.

The Avery situation was the latest of the Lower Down's problems. The exploding chair, as it turned out, was only the first in a series of peculiar incidents throughout Naperville. Bookcases were jumping in Pontiac, maintenance carts were driving themselves in sub-Normal, and Danville reported scores of giggling toilet seats. Everywhere desks were walking off under their own power, and most of the salt shakers had been filled with sugar. Someone had even made off with the Lowest Down's birthday cake.

Individually, these things were little more than practical jokes, but the cumulative effect on the associates was devastating. It called into question Naperville's ability to secure its campus. IA had arrested several associates, but it was mostly for show; they had no real leads.

Then there was the increase in the number of raiding parties. Technically, it was Security's job to defend the perimeter, but since IA had always helped out, the Lowest Down was blaming Hon for the worsening problem. It was just another case of no good deed going unpunished.

Things were not good. Average associates were actually beginning to question the Lower Downs, something that had not happened in Hon's memory. The timing couldn't be worse, coming as it did when the Merger partners were questioning Naperville's ability to complete the last portion if the Transcontinental Merger Project by the May 1 deadline, now just a month away.

More importantly, to Hon, all the setbacks pushed back any plans he might have for ousting the current Lowest Down.

And now Avery was dead.

Or maybe not.

He pulled the pillow off his face and sat up slowly.

"Snoop, how would you like to get some fresh air?" he asked.

"Sir?"

"I want you to go to the Docks and retrieve Avery's body."

"Outside, sir?"

"It shouldn't be difficult. Our agent in Corporate Communications did tag him, didn't he?"

"Uh, yes, sir."

"Take some agents with you. Fully armed: stun rods, sting gas, etc. I want a report within twenty-four hours."

"Sir, I," the young man stammered. "I've never been Outside."

"Excellent – then you can add it to your resume." He lay back down, putting the pillow over his face. "Close the door as you leave, Snoop."

In Facilitator Thomas' opinion, few jobs were as joyful as his. And in the world of SnappyCo, in which all jobs were officially joyful, that was saying a lot.

SnappyCo, unlike the other corporate partners in the Transcontinental Merger, prided itself exceeding the expectations of its employees, if not its customers. If an employee wasn't happy in his work, he was transferred to a job he liked. If such a job didn't exist, it was created for him. If he didn't like his neighbor, he was moved to a new cube (or *creation station*, as they termed it). And if he didn't like himself, they could change that too. Every effort was made to ensure every employee was as joyful as possible so that they could contribute to the progress of the organization. This philosophy was reflected in the corporations's three core values: *Rethinking, Reshaping, Rejoicing.*

Facilitator Thomas loved his job because he got to spread the joy. Right now, for instance, his Reshaping Team was spreading SnappyCo culture throughout the wilderness of Northern Illinois. His team had landed by buzzer some forty miles north of the Naperville corridor in mid-March and already had made excellent progress.

Their primary mission was to eliminate the troublesome Outsiders so the Naperville Corporation could finish their part of the great merger on time and unhindered. This did, regrettably, involve a certain amount of violence and destruction. They had had to level the Native enclave at De Kalb, for instance. But even a joyful job involved some unpleasantness.

Thomas took a satisfying sip of his steaming hot Essbee's mocha latte and looked out over the river valley – the Fox River, he believed they called it. He was a short man, but handsome and sturdily built. SnappyCo did three things – shoes, electronics and coffee – but coffee was what they did best.

He tugged at his ill-fitting flannel shirt which, combined with thick corduroy pants, hiking boots and knit cap, constituted his disguise as a Canadian. This was, after all, a covert mission.

In and around the qwik-huts below him, the men and women of the Reshaping Team were milling about happily. They had made quick work of the villagers in Aurora, despite fierce resistance, and he was giving them an extra day of rest before moving on.

He looked back west at that village. It was hard to tell the charred remains of the community they had just leveled from the decaying remains of the old American city. But it didn't matter. That was why his job was so joyful – soon it would all be SnappyCo. Soon, in a day or maybe two, a Rethinking Team would arrive. It would clean out the old concrete and steel and replace it with clean plastic and synthetics. And a dome, of course, to ward off the Outside. Inside the dome they would build comfortable, modern cubes. And then the anxious settlers would come east. They would make Yike shoes and Snappel ThinkPlops, and sip excellent coffee at EssBee's. They would bring enlightenment and joy.

As for the Outsiders, well, there was always Wisconsin.

In addition to De Kalb and Aurora, they had reshaped the settlements at Elburn and Oswego, always zigzagging to keep defenders off-balance. Not that it mattered much – rifles and mortars were little use against napalm and neurological agents. Still, it was good to stay creative.

He took another sip of his latte, then headed down the slope toward the nearest qwik-hut to meet with his officers. He pushed through the plastic strips that comprised the door. As he did he felt the strong downward stream of air designed to keep out flying insects. It took a moment for his eyes to adjust from the bright afternoon sun. When they did, he saw three senior re-thinkers standing around a projection map of the area. They were in the middle of a heated discussion until one of them spotted Thomas and all three came to attention.

"Carry on," Thomas said. "How's the plan coming?"

"Facilitator – if I may make a suggestion." It was the brash youngster named Jobs. "I believe we should change our immediate objective."

Thomas took another sip. "Go on," he said. *Damn, the coffee was good!*

"As you know, sir, our next target, Naperville, figures to be troublesome. Not in terms of the number of Outsiders, but in terms of geography."

He waved at the projection to zoom in. The area was not the Naperville Corporation, of course, but remains of the town from which, some time in the distant past, it had taken its name. The satellite image showed a band of Interstate lined with large, pre-corporate, steel-and-glass office structures.

"Each of these ancient office buildings is home to a different tribe or family of Outsiders, some Native, some not. Some buildings have as few a one inhabitant. There is constant fighting between these groups."

"We already know this," Thomas said.

"Yes, Facilitator. The problem is that over the years, these people have installed elaborate booby traps and automatic defenses to protect their turf, as it were. Taking these buildings could be costly and – dare I say it? – not joyful."

"And yet they must be taken." Thomas had dealt with such denizens before – office park rats they called them – each one the king of his crumbling domain. They tended to be intelligent, paranoid and heavily-armed – a nasty combination.

"Yes, but I advise we take them later." Jobs zoomed out the image and overlayed a map. "It would be easier to swing around Naperville and go directly to Luckport, then on to our final target – Joliet."

"Facilitator!" another man interrupted. "That would mean days of doubling back on foot. Plus, I don't want to go after the Outsiders' main enclave with this old Naperville at our backs and the Democrats unaccounted for."

"That's why I suggest we call up the buzzers to drop us just outside Joliet," Jobs explained. "It would give us the element of surprise."

Thomas thought for a moment.

"That's good rethinking on your part, Jobs. You've only left one thing out of your plans – we're a *covert* operation. The Lower Downs in Naperville may or may not know we're here, but at this point they can reasonably deny they know about our operation. If we fly a score of buzzers down there, all the corporations in the hemisphere will know about it, and that will cause all kinds of problems for SnappyCo."

Jobs put his head down and took a small step back.

"But cheer up," Thomas continued. "You've given me an idea." He turned to the other man. "Wozniak! Why can't we use the buzzers to destroy these office park rats? Then we'll have none of that pesky building-to-building fighting."

"Yes, Facilitator!" Wozniak replied. Even Jobs liked the idea.

"I'll be in my creation station if anyone needs me," Thomas said, turning to go.

Before he exited, he finished off his cup, rinsed it, and tossed it in the recycling bin. Then he tugged at his shirt.

"Does anyone else find this get-up itchy?" he asked.

CHAPTER 16

"Go back! Go back and die!"

Avery was beginning to realize that surrendering to the Lucks would be harder than he thought.

The battle raged behind him – if scattered rifle shots and the screams of a few hundred men and woman counted as *raging* – but Avery wanted no part of it. He just wanted to surrender.

Only the Luck woman in front of him didn't seem to be cooperating.

"Go on," she said, as if encouraging a child to jump in a pool. "I'll give you a head start."

"No, no," Avery insisted. "I give up. I want to surrender." He was still kneeling in the mud, trying to look as subservient as possible.

"We don't take prisoners."

The woman suddenly lifted her rifle and fired over Avery's head. Avery heard a sound like someone saying "huh" and assumed the bullet had found its target.

"What do you mean?" Avery said too loudly (his ears were ringing from the shot). "You have to. Don't you?"

"You Naps don't," the woman replied.

Avery, having no reply, remained kneeling. The woman, still looking toward the Docks, gestured with her chin.

"Gimme your bag," she said.

Avery complied, tossing the knapsack at the woman's feet. He didn't know if she would simply kill him, but what choice did he have?

The woman squatted down to examine the contents, keeping one eye on the fight. She removed several candy bars and packs of crackers Avery had taken from the vending machine. She was much younger than he had first thought.

"Crap, crap and more crap," she said as she tossed them aside.

"You can have anything in there," Avery said hopefully.

"I know that."

Avery's plan seemed to have hit a snag. Then, as the woman removed an unframed photo from the pack, the young man remembered his ace in the hole.

"Wize!" he cried, pointing at the picture. "Do you know the Wizened Security Guard?"

The woman studied the photo, her face turning serious.

"You know this man?" she asked, indicating Wize.

"Yes. Yes!" Avery replied. "Wize – he's my friend."

The woman frowned. "We know him as Stanislaw. Stanislaw Pink – the great poet." The Luck woman stood up with a grimace. "He owes me 100 bucks Canadian."

"He owes me a chair!" Avery said, hoping to endear himself.

Reluctantly, she led Avery away from the battle, past a splintered line of trees. There, she sat down on a stump, laid the rifle across her lap and proceeded to snack on some of the *crap* she had confiscated from Avery's pack. He watched with interest.

"It must be good to get some real food, huh?" he said at last.

"You think this stuff is real?" she replied between swallows.

"No offense. I mean uncontaminated."

The Outsider gave Avery a sideways glance. "Oh, I get it," she said. "We're all mutants out here."

"Well, I'm sure you've developed certain immunities," Avery said apologetically, "but – yes – that's what I've always heard."

"You Naps are all the same."

"My name is Avery."

"Nice to meet you, Nap," the woman said, rising. "I'm Ted."

Ted tossed the knapsack back to Avery, who dropped it.

"I've decided not to kill you just yet. Come on." She shouldered her weapon and gestured for Avery to follow her.

"Where are we going?"

"Luckport," she called back. "Assuming you aren't eaten by mosquitoes."

They walked for about a mile until they reached an old, buckling paved road, then they headed east.

Walking was nothing new for Avery. Naperville associates did a lot of walking. Bullet trams were expensive and Naperville employees typically weren't in a hurry to get anywhere. But hiking on the Outside was a frightening new experience. The air, although cool, was humid. And he was constantly surprised by the sudden gusts of wind: it was like working under an unreliable air duct. The variety of smells was also new to him. Sometimes the Outside had the aroma of a newly-planted atrium, other times it stank like a backed-up toilet.

The creatures were what disturbed him the most. Unfamiliar species of bird darted about, making him flinch. The sky was a lumpy gray – what they called clouds – and looked unfriendly. The crawlies, though few, appeared menacing and alien. Ted noticed this, and did all she could to heighten Avery's anxiety.

"Keep your eye out for those mosquitoes," she warned. "They'll eat you alive if they catch you."

Assuming Mosquitoes to be a particularly nasty tribe of neoNatives, Avery kept alert for signs of an ambush – at the same time wondering if they could be any worse than the wispy little buzzing insects that kept biting him in the neck and arms.

After about three hours, they stopped for a break on a crumbling black road running over a slow-moving, brownish-black stream. The girl sat down, letting her feet dangle over the edge.

"You thirsty?" she asked, producing a tall clear plastic container..

"Very," Avery said, scratching his neck.

"Don't drink from the creek," she gestured to a stream running under the road. "It's not clean."

Avery looked down. Some greenish fuzz floated lazily by. Drinking from the creek never even occurred to him.

"Thanks," he replied.

Ted handed him a canteen and he took a long drink from it.

"Where do you get your water?" he asked Ted.

"Some people get it from Lake Michigan. Ours is well water."

It took effort for Avery to keep from doing a spit take. He knew what a well was. Did these people really drink water pumped up from the earth? Suddenly, drinking creek water didn't seem farfetched.

Ted arched her back and let out a groan. "We'll walk for a few more hours. Then if we can't get a ride we'll camp for the night," she said.

"What if it rains?"

"It's not gonna rain."

"Aren't those clouds up there?" Avery said, indicating the overcast sky.

"So what if it does? You're not going to melt."

Avery shrugged. It was a good point. Getting wet was the least of his worries. And part of him was curious to see real rain.

They continued on. The path soon turned northeast. They walked through the remains of a small town. Low lines of crumbling concrete outlined where structures had been. Others, made of stone, were better preserved – roofless, with dark rectangles where Avery guessed windows had been. *What must it have been like to live this way?* he wondered, feeling as he did that not completely unpleasant lightness in his solar plexus.

As they passed one such house, a large animal burst from the tall grass and bolted past them. Avery, still worried about the deadly Mosquito tribe, jumped back and cried in alarm. Ted laughed derisively.

"It's just a deer," she said.

"I didn't know. I've never seen one for real," Avery said, collecting himself.

"Come on," she commanded, "the expressway is just up ahead."

The structures changed as they continued. The earth was covered with more broken and uneven concrete with plants and small trees rising through the cracks. Rectangular metal skeletons ran along either side of the road for about a hundred yards. Farther on, isolated wreckage of collapsed brick and metal included large plastic signage, much of it still legible. Avery wondered at the words. What kind of establishment was a Purple Martin? Was there still such a thing as a Bank of America? Was this McDonald the farmer from the nonsense rhyme they sang in daycare?

They marched on. Avery, not used to walking on uneven surfaces, lagged farther and farther behind. Not far ahead, the road rose ahead to cross over another, wider thoroughfare. When they reached the intersection, he noticed two smaller paths that circled down to join the larger road.

"This is the expressway," Ted explained. "If we're lucky, we can hitch a ride with the raiding party. They'll be bringing the grain truck back this way."

They were walking down one of the circular ramps when they heard voices. Ted put her hand over Avery's mouth and signaled for him to move into a nearby ravine. When she was satisfied they were hidden from sight, she turned to him.

"Could be my people. Could be neoNatives," she explained.

A dozen or so young men were coming north on the expressway. Most had bows and arrows, but at least one carried a rifle. They were talking loudly and joking with each other.

Ted sneered when she saw them.

"neoNatives," she spat derisively.

The men veered off on a side path that ramped up to join the road on which Ted and Avery had been traveling, then headed east. Ted waited until the group was out of sight before standing up.

"Are they dangerous?" Avery asked.

"Not really. But it's best to avoid them. I know that one with the pop gun – Illiniwek. He's probably going home to his rich daddy in Joliet."

"Whose side are they on?"

"Their own – like all of us," she said, brushing burrs off a pant leg. "Only that group is more on its own side than most."

"So that wasn't the Mosquito tribe," he concluded. Ted laughed but didn't say why.

They circled down to the expressway and sat down under the overpass.

"We'll watch for a truck from here," she said. "If nobody comes, we'll find someplace out of sight to sleep for the night."

Avery hoped someone would come. The idea of sleeping Outside – *outside* Outside – with all the crawlies and jumping deer did not appeal to him. But as night fell, they were still alone. Ted made camp inside an old brick building on a rise that afforded a view of the expressway one hundred yards away. Avery found some framed boards advertising motor oil and, after checking for crawlies, set them against the windows to keep out the cold night air. Ted built a fire in a corner of the room where there was an opening in the collapsing roof.

"People are always starting fires around here. I don't think ours will arouse suspicion," she explained.

Ted made a meal consisting of dried meat, bread and something that looked like cole slaw. Avery, wary of Outsider food, ate what remained of his candy bars and crackers. Soon they had settled against the wall near the fire, Ted watching the road through an opening in the northeast window. Avery was busy swatting insects, real and imagined. He tried to get his mind off the pests.

"Why do you people raid the Docks?" Avery asked after a while.

Ted looked at him as if he were stupid. "We have to, now that Naperville has cut us off from the south. They divert our grain shipments for themselves – for Naps like you."

"Huh," Avery replied. There wasn't much more to say. He had always thought of the Outsiders as half-human monsters, not people who required food and water. Apparently, there was more to the Outside than he had imagined.

"How many people live in Luckport?" he asked.

Ted's eyes narrowed. "Why do you want to know?"

"I'm sorry. I'm just – " Avery replied. "I'm not a spy. Really."

But Ted's suspicions had been raised. It was getting cold quickly, and Avery had hoped to share the young woman's sleeping bag. Now, however, she made him move to the opposite wall so she could keep an eye on him.

As the fire died out, he could see her, wrapped in her sleeping bag, her right hand on the barrel of the rifle. Suddenly exhausted, Avery lay down on his side, using his knapsack as a pillow. He had forgotten all about the bugs and, indeed, few bothered him throughout the frosty Midwest night.

He awoke from a deep sleep. It was pitch black and he heard no sound, but he was too cold to sleep. He couldn't remember ever being so horribly cold, as if his bones themselves had frozen.

"Ted?" he whispered into the darkness. "Ted!"

"What!?" the woman said a little too loudly. She had obviously been in a deep sleep and was ashamed of the fact.

Avery heard the scraping of metal on the floor and assumed she had grabbed the rifle.

"I'm sorry – but I'm freezing. I've never slept Outside."

Ted groaned loudly. There was a long silence, then:

"Come here. You can sleep next to me – *outside* the sleeping bag."

"Thank you," Avery said gratefully.

He crawled toward her voice in the dark.

"Lie here," she commanded, pulling him over to her left side.

He settled in alongside her, and she spooned him. Eventually, he could feel the warmth of her body and smell the not unpleasant odor of dried perspiration. Sauder came to mind and he wondered where she was sleeping this night.

"I wouldn't want you to die before we get a chance to interrogate you," she explained.

"I understand," he said sleepily.

"And no funny stuff. I've got a knife," she added.

Under different circumstances Avery might have been frightened or aroused or both by this young woman. That night, though, he was just happy to be a little less cold. Within seconds he was sound asleep.

No Outsider city in the Midwest could boast a more vibrant downtown than Joliet. The half-square-mile area was home to seven casinos, a soccer stadium, two concert venues and a prison, not to mention dozens of restaurants, strip clubs and other, more prosaic businesses. With Atlantic City long-submerged and Las Vegas lost to war, Joliet was the place insiders and Outsiders came for fun, moral and otherwise.

It was run by the Illini tribe, and Joe Shabbona was its chief. Over the years, he had done an exemplary job of keeping the trouble to a minimum and profits at a maximum. Joliet was a friend to everyone and a threat to no one, and that was the way he liked it.

But now, as the chief surveyed the casino floor from behind the one-way mirror in his office he knew things were changing. It was a Saturday night, yet the tables were almost empty. The Pentagon soldiers and officials that usually frequented Joliet were conspicuous by their absence. In fact, the few that he had seen around in the past few months he knew to be spies. Even now he could see a man pretending to play a quarter machine while checking out the security cameras.

His secretary's voice interrupted his thoughts.

"Your son is here," she said through the intercom.

Shabbona took a long drag of his last Cuban cigar, then pushed the intercom button.

"Send him in."

"Yes, Chief."

"Oh and Hanna – is everyone packed?"

"Everyone that's going," she replied.

The chief carefully snuffed out the cigar, placing it in the ashtray, and looked himself over in the mirror. He was sharply dressed, as befitted the owner of three casinos. His silk suit was specially made in Buenos Aries, and his shoes were made by Italians in Morocco.

Illiniwek shuffled in. He had the same dark complexion and hair as his father, but his neoNative get-up identified him as a rebellious teen.

"I need money," were the first words out of his mouth.

"Nice to see you too, junior."

"Don't call me that! I'm no longer your son – my name is Illiniwek."

"And yet you come to me for a handout."

Illiniwek plopped himself down in one of the red leather chairs.

"So," Shabbona continued, "what have you and your *tribe* been up to?"

"Hunting, tracking," Illiniwek said. "The things real Indians do."

Shabbona sat down at his desk. "I believe the term is *Native American*."

"Like you'd know anything about it, sitting here in your big office like a white man."

Shabbona, having heard this tirade many times, was not the least bit disturbed. Besides, he had bigger problems.

"You'll be happy to know, junior, that I'm leaving all this behind for a while. Possibly forever."

"What are you talking about?" Illiniwek said.

"Look at the casino floor," the chief said. "Have you ever seen the Al Capone this empty?"

The son craned his neck to gaze out without rising from his chair.

"That sucks," he said with sincerity.

"We're about to be invaded," Shabbona said flatly.

"Get out!" Illiniwek cried.

"I'm not joking. The soldiers have been gone for weeks. And I just got a report that a heavily-armed tribe of neoNatives is heading this way.

"But my Fighting Illini is the only neoNative tribe around here"

Shabbona shook his head slowly.

"They're not neoNatives – they're *dressed* as neoNatives. The fact that they're heavily armed means they're a covert Pentagon force."

"How many?" Illini asked.

"My source with the Independents said about a two hundred, but I don't know how accurate that is."

"And you're running away?"

"Yes. We're retreating to Luckport."

"We should stay and fight."

"If we do, we will die."

"Die like warriors!" Illiniwek said. "Like real Indians!"

"I said they are heavily-armed. We have already sent a scouting party to test their strength," Shabbona said. "There would be no fighting – just death."

"My tribe has rifles," Illiniwek replied, raising his gun.

"That's a bb gun. And not a very good one at that," Shabbona said.

"Nevertheless, we will stay and fight."

Shabbona chewed his lower lip for a moment. He knew not to argue.

"Son, if that is your decision I can't stop you. In fact, I will give you all the supplies we can spare. Just remember that you can retreat to Luckport. We will plan our next move from there."

"With the Lucks," Illiniwek said with distaste.

"With the Lucks, the Democrats and anyone else who will help us."

The young man said nothing. He stood uneasily for few moments, as if uncertain whether to stay or leave.

"You said you needed money?" his father asked.

"Just a few hundred Canadian," he said, looking down at his moccasins.

CHAPTER 17

Avery awoke in a wonderful mood. He felt Sauder's warm body next to his and heard her slow, regular breathing. It was Labor Free Weekend and they had nothing planned for the day. Perhaps, he thought dreamily, they could go to EssBee's and splurge on some pancakes with real soy bacon.

He turned slightly and felt a dull pain in his ribs. In fact, his entire body was sore. Then he opened his eyes and remembered.

Ted woke up and kicked Avery in his left calf.

"Ow! What is that for?" he said, scooting out of range.

"A warning!"

Avery got up stiffly. "I get it. You're a woman. You're afraid I might try to rape you or something."

Ted scowled. "Hmph! I'd like to see you try – I'd cut you!"

Avery watched as she crawled out of the sleeping bag and took his first real look at her. She was tall but well-proportioned. Her hair was cut short, but long bangs fell down over clear gray eyes. She had a smooth, strong jawline and a slight underbite. As she stretched, he could make out the curve of her hips through her loose jeans.

"What?" she asked, noticing his stare.

"I have a girlfriend," he said.

"Is she a Nap like you?"

"Yes, but she went Outside."

"Then she's probably dead," Ted said, pushing her hair out of her eyes.

Avery looked away. He knew she might be right.

"I'm hoping to find her," he said.

Now Ted looked away, south down the expressway.

"Look, I'm sorry," she said, "I shouldn't be mean. It's just that I've never taken a prisoner. I'm a little nervous, I guess."

Avery looked back at her. She really was pretty. Dirty and unkempt, but pretty.

"Thank you," he said.

Ted picked up her rifle.

"We should go," she said.

It took mere minutes to pack, which mainly involved rolling up the sleeping bag. Then, after stretching and drinking some water from the canteen, they walked back to the expressway.

"We'll eat on the way," Ted said as she led them north.

"Will we get a ride?" Avery asked hopefully.

The Luck woman thought for a moment, then said: "I doubt it. If the raiding party got the grain truck they would have passed by here yesterday. And if not, they're on foot."

Nevertheless, after they had walked for a few hours, they heard the high-pitched purr of engines somewhere behind them. As Avery turned, hoping to see a truck, Ted yanked him off the road.

"That's an electric engine," she hissed.

They hurried to a ditch that ran parallel to and under the expressway. It turned out to be a creek. Ted jumped in; the water was up to her ankles. Avery hesitated.

"Get down, before they see you," she said. Then, when he didn't move, asked, "What's wrong?"

"It's icky."

"Oh for – " She reached up and pulled him in. The water was cold and he wondered if there were lobsters.

They could hear the cart pull up almost even with them, but instead of moving on it idled.

"Right around here," a voice said.

"Are you sure it wasn't one of them deers like last time?" a second, female voice asked.

"It was two people. That or bears wearing pants," the man replied. "Come on."

Avery heard the rustling of the tall grass.

"In there?" the woman called reluctantly.

"Hey, it freaks me out too. But if we go back empty-handed we'll be in more trouble than we already are."

The man's voice was close, maybe thirty yards away. Ted pulled Avery down to a kneeling position. Instinctively, he put his arms down to support his body. The creek bottom felt like cold, gritty pudding.

"Shit!" Ted whispered suddenly.

Avery looked at her and realized she did not have the rifle. She shook her head in resignation.

"Just stay down," she said.

Unfortunately, the pursuers walked straight up to the creek.

"Told ya," the man said. "Do they look like deer?"

Avery looked up and saw two security guards from the Docks, the man was holding a stun gun, the woman a pistol. At the same time, he felt something slimy slither under his hand. He rose instinctively.

"Ah, ah – get back down," the woman commanded Avery. "I'll come and get you."

The man leveled the stun gun at them while the other guard climbed carefully down into the creek. As she stepped into the water, she let out an expletive.

"This is grotesque!" she added, pulling up a foot to examine her soaked ankle.

This gave Avery and idea.

"Mud," he said quietly to Ted.

Ted raised a questioning eyebrow.

"Throw the icky mud at them."

As the guard approached to cuff them, the duo in the creek threw handfuls of muck at her. Two shots hit the surprised woman square in the face.

"Ughh!" she cried, staggering backwards, "It's in my mouth!"

The second guard looked confused. "Stop that!" he demanded.

But by the time he turned his gaze back to Avery and Ted, they were throwing at him too. Ted even heaved a rock for good measure. The man dropped his stun gun so he could wipe away the muck with both hands.

"Oh god. I'm contaminated!" he cried.

"It's in my *mouth!*" his partner repeated.

Ted scrambled up the bank and grabbed the stun gun. The guard was too preoccupied to notice.

"Is that a worm?" he asked, looking in horror at some debris he had brushed off his shirt.

Ted knocked down the woman and took her gun before she had a chance to react. Not that the guard cared much.

"I need a wet wipe!" the woman said. "STAT!"

"Let's go," Ted said to Avery, who had climbed up beside her.

They ran back to the electric cart, retrieving her rifle along the way.

"I guess we'll get a ride after all," Avery said, jumping on the front of the three-wheeled vehicle.

Ted climbed on behind him and they motored off toward Luckport.

Back at the creek, the male security guard looked from one muddy hand to the other.

"I feel so dirty," he said.

CHAPTER 18

The Lowest Down sat in the steam room of the executive health club, a towel wrapped around his waist. The skin on his chest and under his arms sagged a little, but he was in otherwise good health for a centegenarian.

Lower Down Hon entered, similarly attired, and sat down a few feet away.

"Things are not going well," the older man noted.

"Uh, huh," Hon replied casually.

"Labor problems out west."

"We're losing the confidence of our corporate partners," Hon added.

"I just spoke to our major shareholders," the Lower Down said. "They're very concerned about our falling behind schedule. Especially the Nigerians."

"Yes, sir. It's looking bleak – "

Just then the door opened.

"Occupado," the older man called out.

The door closed again.

It would have easy for the Lowest Down to conduct virtual meetings without leaving his office. But he preferred meeting in person, especially when discussing matters of a delicate nature.

"You said you had a solution?" the Lowest Down continued.

"I believe there's a way." Hon paused for emphasis. "If there's a will."

The Lowest Down sighed. "Out with it."

Hon grabbed a nearby towel and used it to dab his forehead.

"We know SnappyCo sent a covert force to eliminate the Outside threat. We also know the Pentagon has done the same thing. We also know – thanks to our tracking chip – that a large portion of the Outside force is joining up in Luckport."

"Your Customer Service Rep?" the old man asked.

"Yes. The one Blackball tagged for us. Turns out he led us to much more than a renegade security guard."

"I'm not hearing a solution."

"It seems likely all three groups will engage in battle there. But if the Outsiders somehow win they're still a major problem, and if the corporate forces win Naperville looks extremely weak and ripe for a takeover. My solution is a simple one – we use our cache of missiles."

The Lowest Down coughed vigorously.

"We're not allowed to use our weapons stockpile," he said slowly, as if to a child. "That's the basic tenet of the International Corporate Treaty – no one uses their old government weaponry because everyone has some. It's prevented a major war in this hemisphere for over one hundred years."

"Yes, sir. But desperate times – " Hon threw his hands up. "If we do nothing, Naperville is through as a corporation. The Transcontinental Merger won't be completed on time and we'll be divided up by our partners.

"But a few well-placed – and well-timed – strikes would solve all our problems with minimal risk."

The Lowest Down leaned back.

"We wait until the Luckport conflict resolves itself," Hon continued, "Then we bomb the hell out of the place."

"But if the corporate forces are victorious – ?"

"Sir, there are no corporate forces. Not officially, anyway. So there will be nothing for SnappyCo or the Pentagon to complain about if they are eliminated."

"Yes," the older man said slowly. "Either way, it's a show of strength – to our partners and our stockholders."

He stopped.

"But what about the project?" he asked.

"We free up our conventional security forces – Risk Management and so forth – to handle any problems at the Quad Cities job site. Missiles only take one man to fire."

"Point and click, eh?"

"Exactly."

The Lowest Down stretched his arms out slowly and allowed himself the smallest of smiles.

"I love a good steam," he said.

As soon as Hon had showered and dressed, he placed a secure call to the Lower Down of Facilities.

"Adler. This is Hon," he said. "The LD wants us to recommission the nukes."

He fixed his collar.

"I know it's desperate, but the old guy is dead set on it."

He smiled as he listened to Adler's reply.

"Yes, I think we should make sure his fingerprints are all over this decision."

CHAPTER 19

The ride to Luckport took only forty minutes on the electric scooter. Ted said nothing for the first half of the ride. It wasn't until Avery stopped to wash the dried dirt off his hands in a pond (which was only a little better than the mud, in his opinion) and he saw her clenched jaw and wide eyes that he realized she had been frightened the whole time. He found this odd for a girl who carried a rifle and, allegedly, a knife.

They searched the storage compartment and found a few useful items: water, seaweed crackers, a walkie-talkie and ammo clips for the pistol.

"Are all Naps really that afraid of mud?" Ted asked, referring to their escape from the security guards.

"Oh yeah."

"But it's just nature," she noted.

"Exactly," Avery said. "Are all Lucks really that afraid of scooters?"

Ted tossed her bangs back defiantly. "I wasn't afraid of the machine – I was afraid of your driving."

Avery laughed. He had been taking it slow to conserve the battery.

Ted was more relaxed for the rest of the trip. She held him more loosely, and let her cheek rest between his shoulder blades.

They exited the expressway on a looping incline that fed onto an eastbound two-lane road. After a few miles they saw people in fields on either side of the road. Some walked behind long, V-shaped metal contraptions, which were in turn pulled by horses. Avery recognized the animals from old media he had seen with Sauder. The workers themselves wore baggy jeans and thick, fuzzy parkas and their hair, especially the men's, tended to be long and tied back. There were children in the fields as well, all of whom seemed quite interested in the scooter. Some of the adults too stopped their work to wave at the newcomers.

The people nearer the fence would call out friendly greetings like, *Hey bro! Welcome bro!* and *Hey Ted bro!*

"They seem nice," Avery called back.

"They're idiots," Ted said, spitting out a bug.

As they drove on, the fields were replaced by farmhouses with chickens, pigs and cattle. This surprised Avery. He had always been told that such animals were extinct.

"You must stop up ahead," Ted yelled in Avery's ear.

Avery had already noticed the barricade on the road, the only opening in a four-foot-high stone and brick wall that extended north and south. The vehicle rolled to a stop as two armed men approached – the battery was dead.

Noting Avery's Dock jumpsuit, the men aimed their weapons at him. Ted jumped off the cycle and stepped in from of him.

"It's okay," she said cheerfully. "He's my prisoner."

The men, who seemed to know her, slowly lowered their weapons. One of them signaled toward the barricade, and two more people moved it aside.

"Your father's been worried about you," the armed man said.

They pushed the vehicle through and parked it on the sidewalk just inside the wall.

"Welcome to Luckport," Ted said, grabbing her gear and rifle. "We can walk from here."

She headed quickly down the wide street. Avery had to pick up his pace to keep up. He found he was a little stiff from the previous day's walk, as well as a night of sleeping on the cold, lumpy ground.

The street sloped slightly downward ahead of them, leading to a collection of large concrete buildings. Most were a single story high and some had no roofs. One, though, a long structure with a tall spire at one end, seemed to be well-maintained.

Currently, though, they were passing houses and buildings with shuttered windows. A large group of people was lined up in a field off to the right. Some were practicing archery, others throwing rocks with slings.

"What are they doing?"

"Training for war," Ted said.

Before they could walk any farther, a stocky, long-haired man stepped out from a nearby doorway and blocked their path.

"Theodore!" he said. "Welcome home, bro."

He smiled, revealing two lonely incisors. Then he gave Ted a long bear hug, which she seemed to tolerate more than welcome.

"Who's your friend?" the gap-toothed man asked.

"Bro?" Avery said.

The man leaned his head back and looked at Avery over the bridge of his nose.

"Man, we're all bros," he said.

"I can't stop right now, Reuben," Ted said, nudging Avery along. "This man's a prisoner."

As they passed him, Reuben leaned his head back even more, almost stumbling as he watched them go.

"Prisoner, huh? That's harsh."

"Is he drunk?" Avery asked Ted without turning around.

"He's a Slack."

Reuben called after them. "See you at the Equinox!"

"What's a Slack?" Avery asked.

"Someone who doesn't bathe but hugs you anyway."

Avery shrugged. She was just stating the obvious. Still, as they continued on he saw several Slacks. They weren't hard to distinguish from the regular Luckport residents. All had long hair, either unkempt or carefully beaded. All wore loose-fitting ponchos or wool blankets. And most were extremely friendly if a bit unfocused.

They passed the low concrete buildings Avery had seen from a distance, some with uneven walls, most with stone debris at their bases.

"They used to be office buildings. Like Naperville, I guess," Ted said. "But it wasn't safe to leave them standing. We're using the rubble to build a wall around Luckport."

Ted led Avery up the steps of the well-maintained building they had seen from a distance.

"Dad's usually in here," Ted explained as she pushed open one of the large oak doors.

When Avery's eyes had adjusted to the indoor light he saw a large rectangular auditorium with two rows of benches. At the far end was an elaborate dais. Ted dipped her fingers in a bowl of water by the door and bowed quickly as she touched herself on the head and chest. She then led Avery up one of the side aisles to a door behind the dais.

Ted opened the door. The creaking echoed through the room.

"Daddy?" she called. "Daddy – where are you?"

"In here," came a muffled reply. It came from one of the rooms off the long hallway.

As they approached, Avery heard grunting, followed by a thud and what he knew to be swearing even if he didn't quite catch the words. The room turned out to be a bathroom. A balding, middle-aged man was sitting on the floor, rubbing his forehead. On seeing Ted, his face brightened.

"*Tad-yoosh!*" he said warmly. He rose and gave her a hug, then pushed her back to look at her. His sharp, hawkish face took on a look of reproach. "What have you been up to now?"

"I'm fine," Ted said. "I stayed well back of the raiders, just like you said."

"I said not to go at all."

"Look!" Ted noted proudly. "I brought back a Nap prisoner. His name is – " She looked to Avery.

"Um, Avery," he said.

The man smiled politely. "Well, Um-Avery, it's nice to meet you. My name is Alex Komosinski. I'd shake your hand but mine are dirty. I think it's the pipes again."

There was an awkward pause before the man continued.

"Will you excuse us for a moment, Um-Avery?" he asked.

The father led his daughter down the hall, where they had a short but animated discussion. It was in hushed tones and Avery couldn't catch most of it, but the man seemed to be chastising the young woman. Finally, he heard Ted say, "But daddy – he knows Wize!"

The man looked back over his shoulder at Avery and raised a bushy eyebrow.

"You know the Wizened Security Guard?" he asked.

"Yes. He's pretty much the reason I'm here."

"Well, we'll find out soon enough if you're telling the truth," Alex said.

"I think we can trust him, daddy. He saved me from two Nap soldiers."

Alex's eyes narrowed. "I thought you stayed away from the fighting," he said.

"Oh – this was later."

"Is Wize here?" Avery interrupted.

"He will be," Alex said. "He never misses an Equinox. Until then, my daughter here will keep an eye on you."

Ted hugged her father again, then led Avery out the back way.

"Is that your headquarters" Avery asked.

Ted stopped in the middle of the street to look back at him. A slack riding a two-wheeled contraption deftly swerved to avoid her.

"Our what?"

Avery searched for the right term. "Your board room, um, government center."

"It's our church. You've never seen a Catholic Church before?"

"Not like that," he confessed, thinking back to the Judeo-Catholic services in Naperville, which were held in whatever meeting room was available.

"Hey!" she said, grabbing Avery's wrist. "Are you hungry? I'm starved."

Before he could answer the girl was dragging him down the street. After a few blocks (and at Avery's insistence) they slowed down to a brisk walk.

"So your father's a priest."

"You're funny," Ted said, sliding her arm through his in a very un-guard-like fashion.

Avery wasn't sure what to make of the new, friendly Ted. But at least she wasn't threatening to stab him.

After a block, the buildings changed from stone to wood. Avery was fascinated by these two-story structures. They reminded him of old media stories like *Leave It to Beaver* and *Family Matters*. Most were well-maintained and freshly-painted, although he noticed the whites were not as bright as they were on the surfaces inside Naperville. Also, virtually all the homes had large rectangles of dirt where he expected grass to be.

"There's usually a communal midday meal at the meeting house," Ted explained.

Avery stopped. "You people live outside like this?" Avery asked

"Of course not. We live in houses."

"But the houses are outside," he said.

Ted stepped back and looked steadily at him, as if trying to determine if he were joking.

"So it's true," she said at last. "You Naps spend your whole lives in an office."

"Of course we do. The Outside is polluted – no offense. It's populated by mutants."

"Do I look like a mutant?" Ted asked, insulted.

Avery noted the curve of her torso and the fullness of her hips. She certainly did not.

As they neared the meeting house Avery saw movement out of the corner of his eye. He turned and actually gasped. A black animal had come from behind a house and was moving toward them. He grabbed Ted's arm.

"Um!" he said, pointing with his free hand.

Ted turned as the beast stopped just short of them. It rose slightly on its front legs, shook its head and snorted.

"Hey, Ginger," Ted said, greeting the horse. She took a small object out of her pocket and held her hand palm upward to the animal. It reached over the fence and took the object in its mouth. Avery had not even noticed the fence.

"You're not afraid of horses, are you?"

"What are you giving it?" Avery asked, keeping a few paces back.

"Dried apple. Here, you try."

She handed him a piece. It felt like a piece of nauga leather.

"Hold you hand flat," Ted said. "Yes. Like that."

Avery carefully extended his hand to the anxious horse, which made quick work of the treat. Avery withdrew his hand and examined the wet spot on his palm.

"Wow," he said. "That's horse spit."

Ted stroked the horse's head. It snorted again, but softly. Avery had never been near so large an animal.

"Why keep your palm open?" he asked.

"So she doesn't bite off a finger."

They walked across to the meeting house. It looked to be a new wooden structure, large and square, with a steeply angled roof.

Inside, it was noisy and crowded and filled with the aroma of humanity and baked goods. Pockets of sturdy men, women and children talked loudly in English and some other language Avery didn't recognize. Most greeted

Ted as she passed, though they eyed Avery with a mix of interest and wariness. Only a few Slacks were present.

The food looked familiar: breads and soup, mostly. It was more aromatic than Avery was used to; Naperville food had a uniform smell.

Ted packed food into her bag. She filled two large ceramic mugs with soup and handed them to Avery to carry.

"It's a nice day. We'll have a picnic," she said. "That is, if you don't mind eating Outside."

Avery made a wide waving gesture. "It's all Outside to me," he said.

They walked a few blocks to an open grassy area by a river. The ground, Avery, noted, was dry and surprisingly comfortable. The trees were still barren, but the constantly flowing river fascinated Avery. (It was only much later that he realized the lake under the Docks was a river, possibly this one.)

Ted apologized for the poor quality of the meal, noting that meat was scarce and vegetables hard to come by in early spring. Avery, though, found it delicious: fresh bread and butter, thick bean soup and dried fruit. When they had finished, Ted told him about the Lucks.

The majority of the Lucks originally lived in a larger town upriver. Generations ago, however, some disaster had driven them down to Lockport, where they merged with the few remaining indigenous citizens. The newcomers, who were Polish, were derisively referred to as *Pollacks* by the oldtimers. Over the years, Pollacks and Lockport got combined – hence the name Luckport.

Aside from being fertile land for growing crops and raising livestock, Luckport was important for two other reasons. The first were the locks that gave the town its original name. What water traffic there was between Joliet and the Democrats and Independents had to pass through them, providing tolls and trade for the Lucks.

The second was the oil refinery. The equipment was at least a hundred years old, but the Luck engineers were still able to swap out enough parts to produce a fair amount of diesel fuel.

Ted tossed a few crumbs of bread into an eddy by the bank. Some aquatic birds slid over and pecked at them.

"Of course all that has changed with the Big Wall," Ted continued, referring to the Transcontinental Merger. "We can't ship supplies south, and we can't import crude oil and other raw materials."

Avery watched as one of the birds disappeared under the water. A few seconds later it reappeared a few feet away.

"What about the Slacks?" he asked.

Ted bit her lip and tossed a stone in the river.

"Yeah. The Slacks. They're okay."

A man's voice called from behind them. They turned and saw Alex, Ted's father, walking toward them. A young Slack shuffled along behind him.

"Tad-yoosh," I'm going to have to take you off guard duty," he said when he arrived. "Wize is back and he has news."

"Wize?" Avery said. "Did you tell him I'm here?"

Alex gave Avery a stern look. Avery had seen that look before, usually when he asked the wrong question at a departmental meeting.

"Haven't had time yet," Alex said at last. "But you'll see him tonight at the Equinox. Let's go, Ted. Jackson here will take care of the Nap."

Ted took a step toward her father, who had already turned to go.

"Wait. What's going to happen to me?"

Ted gave his arm a squeeze. "Don't worry about it," she said.

Avery wasn't reassured. He watched them go, then turned to Jackson. The young man wore a worn drab green vest that had obviously once been a jacket. His hair was short on the side and long in the front and back. There was a tattoo on his left forearm of what appeared to be a fierce but scrawny bird. He was smiling broadly.

"Naperville, huh? Dude, I've heard stories about that place."

Avery said nothing for a moment, then:

"So, do you know what's going to happen to me?"

Jackson shook his head in a random fashion.

"Nothing, dude. Unless they think you're a spy. Then they'll shoot you in the head."

CHAPTER 20

"How are your hands, dude?"

Jackson and Avery were carrying planks of wood from the meeting house to an open field behind it. They balanced the plank between two stacks of stone about two feet off the ground. It was part of the stage for the Equinox, which as far as Avery could surmise was an annual spring party having to do with the position of the sun. Avery, who had always gauged the seasons by the merchandise sold at the WaltMart stores and the smaller specialty shops in the Sub-Dwight shopping mall (which were also owned by WaltCorp), didn't really grasp the astronomical details.

He examined his fingers. The weeks in the Docks had accustomed them to hard work.

"You say *dude* a lot," Avery said, rubbing his hands. "The other Slacks say *bro*."

Jackson took a long leathery strip out of his vest pocket and ripped off a piece with his teeth.

"It's my thing, dude," he said as he chewed. "Everybody needs a thing."

They walked back to the meeting house. Jackson started singing, tapping out the rhythm with his hands.

"Aren't you supposed to me guarding me?" Avery asked.

"I am, dude," he said while continuing to clap softly. "I got a gun and everything. Wanna see?"

Jackson pulled out a handgun from the back of his pants and started waving it around.

"I know how to shoot it, too." He took aim at an invisible target. "Blam! Blam!"

When the light began to fade. Avery knew from his experience the previous night that it was the sun setting. He and Jackson sat down in the meeting room and had some tea.

"So, what exactly do you do?" Avery asked.

Jackson leaned his head back in a manner that reminded Avery of the other Slack, Reuben.

"Do? Dude, I don't do. I am."

"But how do you make a living?"

"Dude, I don't make a living. I live."

Jackson gulped his steaming tea and winced.

"How do *you* make a living, dude? What do *you* do?"

Avery told him of his customer service job. Jackson looked confused.

"How do you eat that? How do you wear that?" He shook his head. "Dude, that is messed up."

Avery changed the subject to his immediate future, but Jackson wasn't very helpful. It seemed the party would start soon, basically a feast with entertainment. He knew something big was up, and that Natives from Joliet were straggling into town from the south. But Alex and the leaders were keeping tight-lipped about it.

Avery fished a questionable piece of brown debris from his cup. He had a lot to think about. His old life was over, and he had no definite plans besides talking to Wize and finding Sauder. He had no job and, judging from his discussion with Ted, such things probably didn't exist Outside. Then he thought about Jackson's words: *I don't make a living. I live.* He had heard similar things from motivational speakers in Naperville. It had seemed vacuous then, and only slightly less so here.

One thing he knew for sure: a background in customer service wouldn't count for much Outside.

"Avery, where have you been?"

The voice had an odd yet familiar twitter to it. Avery looked across the table and saw, not Jackson, but a Weed.

"We have been trying to contact you," the Weed continued, its leaves trembling slightly.

Avery looked around. Jackson was nowhere to be seen, and the few Lucks in the room seemed not to notice the alien plant.

"How, how did you – ?"

"Find you? We're fairly advanced, technologically speaking. You have left Naperville."

"Yes," Avery said, expecting at any moment that all hell would break loose. "They transferred me to a very dangerous place. So I ran away."

"This should not happen to someone who is so special."

Avery hung his head and sighed. He noticed his socks were mismatched. "What do you mean by that, anyway?" he asked.

"So you would not know when we will receive our shipment?"

Avery shook his head, hoping to clear his mind. "Your who now?"

"Our payment. We have not been paid."

"What do they pay aliens with? Funbucks?"

"Borax."

"Borax," Avery repeated.

"Naperville pays us in borax."

"What do you do with borax?"

The Weed shook violently, which Avery guessed was a sign of great mirth.

"What *don't* we do with borax?" it said.

"Wake up!"

Avery's opened his eyes and saw Ted's face above him. *Had he been dreaming?*

"What is it?" he said, rising unsteadily.

"You're missing the Equinox!"

She grabbed his hand and pulled him toward the door. It was noisier in the meeting house than it had been at lunch. The smell of fresh bread again filled the room. But Avery didn't notice. He let go of Ted. She turned to look at him. She was wearing a green floral dress, belted at the waist to show off her figure. Her blonde hair, now washed, was straight and almost fluorescent.

"You are lovely," he said.

"Thank you," she said without blushing. "Now let's dance."

She pulled him out into the night. A broad area around the stage was lit by the flicker of torches. Slacks and regular Lucks filled makeshift benches. Avery could smell beer and something else, like burning grass only sweet.

"Can we eat first," Avery said. "I'm starved."

A playful look crossed Ted's face.

"We have a rule," she said, then looked toward the stage where a large group of musicians were playing. Most had acoustic instruments, but a few had electric guitars.

Avery listened for a moment. It was hard to make out the words. He soon realized this was because the singer, a woman, kept stopping. She would look to the musicians as if pleading for help, but they would just laugh. He then noticed the crowd (those paying attention, anyway) were getting a big kick out the performance.

"If you're new you have to sing for your supper," Ted said.

Avery's head jerked back.

"I can't sing!"

"Or something," Ted said. "A poem or a dance. Do you have any talents?"

"I'm a good listener," Avery said without conviction.

He noticed a large tray of bread on a nearby table. In the middle were several small, dark loaves. He smiled.

"I've got a talent," he said.

All in all, it was a good Equinox for Avery. The weather was unseasonably warm. He got his fill of food and beer and something called apple jack. Eventually, the band thinned out so that only a guitar, mandolin and acoustic bass remained. The music was slow and sweet and easy to move to. He and Ted danced, although it was mostly just leaning close to each other. Which suited Avery fine.

When they sat down again, they were joined by two Slacks: Reuben and Jackson.

"Dude, where did you learn to juggle like that?" Jackson asked.

Avery shrugged, and Jackson let it go.

The two Slacks, it turned out, were father and son. They got along very well, even sharing their homemade cigarettes, which gave off the sweet aroma Avery had noticed earlier. They offered Avery a few *tokes*, and he accepted politely. He could tell the smoke was potent, but, being raised on pharmaceuticals, it had little effect on him. The apple jack, however, was a different story; he decided to lay off it.

"You should come out and stay with us," Reuben told Avery. His eyes were red and he was sort of listing to his left.

"Really? You'd let me stay here?"

"Hell yeah, bro," Reuben said. "We're not suspicious like the Townies. Besides, Jackson tells me you're a hard worker – "

"Which you sure ain't, pop!"

"Exactly. You could do chores and keep the old lady off my back. I'll teach you how to farm and raise cattle and make cheese. Gimme back my weed." The latter to his son.

Ted got up.

"Let's take a walk," she said.

"Lucks don't like Slacks, do they?" Avery asked when they clear of the others.

"They think everything will take care of itself. Forget them." She twirled. "Do you like my dress?"

"I love the dress," he said, looking at her eyes. They were in the shadows now, behind a tall concrete pillar or wall. He leaned toward her and she arched her body toward him. They kissed. He had a sudden craving for a bowl of nuts.

"I could live here. With Rueben and Jackson."

He stopped himself. What was he thinking? Live Outside? And what about Sauder? He should be searching for her and instead he was canoodling with an Outsider.

"Did they ask you for money?"

The question brought Avery out of his pondering. "No."

"They will. Believe me."

There as a loud murmur, which Avery realized had been growing for a while now, followed by applause. Ted looked back toward the party.

"Stan!"

She ran toward the stage, once again pulling Avery with her.

Avery looked up and saw a large bearded man in blue.

"Wize!" he cried.

But the Wizened Security Guard was addressing the crowd, which was by now chanting "Stanislaw, Stanislaw, Stanislaw!"

"Thank you, thank you," Stan/Wize said, holding his hands out to quiet the crowd. "I have much to do and not much time in which to do it. You know me: I always have too much on my plate."

He grabbed his ample paunch and the audience cheered.

"Now as you know I am known by many names to many people. Here, I am Stanislaw Pink."

Some of the crowd began chanting again, but he quieted them down.

"In other locales, I am the Wizened Security Guard – "

"Wizened doesn't mean wise, you know!" a voice called out.

"Thank you, Jasper, for the clarification," Wize said without missing a beat. "And you also know I would never come to an Equinox empty-handed. Which is why I have written a poem for the occasion."

The crowd applauded mildly. Then Stan began:

A man from the village of Nap
Went around with a mouse on his cap.
But the man couldn't bake
So he stole a big cake
And brought the whole damn thing on back!

The band improvised a fanfare as four people rolled out a large sheet cake. The message across it, written in frosting, read: "Happy Birthday, Lowest Down!"

"Ladies and gentlemen, Lucks and Bros, I wish you a happy Equinox, compliments of the Naperville Corp."

Avery and Ted waited their turn to see Wize. They had no choice – he was a folk hero and everyone wanted to greet him. As they inched closer, Avery thought about everything that had happened to him in the past month – all of it because of the Wizened Security Guard.

When Avery finally got near Wize, his back was turned. Avery tapped him on the back. Wize turned.

"The kid," he said, eyes wide with surprise.

"Yeah," Avery said. "You remember: the exploding chair?"

Wize put his hands up defensively.

"Hey, don't get crazy now."

Avery lunged for him. But instead of punching him, hugged him.

"Are you kidding?" Avery said. "You're the best thing that ever happened to me!"

CHAPTER 21

"Glad to hear it," Wize said. He was never surprised when things turned out well.

"Stan, do you know this man?"

It was Alex, who had walked up unnoticed.

"Of course," Wize said jovially. "He's one of my contacts in Naperville. Good old Henry – "

"Avery," Avery corrected.

"Exactly. He can be trusted."

"Hmph," Alex said. "Well, I suppose he'd better come to the meeting."

The meeting house was fairly empty when they entered. About a dozen people sat at a long table on one end. Most looked to be Lucks, with a few Slacks. There were also two men with dark hair, ruddy complexions and nice clothes. Everyone bore serious expressions, even the Slacks. Wize and Alex took their seats at the table, while Ted and Avery sat nearby.

Wize gazed around the room with a frown. Suddenly, he jumped up.

"Perhaps I should lighten the mood with a bit of poetry," he said. "There once was a girl from Chunking. And out of her nose hung this thing – "

"Moving on," Alex interrupted.

"Right," said Wize, taken a little aback. "Well. Joliet has been taken by Pentagon forces posing as neoNatives. They will be coming here tomorrow. Bolingbrook has been taken by a SnappyCo reshaping team posing as

Canadians and they will also be here tomorrow. It will take the Democrats at least two days to send the reinforcements they promised. In the meantime, we're kind of screwed."

He sat down, then added: "Oh, and President Adams sends his regards."

"Chief Shabbona – any word from your son Illiniwek?" Alex asked.

Shabbona (one of the nicely-dressed men) sighed heavily. "He insisted on staying to fight. I can only hope he managed to escape. And, barring that, that he died a good death and didn't shoot himself in the toe again."

"I'm sorry to hear that," Alex said. "Nevertheless, we have to plan to save Luckport."

"Most of the tribe came with me," Shabbona said. "That's about eight hundred adults who can fire a gun. Unfortunately, the arsenal was captured so we have no guns."

"We have rifles," Alex noted. "And about six hundred men and women. Assuming we can count on the Slacks."

An old woman with really large earrings rose unsteadily to her feet. She appeared to have smoked one too many homemade cigarettes.

"Although we abhor violence, we will help defend our sisters, male and female," she said. "Although we abhor violence, as I said."

"Perhaps we should abandon the city," Wize said.

"And go where?" Shabbona asked. "There are armies to the north and south, a thousand-mile wall to the southwest, and nothing to the west for hundreds of miles."

"And if we go east they might catch us out in the open. At least Luckport is a walled city."

"Of course, violence is always our last resort," continued the earring-wearing woman, addressing no one in particular. "Maybe we could just make sandwiches or something."

"Yes, the wall will protect us – assuming we are attacked by an army of tortoises," said Wize, who was a little cranky on account of being up past his bedtime.

"But whatever you need," the woman continued. "So, is this, like, next month?"

Ted listened intently as the discussion continued. Avery, on the other hand, knew little about the situation and was soon lost. Ted tried to bring him up to speed, but all he understood was that two covert military units were approaching Luckport from opposite directions, that both had advanced weaponry and that both were expected to arrive the next day. Perhaps that is why it was Avery, his mind uncluttered with facts, who came up with the best idea.

It was a perfectly simple idea, yet he was reluctant to suggest it. First, he was a Nap and therefore suspect. Second, he knew nothing about fighting. Finally, though, he whispered it to Ted. Her eyes brightened.

"Avery has an idea!" she called to the men, almost taunting.

The strategists, who were not getting anywhere on their own, looked at the newcomer as if he were a child asking to go to the bathroom.

"It's kind of a silly idea," Avery stammered. "But from what I understand, neither of these groups knows about the other one – and both are dressed as Outsiders?"

Shabbona nodded slowly.

"Well, couldn't you just get out of the way?"

Wize looked at the other men cheerfully. "I told you we could trust young Chip."

"Avery."

"Whatever."

Avery sat on the floor of the church tower, hugging and slapping his legs.

"Can't I be a Canadian?" he asked. "At least then I'd get a flannel shirt."

"What? You're a natural neoNative."

It was Wize, who was wearing a wool sweater.

"I don't even know why I'm here," Avery said, watching goose bumps appear on the white skin of his forearm.

"This was your idea – you're here to take the credit." Wize spat into a vacant corner before adding, "Or blame."

Avery peered out through one of four windows in the brick enclosure. He saw nothing unusual, but then he really didn't know what he was looking for. He ducked back down out of the wind. It had turned cold and gray overnight, a change that no one but Avery found unusual.

Alex and Wize had climbed up first thing in the morning to watch for the approaching enemy. The tower afforded a view in all directions. A score of volunteers waited downstairs – *indoors*, Avery thought to himself – ready for the day's action. Chief Shabbona had led Ted and the rest of the people northeast. They were due to meet up with a contingent of Democrats at the old Orland Park Mall.

Alex was on the walkie-talkie, getting reports from his scouts. Avery's idea, although simple, needed a strategic nudge or two to implement. The two enemy armies had to arrive at the same time and in the same place – and with any luck that place would be outside of Luckport rather than in it. This meant stalling or diverting the two sides as needed.

Alex looked to the West, where the land rose up slightly on the other side of the river.

"The Pentagon troops are coming up from the south right on schedule," he said at last. "But the Reshaping Team is still too far north." He thought for a moment before making his decision. "We'll send the men across the river to draw the Reshapers south. If we work it right, both armies will meet south of town."

Wize opened the trap door and called down to the men in the sanctuary. "Skins it is!"

Facilitator Thomas was his typical joyful self. He loved his job and he loved his coffee, but what he really loved was an easy victory.

The Naperville corridor had been no problem once they gassed the decaying office structures. Bolingbrook and Romeoville were little more than shanty towns. And now they had caught the neoNative scouts unaware and on the wrong side of the river from Luckport. The Reshaping Team had chased them south, but the savages had managed to cross the bridge before they could be cut off.

Thomas sipped his latte (*or was it a cappuccino – they were all so good*) and reviewed the situation. His team of faux-Canadians were crossing the bridge in orderly fashion. He was confident they would make short work of the neoNatives, then swing back north and wipe out Luckport. After that it was on to Joliet and the reshaping would be done. Once their allies were wiped out, Thomas was confident the Democrats would cause no further trouble. But maybe they'd get the go-ahead to wipe out Chicago anyway.

Thomas smiled and scratched absently through his itchy shirt

Perhaps after this they'll give me my own EssBee's franchise, he thought.

Senior Lt. Grumman led his men north. There had been little resistance in Joliet – only a few tenderfoot neoNatives who had turned and run when the first shots were fired. His men continued to complain about their own scant neoNative costumes, but this was war, damn it. Now they were on the outskirts of Luckport. After that, they would turn west and wipe out the rest of the troublesome Outsiders. The Pentagon was confident that the Democrats would sit quietly by the Lake once their allies had been eliminated.

Suddenly he got a call from his scouts on the left – neoNatives were crossing the bridge. Grumman had his men form lines. But as the newcomers approached and he heard their cries and saw their ridiculous outfits he realized they were his own men – no doubt a wayward platoon.

Rather than stopping, however, the new arrivals ran straight through the Pentagon ranks.

"Canadians!" they cried. "The Canadians are coming!"

Grumman looked west. A group of what appeared to be heavily-armed lumberjacks was crossing the bridge in force. He hawked and spit.

"Prepare for battle, men!" he called. "Let's push these Canucks back to Wisconsin!"

So it was that Avery became the unlikely hero of the Battle of Luckport. The tactic worked better than expected. Both sides nearly wiped each other out, and the few stragglers were quickly eliminated by the small Luck force. Sadly, though, (as one of the Slacks later noted) several cows were victims of collateral damage.

As Wize had predicted, Avery was given full credit for the victory, despite having done no more than crouch bare-chested in a church steeple.

When they marched into Orland Park that evening, Ted was the first to greet them. She ran up to Avery and kissed him full on the lips.

"Now you are no longer a Nap, but a Luck!" she said happily.

Alex approached, frowning more deeply than usual.

"We'd better get to the mall," he said, gently but firmly leading Ted away by the arm.

The mall, at least the part that hadn't collapsed, was not dissimilar to an atrium in Naperville, except that it was only a few stories high. It was open in the middle, with glassed-off rooms around the perimeter. A second floor was accessed by a rusting escalator. The hallways leading away from the area had been recently bricked off.

On one side was what appeared to be a rehabbed cafeteria, and it was to this area they headed. After an impromptu ceremony celebrating the victory, food was served. Ted was busy with her father, so Avery and Wize had time to talk.

"So you have many names," he said as they sat down with their trays of food.

"I am known by many names to many people," Wize said.

"Hey Wize – get your ass out of my seat!" a man called as he approached.

They moved to another table.

"Although I never seem to get the respect I deserve," Wize added quietly.

"But you're not really a security guard from the Docks?"

"Oh, I am!" Wize said through a mouthful of yams. "At least, I was at one point. But that's a long story and, frankly, I don't remember it much."

Avery watched while the big man ate (he could really pack it in). There was so much he wanted to ask him.

"Why did you give me that exploding chair?" he asked finally.

"Mistake," Wize said between gulps of cider. "Big mistake, in fact. The incendiary chairs weren't supposed to be planted until later. Now Naperville is on alert and we've had to take added measures to confuse them." A mischievous look crossed his face. "You ever seen a dancing credenza?"

"A what?"

"It's animatronic stuff," Wize explained. "We get it from WaltCorp Playmation."

Avery shook his head. He was getting nowhere.

"So – what are you?" he asked.

Wize looked serious for a moment, which was difficult with all the gravy stains on his sweater.

"I'm the Chief of Staff. The second in command. I work for President Adams."

"You work for the United States Government?" Avery said, stunned. "But that's not a real entity. It has no power. It's not even a corporation, for Prosperity's sake!"

"It used to be important," Wize said. "And it might be again."

Avery shrugged and sipped his water.

"Let me ask you something," Wize continued. "What do you think will happen to the Lucks, the Democrats, the Tribes – and the peoples north and south of the Transcontinental Corridor once the thing is completed?"

Avery considered this, his gaze straying to a faded sign that read *Orange Julius*. He wondered who Julius had been, and how he got the nickname. He looked back at Wize and shrugged.

"Up until a week ago, I didn't know there were any real people on the Outside. I thought you were all savages and mutants."

"That may soon be the case. For years, the corporations have spread west to east, cutting off trade and travel between north and south. In less than a month the two segments of Outsiders will be cut off from each other completely."

"That'd be May 10. Unification Day," Avery added. "But what can you do about it?"

"Punch a hole in it," Wize said. "Right through Naperville."

Avery looked at a grease stain on Wize's ample stomach and wondered if he was more dangerous than he appeared.

"But – you can't," he said. "I mean – it's Naperville."

"Hey, we have a right to live, same as any associate in any corporation."

Avery, who had experienced only corporate life, knew nothing about rights. Like the chicken bone protruding from Wize's mouth, it was a lot to chew on.

"Wow," he said finally.

"Exactly!" Wize noted. "Hey – you want some pudding?"

Chief Shabbona sat a few tables away, unnoticed. He was dressed impeccably, as usual, but without the usual tie and silk jacket. He took a drag on his Cuban cigar (his last) and nodded toward Avery.

"Have you checked out our new hero?" he asked.

"Yes, Chief," replied John Deere, who was sitting to Shabbona's right. Although young, John Deere was the head of security for Shabbona's casinos. He was busily typing on an ancient laptop computer.

"And would you say he has a chip on his shoulder," Shabbona asked.

"I would say he has a chip in his shoulder *blade*," Deere replied without looking up. "Do you want me to remove it?"

"Any news on Illiniwek?"

"Turned like a dog and ran at the first shot, sir."

Shabbona sighed. "At least he's okay. That's something."

"Yes, sir."

"You look thin, John. Have some pierogi. I recommend the mushroom."

CHAPTER 22

SNAPPYCO: Rethinking, Reshaping, Rejoicing
TRANSCONTINENTAL MERGER PROGRESS REPORT
CLASSIFIED – SENIOR SNAPPYCO PERSONNEL ONLY
April 14, 113 PNYP (Post Ten-Year Plan)
From: Kathie Wozniak, Special Assistant to Sen. V.P. of Tomorrow
To: Andrew Gates, Sen. V.P of Tomorrow

The good news is that the project – with one notable exception – is complete. The Sacramento-Bettendorf corridor is open for business. Likewise, the Pentagon has completed their corridor from Langley to Danville. All that remains to be completed is a short stretch east of the Quad Cities.

Unfortunately, Naperville is still behind schedule. Most of the reasons were outlined in my previous report; however, I was informed today of a few new challenges. Attendees at this morning's project update meeting included: Major Electric (Pentagon), the Lowest Down (Naperville), Bill Smith (Overland Park), President Adams (who was taking minutes) and myself.

WORK SLOWDOWN. It turns out that despite impressive efforts on the part of Naperville's Employee Assistance Program, there has been a work slowdown by the manual laborers. I have again offered our assistance, but their Lowest Down is extremely reluctant to accept it. I think he believes (rightly so) that it would make Naperville appear even weaker in the eyes of its partners than it already does.

Naperville has recently transferred massive numbers of associates to the Quad Cities work site and we can only hope this will have a positive effect. I relayed the strong desire on the part of our stockholders that the project be completed in time for the May 10 Completion Celebration. The Lowest Down said he is aware of the concern since many of these interests also own stock in Naperville Corp.

THE LUCKPORT INCIDENT. Our covert Reshaping Team has met with a challenging learning experience. In light of the misunderstanding at Luckport, the team has thought it best to secure their holdings in the rest of Northern Illinois and take no additional action at this time. To do so might elicit a harsher response from the other North American corporations than the letters of protest sent through President Adams. I'm afraid we've done all the reshaping we can at present.

To end on a note of rejoicing, the Lowest Down seems genuinely confident that these problems can be resolved and the project completed on time. He hinted that the Outsider threat will soon be eliminated. Since we have no alternative at present (unless you can suggest something) we may as well take him at his word.

Did you get the souvenir I sent from Huck Finn Rock? They serve an exotic dish there called Corn Dogs (no, it's not made from *dogs*, silly). When the Merger is completed we can visit there together.

Kathie

p.s.: Have you told your wife about us yet?

CHAPTER 23

Wunderlic, Lower Down of Employee Assistance, stood on a hastily-assembled balcony overlooking the final work site for the Transcontinental Merger Project. He was more than sixteen levels above the ground, if you included the depth of the excavation pit, and hoped no one would notice how desperately he clung to the railing. Wunderlic didn't like heights to begin with – and you never knew when an Outside wind would kick up unexpectedly.

Despite his nervousness, he appreciated the view. It was barely two gigacubes from the Naperville site to its Overland Park counterpart, which ended abruptly over the Illinois bank of the Mississippi. But that still left a sixteen-level, gigacube-wide segment to complete in less than a month. The Lower Downs had sent all nonessential personnel west to work on the project and, thanks to the extremely competent Weeds, that included most associates below the level of director. And even middle managers had relocated near the Quad Cities so they could do eight hours a day of indoor labor. Some complained – until they were given a glimpse of the Outside work site.

Looking out, he could see associates hauling lumber and pushing wheelbarrows with what could truly be called reckless abandon. Even from this height there were clear signs of side effects from the stimulants – a deadly altercation or sudden self-retirement – but all in all things seemed to be moving ahead.

The air in Wunderlic's biohazard suit seemed suddenly hot and stale (the suit was an added precaution; he had already been inoculated). He checked the air hose for kinks; there were none. Still, he could feel the first twinges of panic. He forced himself to breathe steadily and look toward the horizon, a simple relaxation technique.

After a full minute of this, his pulse slowed to an acceptable rate. The panic seemed to be subsiding. He focused on the reassuringly familiar sounds of human anguish coming from the construction site: moaning, cursing, sudden bursts of argument, whistling.

Whistling?

He cocked his head. Amid the normal sounds of construction and misery, a continuous whistle was clearly audible. It was a tune, a bouncy, happy tune!

Wunderlic searched for the source, swiveling his head in an avian fashion. The sound offended him, like a flat not in a symphony. The whistler, it turned out, was directly beneath him, not four levels down. The man stood perilously on an extended girder, hauling up a pallet of supplies. This polo shirt was torn and stained, but still recognizable as the baby blue of Premium Services.

A gust of wind jolted both Wunderlic and the worker, and panic of the former rushed back. He let out a sharp cry, which was muffled by the biohazard suit.

The worker, having apparently heard Wunderlic's cry, looked up and smiled broadly. Then he waved.

"Howdy do!" he called.

Wunderlic gripped the railing more tightly. Then he made the mistake of looking past the worker to the ground sixteen levels below. His legs became margarine. He started to hyperventilate: he couldn't catch his breath, nor could he back away from the railing. Finally, he fell down and crawled back to the storm door.

Once inside, Wunderlic yanked off his hood and gulped the cool, dry indoor air. He used the door frame to pull himself up and looked around the room. There were only a few associates about and none had noticed his behavior, or were wise enough to pretend otherwise. He brushed himself off and headed back to the bullet train.

It had been a bad month for the old Premium Services associates. One day they were the darlings of Naperville, the next they were on a forced march to the Quad Cities. No warning or reason had been given for the transfer, and the Internal Audit troopers who hurried them through the corridors were not exactly talkative. In fact, any time one of the associates stumbled or stopped to ask a question, they were beaten or stunned. The rest soon learned to keep their mouths shut.

They made the seventy-gigacube trek in just three days. Not exactly a world record, but for a group not used to the exertion, it was quite a hardship. About thirty of them – mainly the elderly – did not finish the journey. Upon arrival at the work site, they were inoculated, issued generic work clothes and sent directly to work. This consisted mostly of hauling building materials and digging ditches. The days were long, the conditions were wet and cold and the food inadequate and oddly bitter.

During the first week, several Premium Services employees went into retirement by throwing themselves into the Mississippi River or in front of heavy machinery. It was a behavior not peculiar to the newcomers.

Despite these hardships, many of the Premium Services associates maintained a positive attitude, Kensington being the foremost. They could take away his perks, his luxuries and his easy life, but one thing remained – his self-esteem.

Wunderlic, the Employee Assistance Lower Down, had miscalculated. The Premium Services experiment had not been a complete failure. A lifetime of unconditional positive regard had given Kensington and many of his co-workers a rock-solid self concept. He knew deep down that he was a valuable person, and he would demand respect. It also didn't hurt that he was a born salesman and a fourth-level initiate in Neuro-Synaptic Programming. He can, and had, sold hundreds of extended warranties on broken appliances.

The guards knew he was different sort of worker by lunchtime of the first day when they were slopping a yellow-black muck onto the workers' trays. Most laborers either shuffled along, exhausted, or hopped anxiously from one foot to the other, pumped full of stimulants. Kensington did neither; he simply stopped.

"I can't eat this," he told them.

"Move it or I'll club you," a large, humorless guard told him.

He didn't budge. "I'm serious. I require a vegetarian meal."

Another guard came forward, wielding a stun rod. The other workers backed away in fear, but Kensington did not move. He simply smiled, as if nothing were out of the ordinary and he was merely waiting for an ice cream cone. The second guard raised his rod, but hesitated.

"Sorry to be a bother," Kensington said with the utmost courtesy.

Unsure what to do, the guards huddled in conversation.

"Wait over there," the largest guard told him when they had concluded.

"Certainly," he said.

From then on, Kensington received fresh vegetables and bread, along with some dairy and legumes. He never neglected to say thank you.

The work was grueling, but no one worked harder than Kensington. A few weeks later, however, he decided to take a break. It was late in the afternoon, after one of his best friends (the older woman who had trapped Avery) had tried to kill herself with a nail gun. Kensington straightened up, dabbing his forehead with his neckerchief, and walked over to a hooded Internal Audit trooper.

"Back to work!" the trooper yelled.

Kensington ignored the order. He gazed up at the sky as if it were the most beautiful day he had ever seen – though actually it was cold and cloudy.

"I have an idea I'd like to run by you," he told the trooper, who was just about to club Kensington. "I believe it would increase productivity for my group."

"Your group?" the trooper replied.

"Excuse me – Premium Services. We're kind of a team here," Kensington explained.

The trooper stood motionless. It was hard to gauge his mood through the black hood.

"Look," Kensington continued. "The goal is to complete the project on time, right? We're all on the same page with that, aren't we? I mean, aren't we?"

"Uh. Sure," the trooper said uncertainly.

"Sure we are!" Kensington said. "Now let me outline the problem as I see it: you need us to work hard. That's reasonable. So you put stimulants in the food to make us work hard. Only it makes us die off quicker – or self-retire. I mean, look at these people."

He gestured to the thousand or so workers in the pit beneath them, a hundred or so of whom were currently exhibiting psychotic behavior. One man directly below them was wildly swinging his shovel to ward off an invisible flying pest.

"It's not efficient," Kensington continued. "So here's my idea, um – what's your name again?"

"Fellowes," the trooper replied softly.

"Fellowes. Great. I'm Kensington, by the way. Anyway, here's my idea, for what it's worth – stop giving us the drugs. Not everybody. Don't want to rock the boat. Just Premium Services. Give it a try. See if we don't get a lot more done than our doped-up comrades. Not that there's anything wrong with that. It'll make us look good. It'll make Fellowes look good. We'll meet the deadline. And everyone's happy."

Fellowes made no reply.

"Well – just an idea," Kensington said. "Just thought I'd run it up the flagpole and all that. Thank you for listening, Fellowes. I've got to get back to work now."

The next day all of Premium Services was on the vegetarian plan. And, as Kensington had promised, they were twice as productive as the other workers.

But Kensington had bigger plans.

Because Kensington was not really happy. In fact, he was very angry. The corporation had transferred him, and he could live with that. They had tried to drug him and retire him, and he understood that. They had turned their backs on him and his co-workers, but that was business. However, Naperville had done one other thing, one unforgivable thing that made him their enemy for life.

They had killed the love of his life – his dog Queenie. And for that he would make them pay.

Three Lower Downs stood impatiently around a console in the Internal Audit control room. Hon and Adler (of Facilities) were patiently explaining the panel of lights and buttons to the unusually impatient Lowest Down.

"All right, all right – so each of these buttons fires one of our surface-to-surface missiles, correct?" he said, reaching toward the panel.

Adler brushed his superior's hands away as politely as possible.

"Yes, sir," he explained. "We just have a few more adjustments to make and we're all set – "

"Got it," the Lowest Down said, cutting Adler off. "So you press once to arm it and twice to fire it – "

He pressed one of the glowing buttons. Adler's eyes widened. Hon, however, maintained his composure.

"You just launched a missile," he said.

The Lowest Down almost looked up with an expression of curiosity, which was the closest he came to remorse.

"Where was it aimed?" he asked.

"Southern Indiana, fortunately. I don't think anyone will notice. Besides, these are just tactical weapons, not the big boys," Hon said.

"I'll take the blame on that one," Adler said diplomatically. "We haven't retargeted the missiles yet."

Bush, manning his monitoring station nearby, cast a quick, impish glance at his co-worker, Snoop. The other man, however, was in no mood for humor. His short trip to the Outside had been very unlucky for him.

For one thing, he hadn't enjoyed the company of the IA troopers, who had somehow discovered his nickname. *What's the matter, Snoop – break a fingernail?* they would say. Or, *Hey Snoop – can you see which finger I'm holding up behind you?* And that was nothing compared to the inappropriate use of the stun rods.

Then there was the Outside itself: the bugs and the mud and all that wild vegetation. And the whole time he was completely exposed. Just thinking about it made him shudder involuntarily.

The worse part was being bit by the wild dog. At least it was the size of a dog. The troopers gave him no sympathy, of course – no sympathy for Snoop – as they dragged him back to the Docks where a business-like medic roughly stitched the wound and gave him a series of painful shots.

"And when can you get us the new coordinates?" Adler was asking Hon.

"We know where the Lucks and Natives are, thanks to the tracer we implanted on the customer service associate, Avery. We're just waiting for the Democratic Army to join them."

That's right, Esselte fumed. *All my misfortune had been for nothing.* The suspect was long gone, just as Hon knew he would be. He cast a malevolent, sideways glance at Hon. He now realized he was in a dead-end job. Sure, he was a direct-report to a Lower Down, but he would never advance beyond being what he was – a Snoop.

"Yes," the Lowest Down said. "I've also got my sources. Hon and I will provide you with the coordinates when the time comes."

"Yes, Lowest," said Adler.

"In the meantime let's keep this room secure," the Lowest Down added. "We don't want any more accidents."

"That shouldn't be a problem, sir. We're virtually the only people on this end of Naperville."

"So, any other pressing business?" The Lowest Down seemed anxious to leave.

Hon hesitated. "Just that, um, we've been receiving a lot of calls from the Weeds."

"Tell them to wait – we'll soon have plenty of work for them."

"It's not that. They're worried about Avery," Hon said. Then seeing his superior's look of confusion added, "The customer service rep – he was training them."

"Hmm," the Lowest Down said, looking incredibly bored.

When the Lowest Down arrived back in his first-level office, a sad young man in tattered buckskins was sitting in the reception area. The executive ushered him in.

"What have you got for me?" the Lowest Down said as he closed the door.

Illiniwek plopped down on a guest chair. "The Pentagon forces have taken Joliet," he stated.

"The Pentagon forces have been wiped out by the SnappyCo forces," the elder man replied. "They destroyed each other in Luckport. Where the hell have you been?"

"I've been," he looked down at his belt, "on the run."

"Running from a fight is more likely."

"I need money," Illiniwek said. "And another gun."

The Lowest Down looked Illiniwek over.

"I'll give you a little more money," he said at last, "but you're not getting another gun until you bring me back some useful information."

"How am I supposed to do that?"

"Go back to your father. Find out what they're up to."

Illiniwek nodded, but made no move to get up.

"What are you waiting for?" the Lowest Down asked.

"Can I use your shower?"

"Hell no!"

The Lowest Down watched as the young neoNative shuffled out of the room. The wrinkles on his oddly-tanned face sharpened into a pensive expression. Illiniwek had thus far proven to be useless. He wondered if it was time to retire him. Then he wondered if Outsiders even used that term.

No wait, he remembered, *they call it* killing.

May at the Quad Cites work site was, after eight days of rain, sunny and warm. With the deadline only weeks away, the drug-addled associates were working even harder than ever, although the results were somewhat mixed.

Premium Services was the exception. Fortified with healthy, stimulant-free meals and motivated by Kensington, the little crew of formerly unskilled laborers was clearing debris and pouring foundations at an above-average pace. On the surface, it was a win-win for Kensington's group and their IA overseer, Fellowes.

Kensington looked out over the work pit. The gigacube-wide, sixteen-story Grand Atrium, the ceremonial junction of the Transcontinental Merger Corridor, was nearly complete; a hundred-cube gap was all that remained to be built. Despite the dry air, Kensington was drenched with sweat from that morning's exertion.

"We need more dynamite," he said.

Trooper Fellowes, standing nearby, groaned audibly. It had been in his best interest to ensure that Premium Services excelled, and that often meant providing special materials the other teams didn't have access to; but he wasn't sure his superiors would look kindly on his providing explosives to what were for all intents and purposes slaves.

"Listen, I appreciate everything you've done for us," Kensington said smoothly. "You stuck your neck out for us on the meals, and we appreciate it. I mean, we've only had two of our people retire in the month we've been here. And we've held up our end of the deal by getting twice as much done as any other team – "

"Yeah, but if I get caught – "

"Think about it this way," Kensington replied, looking the hooded man in what he assumed were his eyes. "What happens to you if we miss the deadline?"

Fellowes didn't reply, but the other man knew he was weighing his options.

Kensington descended back into the pit, where his team was laying the charges to blow a hole in the ground that would hold the foundation for yet another girder.

"Don't put it too deep!" he hissed to one of his co-workers. "We just want it to look good."

Indeed the dynamite, which was buried under a foot or so of loose dirt, made quite a show when it exploded, yet barely put a dent in the ground. Most of the excavation was done by shovel.

Kensington always made good use of the leftover dynamite, although what exactly he did with it late at night he told no one but LePage. And since LePage had retired he carried on the nocturnal project alone.

CHAPTER 24

Avery never ceased to be surprised. He was just getting used to losing his career, and adjusting to Outside life – and now he was suddenly a hero. It was pleasant, to be sure, but a new experience nevertheless. People were always giving him gifts, old women giving him bread and Slacks giving him slaps on the back.

But it wasn't all fun and gluttony. The Democratic leaders had arrived and preparations had to be made for a strategy meeting. Avery, despite his new-found reputation, didn't know an enfilade from a flank. He volunteered to help set up chairs.

"That's good," said Ted as they unloaded folding chairs. "You aren't letting success go to your head."

"I didn't really do anything."

"You had the right idea at the right time – that's important," she noted, and kissed him on the cheek.

Ted's affection was another surprise that took getting used to. He was so distracted with everything else that he didn't quite know how to react. He thought of telling her about Sauder; finding her was, after all, the reason he escaped the Docks in the first place. But he didn't know where to look for her. Or how. And, if he was honest with himself, he was physically attracted to Ted in a way he had never been to Sauder. Her body was like a magnet.

Avery's biggest surprise came when the Democrats arrived. The mayoral team arrived on bicycle, a group of fifty or so. Being a hero, Avery was introduced to the Mayor himself, a stocky, sweaty man named Michael John Daley. As he was shaking the man's hand, his eyes spotted a familiar face in the delegation.

"Sauder!?" he cried, forgetting the politician completely. She looked different – longer hair and dressed in spandex – but it was her. He picked her up and hugged her.

"You'll have to excuse our hero," Shabbona said to the Mayor. "He seems to have run into an old friend."

But the Mayor was not one to stand on ceremony. He merely smiled.

"Gentlemen," he said, "let me proudly introduce the newest proud member of my *mayoral* team. Sauder is our City Historian. She's been doing a lot of research for us at Hyde Park University, as well as in writing a history of my family tradition."

Sauder bowed slightly.

"Go on," Daley said. "Go catch up with each other. I'll call you when I need you."

Avery and Sauder hadn't wandered far when they ran into Ted.

"Oh – Ted!" Avery said, running his hand through his red mop of hair. "This is Sauder. We both escaped from the Docks – well, not at the same time – "

"So she's the other Nap," Ted said coolly.

"Well, yes. But she's more than that. She's my – " It suddenly occurred to him that this was an uncomfortable situation. "She's, uh…"

He looked to Sauder.

"Yes," she said, "I'm an, uh, what?"

Both women waited. Avery stammered nervously, "She's the one I came to save," he explained weakly.

Ted's eyes narrowed to slits.

"Well. I guess you can both go home now!" she said, then stomped off.

Avery watched her leave. Then he turned to Sauder, but he couldn't read her expression. This was not the reunion he had imagined. *Did things always change so quickly on the Outside?* He wondered.

"She, uh, tried to shoot me," he said at last.

"I can see that," Sauder said.

The two retired to some folding chairs at the back of the atrium. Avery recounted his journey to, and escape from, the Docks. Then it was Sauder's turn.

She had indeed taken the Short Brothers' boat and headed northeast. It was a strenuous trip upstream, but Sauder was in good shape and made steady progress. One of her books had had a map of the Chicago area, so she had a vague idea of where the river would lead (unfortunately, the other books were still somewhere in the Docks).

She bypassed the Casino town of Joliet, which looked like a good place to get robbed or worse, and was going to do the same at Luckport. But Luckport had locks on the river, and she was apprehended while trying to portage around them. They took her to the church where she, having read of the practice somewhere, threw herself on the altar and begged sanctuary. Alex wanted to kill her, but the Slacks talked him out of it.

There followed an intense interrogation over tea and cookies, during which Sauder described her escape. Alex, however, still felt she might be a security risk, possibly even a Nap spy.

Fortunately, Wize dropped in just at that moment, having smelled the freshly-baked cookies.

It turned out that Wize had heard from President Wilson about Sauder's misfortune and had decided to help her if he could. Her transfer to the Docks was, after all, indirectly caused by the guard's gift of the exploding chair to Avery. She told him of her desire to reach the great university in Chicago, if it still existed. Wize offered to drive her to Chicago himself, since he had business there.

She was disappointed by her first glimpse of the once-great city.

"We could see the ruins of the Sears Tower almost as soon as we started," she said softly. "And along the route there were a few intact exit signs – large faded green rectangles – pointing the way to Indiana, Wisconsin and Midway Airport.

"As we neared the city, more ruins were visible – towering metal skeletons. I could see the old Standard Oil Building in the distance. It looked like a broken tooth.

"As we neared downtown – the Loop they used to call it – the damage and decay became obvious. Square miles had been burnt out long ago, then rebuilt, then abandoned. Prairie grass had overgrown most of the blocks, and there were few people to be seen."

Downtown itself was thriving. A permanent market had been set up around a queer steel statue in a place they call Daley Plaza, and there was active trading of grains, produce, livestock – and books! The streets were orderly and the buildings (at least the first few floors) seemed well-maintained."

Sauder said she had wanted to explore immediately, but Wize insisted on taking her directly to the Mayor's office. They had a long wait, since the main corridor was filled with favor-seekers and other party officials. Finally, one of the clerks escorted them to Mayor Daley himself, who was sitting at his paper-strewn desk, wolfing down a corned beef sandwich. He quickly read through the messages delivered by Wize and was about to dismiss them when Sauder decided to speak.

"I've seen media of the original Mayor Daley," she blurted, "and I can see the family resemblance."

That was all it took. Daley handed her the other half of his sandwich and insisted she join him for lunch. They spent the next two hours discussing Chicago history (much to the annoyance of the lobbyists who were kept waiting). He put Sauder and Wize up at the best hotel, the Viceroy.

The next morning, he took her on a bike ride along Lake Michigan (Sauder rode in the back). Having never seen anything bigger than a small river (and that only recently), Sauder was overwhelmed with the choppy expanse of water that extended to the eastern horizon. The Mayor was so impressed with her knowledge of history he appointed Sauder City Historian.

"But what about the university?" Avery asked.

"His Honor said once the present crisis is resolved, he'll do what he can to get me in. It's a little tricky because Hyde Park University is technically in Independent territory," she explained.

Avery frowned. "What are they independent *of?*"

"Don't know yet," Sauder laughed. "His Honor says I should fit in because there are a lot of other black people."

"What does that mean?"

"Don't know that yet either. I think it has to do with skin color."

"That seems arbitrary."

They watched a young Slack walk by carrying a burlap sack filled with rifles. Avery remembered Jackson's careless handling of a pistol.

Chris Bittler

"Do you know what they're planning to do?" he asked, waving his hand to indicate the whole collection of Outsiders.

"I guess that's what we're here to decide."

Sauder crossed her arms and looked up at him. "So … , tell me about this Ted."

The convention of Outside tribes was delayed several times due, apparently, to extensive backroom negotiations. Avery and Sauder, who were left out of most of these unofficial talks, found themselves with time to kill. They explored the land surrounding the mall, avoiding the crumbling commercial structures. As they did, Avery grew more accustomed to being Outside (though Avery still preferred having a roof over his head).

Sometimes Ted joined them, and sometimes she took them hunting. Avery would neither hunt nor fish, but Sauder actually caught a small-mouth bass and pulled the hook out of its mouth herself.

Despite Ted's initial coolness, the two women were getting along well. Avery let it go, hoping to avoid – or at least delay – any unpleasantness.

Finally, about a week before the May 10 Completion Day Ceremony, the Outsiders had their official confab. Most of the Lucks and Slacks were in attendance (although the Slacks tended to nod or wander off), along with virtually every member of Shabbona's Illini. The Democratic Army marched in, two thousand strong. The force included everyone on the city or party payroll, from precinct captains on down to superfluous maintenance workers.

The leaders assembled on a hastily-constructed platform in the mall atrium: Alex and the Luck elders, Shabbona and his assistants, and Mayor Daley and his chief of staff. Also on the platform, off to the side as if an afterthought, the Wizened Security Guard sat drinking a can of soda.

Avery joined Ted and Sauder in the front row. Farther down was a sullen, shirtless young man who had introduced himself as the Chief of the Fighting Illini.

Alex was the first to step to the microphone stand, amid cheers from the Lucks.

"We Lucks are a peaceful people, a hard-working people . . . above all, a good people. *(Cheers.)* Many of our ancestors came from Northern Eurafrica to build a better life here. And we did just that. Long ago, we helped build this great state – and with our bare hands we rebuilt Luckport! *(Cheers.)*

And through it all we have strived to live at peace with our neighbors: the Joliet tribe *(cheers)*, the Democrats *(cheers)*, the Independents and others.

"But the corporation to the south has not been so neighborly. *(Boos.)* They have stripped us of our resources and stolen our shipments. The corporation to the south has sent its allies to wipe us out in an unprovoked attack – which we only avoided through the bravery of our men and the quick thinking of our new hero, Avery!"

At this, the crowd began cheering and wouldn't stop until the hero in question reluctantly stood up and bowed.

"And now this so-called neighbor, this *Naperville* wants to cut us off completely! *(Jeers.)* Well, I say the time for peace is over. It is time to take back the State of Illinois and the United States of America! *(Cheers.)* Luckporters – it is time to fight!"

The convention went on like this most of the day, with stirring speeches from the leaders. Chief Shabbona emphasized the importance of free access to the Illinois River (and thereby the Mississippi), noting that the legendary Abraham Lincoln (whom Avery had always thought as fictional as the Wizened Security Guard) started a war over the issue. It was Mayor Daley's speech, however, that provided the most entertainment, albeit unintentional.

He started smoothly enough, with only a smattering of malaprops and spoonerisms. And his loyal patronage army didn't seem to notice, cheering him on with gusto. It was only toward the end that things got a little dicey.

"Our enemy is aggressive," he read woodenly, squinting at his notes, "but we will be *over*aggressive! They are smart, but we will be, uh – too smart! We will fight each other – uh – with each other – "

Confused, the once-cheering crowd quieted down.

"I mean – we will each keep fighting until each other has defeated Naperville once and for all!"

There was a smattering of applause, and the determined politician stumbled on.

"As the great Revolutionary leader Benjamin Franklin once said. . ."

"I gave him this quote," Sauder whispered proudly to Avery.

". . . if we all hang separately, we will surely hang together."

The crowd was silent. The mayor cast about for something to add. The crowd grew restless. Suddenly, the mayor's eyes brightened.

"Go White Sox!" he cried.

The crowd burst in applause. This was followed by a half an hour of the kind of chanting and chest-thumping that occurs just after war has been declared but before it is actually experienced.

The unanimous decision had been reached – they were going to war with Naperville. With the Completion Ceremony just days away, there was no time to waste; they would march out the very next day.

After the chanting, Wize took the stage and tried to lead the crowd in something called *The National Anthem*, but since no one knew the words, he quickly switched to *Take Me Out to the Ballgame*, followed by *The Mickey Mouse Club* and something called *YMCA*. It was a rousing success.

Meanwhile, one little shirtless Indian sat brooding.

The specific battle plan was left to Alex, Shabbona and the Mayor. Sauder, although officially a member of the mayor's staff, was again left out. Not that she felt she had much to contribute.

The plan of battle turned out to be relatively simple. The army was divided into two groups of about two thousand each. The first contingent would be jointly led by Wize and Vince Daley, the Mayor's brother. Avery and Sauder would accompany them and serve as guides. Their mission was to enter Naperville through the Docks and fight their way west.

The second group, led by Alex and including Shabbona, Mayor Daley and Ted, would attack the corporation about seven gigacubes to the west.

Four thousand soldiers seems a woefully inadequate number for an attack on a modern corporate campus containing millions of associates. But there were several factors that made such an attack, if not easy, at least feasible.

First, most of Naperville's associates were not used to any type of physical exertion, much less fighting and killing – and nearly all of them had by now been sent to the Quad Cities to help finish the Transcontinental Merger Project. The Outsiders, on the other hand, were used to manual labor and many, when necessary, fighting.

Second, the number of actual security forces in Naperville (security guards, Internal Audit troopers, Risk Management officers) was relatively small. Security cost money, after all.

Third, the Outsiders had been preparing for war for several years. The Lucks had become adept at the use of bows and slingshots (both fierce weapons in ancient times), and the Democrats had produced munitions launched primarily by trebuchets. In addition, they had smuggled in a large cache of standard weapons.

Finally, the Outsiders' goal was not to destroy Naperville, but merely punch a whole in the sixteen-story, 150-mile-wide structure. Their secret weapon in this quest was the office chair.

In recent years Wize and other rebel security guards had been planting exploding chairs in the Naperville Campus (one of which, unfortunately, ended up in Avery's cube). They had been strategically placed in a line running north and south through the heart of the structure. This was where Alex's army hoped to enter Naperville. From there, the plan was to secure a large swath of the campus and force an agreement with the corporation.

Exploding chairs don't grow on trees, of course. They had been graciously provided by Halliburton and smuggled in from the south by WaltCorp with their regular deliveries to WaltMart stores. The fact that an attack on Naperville also served those corporations' interest was just a happy coincidence.

Wize explained this to Avery and Sauder as they marched back toward the Docks at the head of their army a few days later. It was a ragtag bunch, lightly provisioned and not especially disciplined; but, a half day into the march, they seemed enthusiastic.

"Didn't my chair exploding tip them off?" Avery asked.

"We were afraid of that," Wize wheezed between gulps of breath (walking had never been his favorite mode of transport). "That's why we sent in the animatronic furniture – to throw them off the scent. Hopefully, they thought the chair was just another piece of defective WaltMart junk."

"I don't know. I'm sure they suspect something," Sauder said. "I mean, they sure thought you were a threat – and they knew you had contact with Avery."

Wize sighed. "If we had had more time, we would have had a better plan."

They stopped for the night at the interchange for an old east-west road. A broken white sign indicated it was Rt. 52. The weather was clear and the army made camp wherever it could.

Sauder studied the group from her perch atop the overpass. Vince, the mayor's brother, was sitting next to her. He had taken a shoe off and was examining a blister on his toe.

"Did you train this group?" she asked him.

161

Vince looked up in surprise. "Me? Hell, no. I don't know nothing about that stuff." He resumed his foot inspection.

"But you're their leader, right?"

"I guess," Vince answered vaguely. "Mike said not to worry too much about it. It would all work out."

Sauder looked out over the group. In the fading light she could see confrontations breaking out as people argued over food and blankets. She hoped they would fight better than they camped.

It was pitch black, and the only sounds were the soft breathing of Ted and Vince – and Wize's nasal whistling. Avery was warm and cozy inside the large tent, wrapped in a thick wool blanket. But he couldn't sleep.

It wasn't the imminent battle, though, that weighed heavy on his mind. Nor was it his intense dislike for the critters that could be (and probably were) creeping nearby. No, Avery's insomnia was directly tied to a growing soreness in his upper back. He had first noticed it while working on the Docks, but had brushed it off as one of the miscellaneous injuries he daily incurred there. After escaping, he was too preoccupied to think much about it.

Now, though, in the quiet of the night, he could think of little else. It was a sharp, throbbing pain on his shoulder blade, just beyond his reach. And it was getting worse. He tried to ignore it, but after a few hours it was simply unbearable.

He climbed out of his sleeping bag and felt around for something with which to scratch the spot. In the process, he woke Sauder.

"What is it?" she whispered, fearing trouble.

"I think I've got a bug bite."

"Where?"

"On my back."

A blinding light cut through the tent. Sauder's flashlight.

"Let me see," she said.

Avery took off his shirt, revealing his skeletal back. A nasty red bump was clearly visible on the pale skin.

"It looks infected," Sauder said, frowning. "Did you have anybody look at this?"

"Yeah," Avery replied, wincing as Sauder poked the sore. "Shabbona's guy – John. He said not to worry about it."

"That's odd."

"Hey kids – no hanky-panky in my tent!" Wize said groggily.

"Look at this," Sauder said. "It's all red and blotchy."

"Yeah, that really sounds like something I want to see."

"Get over here and hold the flashlight," she commanded.

"What are you going to do?" Avery asked nervously.

"Just clean it."

Avery heard her open a plastic case and rip open a package. He felt a slight sting, followed by a cool sensation.

"Just some alcohol," Sauder said.

"Here – I got it," Avery heard Wize say, followed by a stab of pain.

"Ow!"

"Wize – I sterilized it for a reason!" Sauder said.

"Hey, it needed popping – I popped it."

Avery felt Sauder's fingers on his back.

"He's probably right," she told the patient. "I'm just going to clean it – *again* – and put some – " She paused.

"What?" Avery asked. "What is it?"

"Wize, is there something in there?" she asked.

"Let me take off my glasses," Wize said. "These things are practically useless."

Avery's thought of the terrifying possibilities: leeches, burrowing insects, possibly even lobster eggs.

"Probably a sliver," she reassured him. "I'm just going to pull it out."

Avery felt Sauder digging around with what felt like a large knife but was actually a pair of tweezers.

"Got it," she said.

Avery turned around and the three examined the object. It was smooth and gray and looked to be about a quarter inch square.

"That," Wize said definitely, "is a tracer. An Internal Audit tracer."

Sauder put the tiny device on a rock and was going to crush it with another. Wize stopped her.

"Wait," he said. "Let's think about this."

"But they know where we are – right now!" she said.

"Yeah, but if we crush it they'll *know* we know."

"So?" she asked.

"I don't know," Wize mused. "That's why we should think about it."

Avery gestured toward Vince, who had been sleeping soundly through the whole conversation. "Should we tell him?"

"In the morning," Wize said, lying back down. "In the morning."

CHAPTER 25

While Wize was prodding Avery's shoulder blade with a knife, the other half of the Army was sleeping comfortably in Luckport. Even though they had a longer journey to their point of attack, the leadership was in no hurry.

"The vehicles are fueled and ready," the Mayor's aide reported.

Alex, Shabbona, John Deere and Mayor Daley were in the meeting house, drinking coffee and making final plans for the attack. Ted and Illiniwek sat in the first row of benches.

"Thank you, Burke," the Mayor said. "What about the men?"

"Lights out was at 2200, with reveille at 0600 hours," Burke reported crisply.

Daley frowned at him. "We're not a real army, Burke. Just give me it to me in people time."

"A six o'clock wake-up, sir."

"We have enough supplies for ten days, which will be more than enough," Alex said.

The Chief examined the old maps in front of him; the outline of Naperville had been drawn on with red marker.

"What's the status of the radio detonators?" he asked.

"They worked perfectly in our field tests," Alex noted. "They have a range of 110 miles, which means we should get as close as possible to Naperville before detonating the line of chairs if we want a clean break all the way to the south end."

"And the trebuchets?"

"Don't worry about that," the Mayor said. "We've got forty of those babies, all mounted on flatbed trucks. They'll hurl anything from rocks to grenades."

"We've also got three howitzers in working order, with about 100 shells."

"Still, it'll be sticks and stones for most of us," Alex said.

"And Avery's army didn't even get that!" Ted said, rising.

Alex crossed to his daughter and put a reassuring hand on her arm.

"I've explained this already, *Tad-yoosh*. They have a very important job – they're the diversion. While the Naps are busy fighting them off at the Docks, we can punch a hole right through the corridor."

"But why Avery? Why Uncle Stan?"

"It has to be convincing," Shabbona said. "That's why we sent so many men with them. The mayor even sent his own brother – "

"Big loss," Daley said with a noticeable lack of fraternal concern.

"Plus, Avery has that tracker in him," Alex said. "And you know how much they hate Uncle Stan. The Naps think he's a big deal."

Ted folded her arms and sat back down. The leaders went back to their planning. Only now it was Illiniwek who interrupted.

"So you're saying," he said slowly, "that your force is actually the *main* one."

"See," Shabbona said to John Deere. "I told you he was bright."

Late the next morning, Vince Daley's diversionary army had assembled – or rather was milling about – on the interstate. With this group, an 0600 reveille was out of the question.

"Okay," Wize called out. "Anybody who has a weapon that is not a shovel or a baseball bat, please wave it in the air."

A woman in the front waved a metal tool.

"What is that you're holding up?" he asked her.

"A shovel," she called.

"Exactly," he said, then called out again: "If you have a weapon that is not – repeat, not – a shovel or a stick or a handle or a club or a bat, wave it in the air.

Fewer people waved items in the air, though most were still of the stick genre.

166

"We are completely screwed," Sauder said softly.

"Totally hosed," Avery agreed.

"Okay," Wize called out. "We're going to camp here for another day. So go out and forage. You know – look for stuff." He turned to the others. "So, who's hungry?"

The four leaders talked over an early lunch (Wize, at least, was not lightly provisioned). Avery hugged his knees moodily, and Sauder looked nervous. Even Wize ate in a more distracted manner than usual. Only Vince Daley seemed blissfully unconcerned with the situation.

"Vince, what exactly is your area of expertise?" Sauder asked finally.

"You mean, currently?" he said, choking down a mouthful of bread. "I'm Director of Tourism."

Sauder and Wize looked at each other.

"Do you get many tourists in Chicago?" Sauder asked.

Vince became defensive. "How should I know? I just started the job. I used to be Assistant Director of Public Affairs, and before that Special Maintenance Liaison."

"None of those sound like useful positions," said Avery, who understood neither patronage nor nepotism.

Sauder ignored the comment. "Those people out there – what do you make of them?"

Vince looked down uncomfortably. "There's screw-ups. Like me."

The wind picked up, blowing away the remains of Sauder's meal and knocking over her canteen. She didn't bother to pick it up.

"So – we are what? Cannon fodder?" Wize asked no one in particular.

"Looks like," Vince said, ripping off another piece of bread.

"This blows!" Wize said, getting to his feet. "Why would they waste me? I'm a legend. I'm important. I'm the Wizened Security Guard!"

"That doesn't mean wise, you know," Vince said.

A look of realization crossed Sauder's face. "You're a legend – but you're not important. Same with Avery. That's why you're both here."

Wize raised an eyebrow but said nothing.

"Have you ever heard of D-Day?" she asked them.

"Yeah!" Vince said. "Famous stripper in Joliet. Great big – "

"World War II?" she continued. "The invasion of Europe by the Allies?" The blanks expressions told her they hadn't. "Anyway, there was a famous general named Patton. The Germans thought he was the Allies' best commander and that he would be leading the main attack. But the Allied commanders were not as keen on Patton as the enemy was. So they put him in charge of a diversionary force. They figured the Germans would throw the bulk of their force against Patton rather than the main Allied invasion force.

"Wize and Avery are Patton. Naperville will think we're the main force because you two are leading us."

"Son of a buck," Wize said. "I'm a diversion."

"Then why send you and Vince?" Avery said.

Sauder shrugged. "I'm probably here to convince you two this is a legitimate army. And Vince?" She looked at him.

"I totaled my brother's limo," he said.

Wize was still confused. "So we're a fake army?"

Sauder nodded. "Just like Patton. Only instead of fake airplanes and inflatable tanks, we've got two thousand inveterate gamblers and expendable city workers."

"And black sheep," Vince added dourly.

Avery looked out across the rolling prairie, still brown from winter. It was a clear but blustery day. Lumpy cumulus clouds raced across the sky from south to north.

"I gotta think about this," he said. He climbed to his feet and ambled away. As he walked, he picked up four smooth stones and began juggling. He found that doing so calmed him and cleared his mind.

He had already been troubled about the whole war business. Finding out he was merely a decoy was just another point to ponder. *Another ball to juggle*, he thought grimly. Naperville had treated him poorly, to be sure; but he had no desire to destroy the corporation he had called home. On the other hand, the Outsiders had every right to do just that – they would die if cut off from the South. Besides, he was a Luck now.

"Wherever did you learn to do that?"

Sauder had come up behind him.

"Just something I picked up on my way to rescue you."

He was glad to see her. She was probably the only one who could understand what he was going through.

"I learned to row a boat," she said, sitting down on the trunk of a fallen elm tree.

Avery stopped juggling, neatly catching the stones one by one. "So what do you think?" he asked.

"About what?"

He shrugged. "Everything."

"Yeah," Sauder replied. "Things really got complicated in a hurry."

Avery sat down next to her.

"It's probably not the right time," he said, "but I, uh, think I'm going to ask Ted to marry me. Or whatever they do on the Outside."

Sauder watched a black bird with red on its wings fly by.

"Like you said, it's probably not the right time to talk about it."

"I just wanted to be honest with you."

"Uh, huh."

He tossed the stones away.

"So, who's side are you on?" he asked.

"Oh, I'm definitely an Outsider now. After what Naperville did to me, and what they're doing with this TransContinental Merger Project – they're going to divide the continent in two." She looked at him. "What about you?"

He thought back to their hike from Luckport, when he had seen his first dead person. It was a corporate soldier, his body twisted at an impossible angle and one foot bent the wrong way at the ankle. His abdomen was open on one side, revealing part of his rib cage. His expression was not a peaceful one.

"I think I'd just rather not fight."

"You're not thinking of providing information to the Lower Downs, are you?"

"Prosperity no," he said.

"Good," Sauder said, jumping up. "Because then I'd have to kill you." She started walking back toward the interstate. "When you're ready we should talk things over with Wize."

"And Vince," Avery added.

"I think he's already deserted," she called back.

When Avery returned he found Wize and Sauder talking. Wize, as it turned out, was in an uncharacteristically serious mood. He had decided that, diversion or not, it was his duty to lead the attack on the Docks as planned. Sauder was in agreement.

"So," Wize said, turning to Avery, "are you ready for battle?"

"No," Avery said. "But I have an idea."

Avery's plan was to sneak back into the Docks the same way Sauder had escaped — the river. Once inside he could sabotage as much of their defenses as possible, which, he reasoned, would save lives on both sides. He was also hoping to get the Short Brothers out of harm's way.

"There's just two problems with that," Wize said. "You can't swim and we don't have a boat."

But these problems were quickly solved. Sauder's boat, it turned out, was stashed just a few hundred yards from their present location. The next morning, just two days before the Unification Ceremony, they set out for the boat. Wize gave them a walkie-talkie that would allow them to contact him when the army approached the Docks. He kept the tracer. After watching them head west on Rt. 52, he and the army shuffled south along the interstate.

The trip downriver had been relatively uneventful, despite Avery's fear of deep water. He and Sauder had stayed on the west bank when passing Joliet, but had seen no Pentagon soldiers. Avery had been more disturbed by the two rat-like creatures that had swum near the boat, smelling of wet socks.

The pair had made good time traveling downstream and passed out of the gray daylight into the bowels of Naperville by mid-afternoon. The lighting was poor and there were few signs to indicate their location. After stopping to check a few familiar-looking piers they had come upon one marked "Docks." They had climbed the stairs, using their flashlight sparingly. But the door at the top was shut tight.

"Should we knock?" Sauder had said.

"No. The Short Brothers won't hear us from the Factory. Let's wait until five o'clock. Shouldn't be more than a few hours."

Sauder had been amused. "You call them the Short Brothers?"

So they sat in the dark and plotted. Avery, it seems, had not exactly worked out the details of his plan.

Avery awoke to see a vertical strip of light. Sauder's cry suggested that she too had nodded off. Two forms stood in the now-open doorway.

"Book Girl!" a happy voice chirped. "And Special Guy too!"

"Special Guy?" Avery repeated, taken aback.

"Where's Santa?" asked the other, slightly taller figure.

Sauder jumped up and hugged both of the little men.

"We've brought your boat back," she explained.

"*Special Guy?*" Avery said to himself.

"Is Santa with you?" Fester insisted.

"He's outside the Docks," Sauder replied.

"Let's go meet him!" Lance suggested to Fester.

Avery stopped them. "Santa told me to thank you for letting us borrow your boat. And as a reward, he wants you to take a nice boat ride. A long boat ride. And when you return, there will be a present for both of you."

"We can hunt for water-rats!" Fester cheered.

"Why did you tell them there'd be presents?" Sauder asked.

They were sitting in the Factory cafeteria, where Avery had finessed some snacks out of the vending machines.

"Because I have presents." He produced two autographed photos of Uncle Bobbie, only slightly dog-eared from the journey.

After filling their pockets with snacks, they headed for the supply room. It was after hours, but Oink was still at her desk, asleep. Quietly, they searched for the necessary supplies. They were about to leave, when Avery thought better of it.

"Oink," he said, shaking her gently.

She looked up groggily, then seeing who it was, put her arms up defensively. Before she could speak, he continued.

"If you can, I'd leave the Docks for a day or two. It's not safe here."

Oink looked up at him, uncomprehending. "But my job," she protested. "My *credenza.*"

"At least move as far up the entrance corridor as possible," he added.

"I go nowhere without my credenza," the small woman insisted.

"Come on," Sauder said to Avery. "You've done what you can."

At about the same time, another Outsider had infiltrated the shiny walls of Naperville, and for a different purpose.

"Thank you. You've been very useful," the Lowest Down was telling the visitor. He was dressed casually, in expensive SnappyCo jeans and a denim shirt. But the carefully coifed man never really appeared casual.

Illiniwek slouched in the love seat opposite the Lowest Down.

"I'll take the money now."

"As agreed." The Lowest Down picked a duffel bag off the end table and tossed it on the young neoNative's lap. "Five hundred thousand Canadian: that's equal to three and a half million funbucks."

"My tribe will put it to good use," Illiniwek said.

He zipped open the bag and rifled through the bills. They looked legitimate.

"Yes," the Lowest Down said. "I'm sure."

Illiniwek looked up, but he decided to let the perceived insult pass.

"I can get out the same way I came in."

"Please do," the executive said. "I have to get up early to catch the bullet tram to the Quad Cities." He sat down at his writing desk and turned his back on the visitor. Illiniwek rose to leave.

"Oh – one more thing," the Lowest Down said.

Illiniwek turned to see the other man opening his desk drawer. *Did the Nap want to give him a document? A bonus, perhaps?*

But it was just a bullet in the chest.

The young man looked down at the red dot forming on his buckskin pullover. He tried to object, but no words came out. Three more shots hit him, and he had nothing to say about those either.

The Lowest Down looked at the gun. It was an old automatic, fitted with a silencer. *Like something from an old media story*, he thought fondly. He had ordered many people retired in his career, but he had always wanted to retire someone personally.

There wouldn't be any fuss, of course. First because the victim was technically an intruder, but mostly because *he* was the Lowest Down.

He dropped the gun on the carpet and left the room, closing the door behind him. He'd let Hon take care of the disposal.

CHAPTER 26

The day of the Completion Ceremony was a busy one for everybody. Wize was assembling his inept force outside the Docks, just beyond the broken tree line. To the west, Alex's main force had gathered a mere one hundred yards from the Naperville campus, an endless, sixteen-story wall of composite and glass. In the Docks, a formidable security force had assembled to repel the expected attack, while a bigger one was stationed farther west. Deep inside Naperville, Snoop was left to man the missile controls. Virtually all the rest of the associates, including Hon and the other Lower Downs, were at the Quad Cities site, awaiting the official opening of the Transcontinental Merger, a shining corporate structure stretching from sea to sea.

Meanwhile, back in the Docks, two former Customer Service reps were preparing to put their plan into motion.

"Why did they call me Special Guy?" Avery asked Sauder.

"Because you are. You're a special guy. Oops!"

Avery was giving Sauder a crash-course – literally – in driving a forklift.

"That's okay. Just back it up."

She was doing well, certainly well enough for what they had planned.

"The Weeds called me special too," Avery noted.

"I wonder what they think of all this," she said, followed by a quick *sorry* when she nicked a pallet.

Wize stood outside his campaign headquarters, in this case a large tent. It was the most important day of his life and he was dressed in full regalia: light blue shirt, navy blue slacks, sensible black shoes and a paisley clip-on tie. Around his belt hung the accoutrements of his position: walkie-talkie, key card ring, mace canister and oversized flashlight.

He lacked but one accessory to complete the ensemble: a new cap. He opened the cardboard box on the table in front of him, a good-luck gift from the COO of WaltCorp himself. At first take, it looked exactly like the caps he and president Wilson had worn before – only there wasn't a cartoon duck or dog on the crown. No, this was the image of the Big Mouse himself.

Wize donned the cap with immense pride. He had nothing but contempt for WaltCorp – they were merely a convenient ally for restoring the federal government – but who didn't love the Big Mouse? When he turned toward his army and they saw the image, a spontaneous cheer rose up. The Wizened Security Guard didn't waste the opportunity.

"Men!" he cried in a voice that was an octave higher than he had planned, "today is the greatest day of your lives!"

The men and women of his army stopped cheering and began to listen.

"We are not well-armed. We are not well-trained. Heck, most of you aren't even listening to me right now." He got a few chuckles with that. "Not much is expected of us. In many ways we are like – the Big Mouse!"

He held up his cap for emphasis. The troops nearby roared their approval.

"Yes – the Big Mouse!" he continued. "The Big Mouse was funny. The Big Mouse was tiny. The Big Mouse ran around singing and dancing in little red shorts. But the Big Mouse took over the world, didn't he? He showed them what a little mouse with a big heart could do. And today – *we are that mouse!*"

Cheers rang out, even from those who couldn't hear.

Wize looked at them all with as serious and stern a face as he could muster. Fire was in his eyes, and a half-eaten piece of beef jerky in his pocket.

"We go to fight for honor," he cried. "For justice. For our very existence!" He paused. "But mostly we fight because there's a crapload of great stuff in there – and we get to keep anything we find!"

Nothing could have been more motivating to a group of ne'er-do-wells than that. Judging the cheering assembly to be as ready as they'd ever be, Wize led his army through the broken trees. Ahead lay the dark maw of the Docks.

As they charged, Wize could make out the glint of rifle barrels ahead of them. As if on cue, he heard the *whiz* of bullets. Reports of the shots echoed across the broken field. Three people cried out near him, then fell, victims of enemy fire.

The shots had an immediate effect on morale, and the troops fell to the ground almost as one. They were a good fifty yards from the Docks. Wize crawled to a nearby rise of earth and crouched behind it for cover. Beside him, a man in a powder blue jogging suit cowered in fear.

"Frankly," Wize told him between gasps, "I didn't think we'd make it this far."

Inside the Docks, on the highest level of the storage floors, Avery and Sauder heard the shooting and waited. After a few minutes, they crept to the edge and peered down. There was no sign of the Outsider army, and the snatches of conversation from the defenders were not encouraging.

"Can you make anything out?" Avery asked.

"Something like 'Look at them run,'" she reported. "Oh, and 'This should be a rout.'"

Avery frowned. "I hope we're not too late."

They ran back to their respective forklifts, each in a different aisle, and started moving them forward. The drums in Avery's aisle started cascading down to the floor below, Sauder's following soon thereafter. The drums burst open as they landed: Avery's spewing out ball bearings and marbles, Sauder's spilling out corn oil.

The Dock forces, assuming they had been outflanked, rushed back and slipped in the unstable mess. The saboteurs jumped off the forklifts and lobbed smoke grenades down on the defenders.

Wize noticed the shooting had subsided. He risked a peek over the ridge and saw smoke pouring out of the Dock openings. Seizing the moment (and hiking up his pants), he leaped up and called out.

"It's a rout, Men! Follow me and we'll mop 'em up."

This time there was no enthusiasm.

"I'm serious, folks. They can't see in there. All we have to do is wait outside and club them as they emerge."

This seemed like a reasonable plan to many, and most of the army followed their chunky leader, albeit at a more cautious pace than before.

Lower Down Hon stood on the reviewing stand inside the newly-completed Grand Atrium. It was a magnificent structure: mostly glass with crisscrossing girders. Even the floor was translucent, affording a view of the Mississippi below. Around him were other Lower Downs in their finest corporate dress. To their left were arrayed Major General Electric and the other Pentagon bigwigs; to the right, the trendy SnappyCo leaders and the Overland Park contingent.

Festive music played over the PA system, and bright banners hung from the ceiling high above. There was a general buzz of excitement from the thousands of associates lucky enough to view the event in person (the rest would have to settle for nearby viewing screens).

But Hon was more interested in the events to the east. He had a big surprise for the armies of the Outside, and he wished he could witness it in person. The last-minute intelligence supplied by the old man's spy had finally proved useful.

His thoughts were interrupted by an incoming call on his in-headset. Annoyed, he tapped his temple to answer it. "What is it, Snoop?"

"Sorry to bother you, sir, but we've got a situation at the Docks."

"Just spit it out," Hon said. A SnappyCo dignitary gave him a disapproving look. He shrugged an apology.

"The Outsiders are winning. They're invading the Docks."

Hon bit his lower lip in anger. He tasted blood.

"Snoop — are they *inside* the Docks?"

"Some, some are. But it sounds like most are just outside."

This was bad, Hon knew, but not hopeless. "Fire the second bank of missiles," he ordered. "The *second* bank, understand?"

"But sir," Esselte protested. "Won't that mean collateral damage to associates in the Docks?"

"Yes."

"Including security personnel."

"Snoop. *Esselte*," Hon said in a low hiss. "Fire the missiles. Fire them now!"

There was a pause on Snoop's end, then: "They're off, sir."

"Good. Don't call me back unless there's a problem. And be ready to fire the first bank."

"Yes sir." The call terminated.

Hon glanced down through the floor and noticed movement. A lone worker seemed to be manipulating something on one of the massive support columns. *Probably scratching his initials in it*, the VP thought to himself. He made a mental note to have the man interrogated.

CHAPTER 27

The Wizened Security Guard was so pleased with his victory he considering giving himself a medal. Then the explosions started.

The Naps, blinded and confused, had been easily defeated: the Dock workers had given up almost immediately, and the vastly-outnumbered security force soon after that. The rag-tag victors had just finished rounding up the prisoners outside and were about to commence some serious scavenging when they were rocked by a series of concussions.

Inside the Docks, much of the storage structure collapsed, raining crates on the unfortunates below. Wize staggered to his feet and looked out. Where there had once been about one thousand prisoners and Outsiders, there was now an irregular patchwork of craters. Odd stick shapes, some recognizable as bodies, were strewn across the uneven landscape.

As if waking from a dream, the bearded old man heard someone calling his name.

"Wize! Wize! What was that?"

Wize turned to see Avery and Sauder running toward them. The latter was limping.

"Did *we* do that?" Sauder asked, referring to the Outsider army.

"I think those were missiles. Government missiles." Wize's own voice sounded flat and distant.

The three stood motionless. The few remaining Dock medics hurried out to help the wounded and dying. Avery hoped no more missiles would fall.

"But, they can't use their weapons stockpile," Sauder said at last. "It's against all the treaties. The ramifications would be – it's just crazy!"

"The Lower Downs must think they have nothing to lose," Wize said softly. "Or they just don't care."

Avery steadied himself. He felt the nausea rising within him. But he knew he had to act.

"Let's see if we can help," he said. He took a step forward, but Sauder grabbed his elbow.

"Wait," she said. Then, turning to Wize, asked, "Are there more missiles, do you think?"

Wize twisted up his mouth, trying to think. "I'm not the guy to ask – but yes, I bet there are."

"Then we have to find them," she said, "before they're used against Alex's army."

Avery looked at her with renewed admiration. He could never think that clearly under pressure.

"No," Wize said. "We have to find the control room."

After a quick but heated discussion, it was decided to head for the Internal Audit surveillance room. It was likely that the missiles were controlled from that location and, if not, they could use the monitors to locate them. In addition, both Avery and Wize knew how to get there.

Wize quickly rounded up a handful of his soldiers who didn't seem completely useless. Avery and Wize, meanwhile, grabbed what weapons they could from the security guards' cache: three shotguns, two pistols and several stun rods.

It took some doing to open the large warehouse doors leading to the main campus. But a few shotgun blasts and a crowbar finally did the trick. They hopped on two delivery carts and headed for the main corridor.

The campus was eerily empty as they raced through it. The Outsiders who came with them were awed by the endless rows of cubicles. The only sound was the blaring of the giant view screens, heralding the Unification Ceremony.

"Where is everyone?" Wize wondered.

"Boy – you're gone for a few weeks and look what happens," Avery joked. But no one laughed.

"Do you think they're all at the ceremony?" Sauder asked.

They took a freight elevator down to the third level, the level of the surveillance room. When they emerged, the view screens were silent. The images, however, showed a collapsed portion of the campus.

"That'll be the exploding chair line!" Wize said, slowing his cart to get a better view.

They watched the images, trying to determine the extent of the damage. The announcers, jubilant only minutes before, were cautiously mute. Sauder was the first to realize that this was not the result of the chair bombs. It was something unexpected.

Kensington was no structural engineer, but he recognized a support beam when he saw one. He was also not a demolition expert--which was why he had used much more dynamite than was actually needed.

The first hint the assembled corporate partners had that something was amiss was a series of low pops, like the implosion of several massive subterranean balloons. This was followed by a strong yet gentle shock wave. It was, in fact, not until the ensuing grinding and shattering of glass and composite began that anyone in the Grand Atrium realized that they were in big trouble.

The Lowest Down's last thought was a religious epiphany. He had been about to cut the ceremonial ribbon when the disaster struck. Ridiculously, he tried to finish the job, but fell to the floor, the scissors bouncing away.

"It's God," he thought, as the floor tilted and cracked. "I finally pushed it too far." Then the floor shattered and he was gone.

Hon's musings were more practical than his superior's. Holding onto the review stand for stability, his mind was already considering how to turn this unexpected disaster to his advantage. He had come so far, after all, and accomplished too much to give up now. He had already deactivated the chair bombs, for instance. And the missiles would eliminate both Outsider armies once and for all. *Concessions will have to be made to the merger partners, of course, but ah – we'll need a new Lowest Down*, he noted as he saw the white-haired man slip through a hole in the floor.

Then he slipped through himself.

Each person in the atrium, corporate movers and shakers all, had their own unique thoughts as the structure collapsed around them.

Major General Electric was outraged. "Somebody fix this!" he barked just before a section of glass sliced his festooned uniform (and his torso) neatly in half.

Andrew Gates, SnappyCo's Senior Vice President of Tomorrow, was philosophical. *This is extremely unjoyous*, he thought as a girder crushed his skull. "I love you, Lambykins," cried his paramour, Kathie Wozniak, as she slid away down the now-tilted floor. *I should have known*, mused his wife before she lost her balance.

Down they fell, whoever they were and whatever they were thinking. Down, down they fell into the mud and the muck and the misery of the Mississippi.

And far away, watching on the view screen in his office high atop the southest corner of Naperville, President Adams too had a thought:

I'm glad I wasn't invited.

CHAPTER 28

"I said drop it!" Wize smacked Mario's hand with his flashlight, causing the man to release the portable projector he had just stolen. "This is not a scavenger hunt."

Mario rubbed his hand moodily and climbed back on the delivery cart.

Sauder sighed. It had been like this ever since they saw the destruction of the Grand Atrium on the view screen. The men they had brought with them were getting out of control, especially the tall blonde one with the unlikely name of Mario. The missiles were still a real and immediate threat, but the titular soldiers were convinced the war was over – which for them meant it was time to begin looting.

"I'm not going to be able to keep them in line much longer," Wize told her. He had pulled up his cart even with Avery's so they could discuss the situation.

"Oh man," Mario yelled, looking longingly at a low cubicle they had just passed. "Those were malted milk balls. A whole carton!"

Avery gestured back to their passengers, but addressed his comments to Sauder and Wize. "This is not the time to make a point. I say we cut them loose."

Wize took his foot off the accelerator, and his cart rolled to a stop. Avery hit the brakes. The guard jumped out of his cart, then gestured to the soldiers.

"It's all your, boys. Thanks for following us this far."

Without so much as a thank you, the five men turned the cart around and drove off, hooting and arguing. Wize jumped on Avery's cart, which rocked like a hobby horse.

"Internal Audit is up ahead," he told them.

The secretive department was easy to recognize, surrounded as it was by walls of dark glass. They pulled up to the main entrance, a set of glass double doors of the same material, and were only slightly surprised to find them unlocked. Avery was about to enter when Sauder stopped him.

"Just what is our plan?" she asked.

Avery thought for a moment. "Head straight for the surveillance room, which is – ?" He looked to Wize for confirmation.

"Fourth door on the right, just past the break room." Then, noticing their questioning glances, added, "What? I get hungry when I'm snooping."

"Then grab the controller," Avery concluded.

"This is assuming there aren't several IA troopers waiting on the other side of the door," Sauder said.

"Obviously," Avery said uncertainly.

They each took a pistol and a stun rod. Wize gave them a quick lesson in marksmanship (*'Make sure the safety is off and aim for the middle of the torso'*), then he grabbed a shotgun and a stun rod for himself.

They were bracing themselves to go through the door when they heard a dull thud from the other end of the hallway. They looked back and saw that the wall had collapsed. Behind it were two storm troopers on armored battle cycles.

"Look who we got, Rambler," said one through his hood. "I don't think the fat guy's going to escape to Seventeen this time."

They revved their cycles; a fierce sound considering they were electric-powered.

Sauder took a step toward them. "This is senseless," she cried over the humming. "The Grand Atrium is destroyed. The Lower Downs are all dead."

"Then they won't mind if we beat you to death," Rambler noted.

Wize threw Sauder back behind him. He cocked his shotgun and stood facing the troopers.

"I'll handle these toads," he said over his shoulder. "You two go save the day."

"But Wize – " Avery objected.

"Remember I told you I couldn't remember some things about myself? Well, one thing is coming back to me. For a time I was really, really bad. And it's still in me."

Avery was about to say something when he noticed Wize's eyes. They were icy and gray and devoid of humor. This was not the carefree Wizened Security Guard – it was something fearful and emotionless.

"Go!" Wize repeated

Sauder tugged at Avery's elbow. "There's no time. The missiles."

The cycles flew down the hall towards them. Wize fired once, the sound roaring through the hallway. There was no effect at first, then Rambler's bike skidded and fell. Sauder and Avery opened the door and, seeing no one inside, entered quickly.

The last sound Avery heard from the Wizened Security Guard was a feral growl.

They ran down the hall, seeing no one. Sauder noticed that the dark glass was transparent from the inside, though she didn't have time to look back to see how Wize was faring. They reached the fourth door on the right (just past the break room, as Wize had predicted). It was locked. What's more, it was made of the same one-way opaque glass that surrounded the department. They couldn't see inside – but anyone inside could surely see them.

Avery looked at the door, at a loss.

"Shoot it," Sauder said.

They backed up. Avery brought up his pistol with both hands and fired at the door handle. The door shook, but didn't even crack. The bullet, however, ricocheted down the hall and broke a pane of glass on the opposite side. He fired again and this time shattering the pane of glass directly behind them.

"Stop!" Sauder cried.

As they stood there, they heard a voice from inside the room.

"It won't break. It's bulletproof. Heck, it's bombproof," the voice said. It was a young man's voice, high and wavering.

"Can you let us in?" Sauder asked in the tone of a kindergarten teacher.

"No, no NO!" the voice replied. "No one is allowed in the surveillance room without top security clearance. And I'm the only one alive who has that clearance. Just little Snoop –" The voice broke off in a sob.

Avery and Sauder looked at each other.

"It sounds like you're upset," Sauder continued. "Do you want to talk about it? My name is Sauder. And you're Snoop?"

"Don't call me that!" the voice cried angrily. "That's not my name!"

"I'm sorry. What is your name?"

"Esselte," the voice said softly, barely audible.

"Esselte," Sauder said carefully. "Are you alone in there?"

"Yes. Alone. All alone."

"Esselte, you don't have to be alone. Why don't you open the door and talk to us?"

"Who's with you?" Esselte asked suspiciously.

Avery was about to say his name, but Sauder stopped him. "Just a friend," she said. "He's nice."

"Which one of you has the gun?" he asked evenly.

"We both do," Sauder admitted. We're putting them down right now."

They did so.

"That was smart of you," Esselte noted. "Because I can see you. I can see *everything*." There was a disturbing lilt in his voice.

"Yes. Now you know you can trust us, Esselte. Do you think you could let us in now? It's important."

"Is it about the missiles?"

"Yes. Have they been launched yet?"

"No," he replied. There was a pause. "Not yet."

"Esselte, listen to me," Sauder said. Although it was difficult, she maintained an even, reassuring tone. At least her customer service training had been useful for something. "Before you do anything – I really need to talk to you."

"You're going to hurt me!" Esselte said accusingly.

"No. We don't want to hurt anyone. That's why we need to talk to you before you do anything."

There was a long silence.

"Esselte," Sauder continued. "You say you can see everything. With the monitors, right? Then you know the Lower Downs are dead. The Atrium has collapsed. Everything has changed – and change is scary. But we don't want to make things worse, do we?"

Another pause. Then, "I guess not."

"Open the door and let's talk things over, okay? Look, we're sitting down on the floor, away from the door."

They sat down, leaning against the far wall, below the shattered pane of glass. They waited for a long moment. Then there was a clicking at the door and the handle turned slowly. A nervous young man appeared. He had a handheld device in one hand. Seeing Sauder, he smiled weakly.

"See?" Sauder said cheerfully. "No tricks. We just want to talk things over. Are you – ?"

But when Esselte looked at Avery, his expression became one of shock, then betrayal. He knew that face. He had not recognized him on the monitor – and the tracer indicated he was somewhere else. It was the customer service rep. The exploding chair guy. The friend of the Wizened Security Guard.

"You!" he cried. "You!"

"What's the matter?" Sauder asked. She started to rise.

"Get away!" Esselte said. He stepped back, his lips curling into a grin.

"Nice try," he giggled. "But you can't fool Snoop that easy."

Then, as Avery and Sauder watched, Esselte began punching furiously at the controller.

Seeing this, Avery jumped at him. Both men fell to the ground, wrestling for the device. Avery managed to get on top, and was soon holding Esselte down by the wrists. Sauder dashed over and grabbed the controller.

"Too late," Esselte screamed in a laughing sob. "Too late now!"

Sauder looked at the readout and realized it was true. The missiles had been launched. She looked at Avery and shook her head gravely.

"How long?" Avery demanded. "How long until they hit?"

"Five minutes," Esselte muttered miserably. "Ten minutes. I don't know."

Avery raised the man by the collar and shook him.

"How do we stop it?" he asked.

Esselte merely laughed in reply.

Sauder studied the device. She punched the screen a few times, tentatively, then gave up.

"It's beyond me," she said, handing it to Avery.

Avery looked at the readout, but could make nothing of the graphics.

They both sat down on the floor, backs to the wall. Esselte rocked gently on the floor, mumbling.

Avery noticed the crumpled corpse of what had once been Esselte's co-worker inside the surveillance center.

"Any ideas?" he asked Sauder.

"I got nothing," she replied wearily.

Avery sat, exhausted and sick with despair. His new friends would soon be blown to bits, and there was no way to warn them. He had no idea what would become of Naperville, either.

Sauder was apparently thinking along the same lines. She suddenly turned Avery's head toward her and kissed him. He wrapped his long arms around her and pulled her close. She was warm and comfortable. When the kiss was over she looked in his eyes.

"I'm moving in the the Mayor," she said.

"Things worked out well for both of us," he said. Then it occurred to him that Ted and the Mayor would probably die with the rest of the army. "If only there was *some* way to warn them."

"At least we can warn Customer Service. If one of those missiles strays, they might get hit."

The two got up and searched for an audio line (Sauder's internal headset having been removed when she was transferred to the Docks). Avery called the service line; a voice immediately answered.

"Customer Service," a stiff, filtered voice replied. "How may I please you?"

"Weeds," Avery told Sauder. Then: "Yes, this is Avery. I – "

There was a pause. Avery imagined the odd creatures were engaged in the odd murmur/laughter he seemed to inspire in them.

"Avery," the voice returned. "We were very happy to receive our borax shipment today. It came by rocket from a place called Kamchatka. Now – how may we brighten your day?"

"I wanted to warn the associates in Customer Service that they may be in danger."

"The associates have gone to the Unification Ceremony. We are handling requests at this time. Will there be anything else today?"

"No," Avery said flatly. "Unless you can stop a missile attack."

"The missiles that were just launched?" the voice asked.

"How did you know?"

But he now hearing a bossa nova version of the motivational standard, *How May I Help You?* The Weed rep had put him on hold. He looked at Sauder and shook his head in confusion.

The Weed came back on the line. "Thank you for holding. Yes. We can do that."

"Do what?" Avery asked, perplexed.

"Stop the missile attack."

"You can do that?"

"We can do that."

Avery shrugged. "Then please do that."

Another pause. More bossa nova. Avery put the phone on speaker.

"They say they're going to stop the missiles," Avery told Sauder, his voice giddy.

"*Can* they?" she asked, incredulous.

"Who knows what they can do."

The voice returned.

"Avery, we can stop the missiles."

"Great – "

"But we won't."

Avery practically screamed. "You won't!? *Why the hell not?*"

"Stopping the missiles would be helping you," the voice continued evenly. "You told us we should never actually *help* the customer."

Sauder jumped in. "Please," she said. "This is incredibly important. Thousands of people will die! You have to stop the missiles *NOW!*"

Another pause. "Avery told us *not* to help the customer."

"But that's crazy!" Avery screamed.

"I understand your anger," the voice said in its best customer service tone. "I empathize and sympathize with it."

Alex, Ted, Chief Shabbona, Mayor Daley and the rest of the main army of the Outside watched intently as absolutely nothing happened. They had been watching nothing happen for the past fifteen minutes, their anxiety growing as each second of the non-event ticked away.

The army was arrayed in a crescent, like horns of a bull, a mere 100 yards north of the looming Naperville edifice. The archers and marksmen were at the ready. The trebuchets bent back and ready to launch. The infantry assembled in lines of battle. But there were no orders to attack.

Alex had sent the radio signal to detonate the chair line, had sent it several times in fact. But there was no boom, no sound at all but that of dry leaves in the wind.

"Maybe something's wrong," the Mayor offered.

Shabbona rolled his eyes. "Of course there's something wrong! But it's not the radio signal; we've triple-checked it."

Alex handed the useless transmitter to the chief and stared grimly at the endless corporate campus

"If the Naps attack us now – and in force – we're sitting ducks here," he concluded.

"Just like Uncle Stan," Ted said pointedly.

They waited longer. Then something did happen. It was just a sound at first: a distant whooshing of air, like a tornado. They searched the sky for the source, but saw nothing. The whooshing became louder. It seemed to come from all around them.

Finally, they saw the first of the missiles descending.

"They *can* stop the missiles," Sauder said, her voice toneless.

"Yes," Avery agreed.

"But they won't."

"Exactly."

"Because you trained them to *not* help the customer."

Avery shrugged. "Precisely."

They were silent.

"Hello?" the voice continued. "Is there anything else I can do to brighten your day?"

Suddenly Sauder's smiled. She turned to Avery.

"You're not a customer!" she said.

"I'm not?" he replied, confused. Then he understood.

"Customer Service!" he cried. "Customer Service – are you still there?"

"Of course," the voice replied.

"I'm not a customer," Avery practically shouted. "I am *NOT* a customer and I'm asking you to stop the missiles! Do you understand?"

There was a pause, followed by more music. Avery and Sauder paced nervously. After what seemed like minutes, the voice returned.

"We have done that," it stated flatly.

"You've done that?" Avery repeated, his heart pounding.

"Yes. And in the future, Avery, please do not use this line for personal calls."

"Just my dumb luck," the Mayor said as the missiles streaked toward them from the southern sky. Then, realizing his poor choice of words, he said to Alex and Ted, "No offense to you Lucks."

The murmur rose from the army, half awe, half dread, as they recognized the horrible volley.

Alex hugged Ted and kissed her forehead. They closed their eyes and waited.

But instead of the blast of heat they had expected, they heard a strange sound, exactly like a cartoon anvil dropping on someone's head. Only much louder.

Chief Shabbona saw it first. He refused to close his eyes, thinking it might be bad form for a Native to do so, casino owner or no. As the first missiles came within 1,000 feet of the ground, they exploded, creating a deafening metallic thud. The noise was repeated over and over as the entire arsenal slammed into an invisible, umbrella-shaped shield.

When it was over there was a long silence as people looked around, amazed to be alive.

The Mayor scratched his head.

"So," he said, "Did we win or lose?"

Shabbona pressed the detonator button. Seconds later, a muffled *whumff* came from the direction of Naperville.

"Let's go find out," he said.

CHAPTER 29

Victory has a way of being more trouble than defeat, and so it was for the Outsider Coalition. The corporate wall had been breached or kept open in three places: the Mississippi River/Quad Cities and at the middle and eastern end of Naperville. But the corporation was, after all, a small component of the Transcontinental Corridor, and were it not for the Weeds, SnappyCo, the Pentagon and the rest would have scattered the Outsiders and finished the corridor in short order. And it was not certain if the aliens were on anyone's side but their own. In fact, the only thing anyone knew for sure about the Weeds was that they were as dangerous as had been feared and nowhere near as naïve as had been hoped. During the ensuing power vacuum, the Weeds had taken control of Naperville, on the grounds that "somebody had to answer the phones." In short, no one trusted them, but neither could anyone fire them.

Months later, the Coalition convened a summit of sorts in the hope of reestablishing the federal government as a viable entity. Parties sending delegations included the Downstaters (who had already made the trip), the Chicago Democrats, Hyde Park scholars, tribes of neoNatives from as far away South Dakota and Lucks (the Slacks had no interest). The summit was held in June in Joliet, and it is safe to say a good time was had by all. There were several days of speeches, several nights of carousing, and even a bit of flag-waving (mostly by President Adams). After a few days, representatives from WaltCorp, Halliburton and the other corporations showed up, sniffing around the periphery for opportunities or perhaps weaknesses.

And weaknesses there were. It turned out Outsiders didn't want to be governed by a central authority any more than the corporations did. They approved the office of president, but afforded it no real powers – not even the ability to make treaties with other nations. (This caused Yves Charboneau, the low-level envoy from Canada, to wonder loudly from the podium why he had even bothered to make the trip as they had better casinos and strip clubs in La Crosse.)

Sauder covered it all, gavel to gavel (a rare item, provided by Mayor Daley for the occasion). As did Frederick Douglas VIII, dean of the Hyde Park Campus. Avery, the reluctant hero, ran into them on the first day, on a terrace overlooking the river. Sauder, in baggy jeans and a slim yellow tee, was talking and gesturing to something on the opposite bank. Avery could tell by the way she kept cocking her head sideways for emphasis that she was in lecture mode and it made him nostalgic. In the corporate world, where history was deemed unnecessary and potentially troublesome, everything his bookworm former girlfriend had to teach was breaking news.

" ... right around there. That side of the river, at any rate," she was saying as he approached.

"Huh. I'm not sure I ever got the whole story on your escape from the Docks," Avery said. He leaned on the railing. Polished bronze metal without a blemish. The terrace was part of the convention center, which was part of the casino, which was by far the most antiseptic institution he had encountered on the Outside.

"Avery!" Sauder threw her arms wide to hug him, hesitating only momentarily to give a quick sideways glance to the other man. The crushing grip around his waist, like the lecture, gave a second sweet pang of nostalgia.

Frederick Douglas VIII looked on, impassive.

Sauder stepped back and looked Avery up and down, affording Avery a chance to do the same to the other two. Sauder's short, curly, black hair was fuzzier, less meticulously tended. Indeed, she seemed less tense, less driven. Her chocolate brown skin looked a shade darker, but didn't betray its exposure to the elements as much as other Naps.

"Avery, this is Frederick Douglas VIII. He's my, um ... "

"Boss. Among other things," the other cut in. He was tall, also dark-skinned, with a short-cropped beard touched with gray. "Call me Freddy," he said if the idea pained him greatly.

The two men shook hands. Freddy wore the same style of jeans as Sauder, but opted for a bright white oxford dress shirt, sleeves carefully folded twice up the arm. Avery knew he was management by the way he wore his "casuals" – like a kid showing off his new Halloween costume. His grip, too, was management – too firm by half.

"I've heard much about you," Freddy noted with a knowing look that could have meant anything.

Avery shrugged. He was getting used to the comment, even though by his own reckoning there was little to tell. His story, as he imagined was true of most humans, was one of dumb luck. In point of act, he was staring at their feet; both were shod in soft brown leather.

Sauder noticed. "We bought genuine moccasins at a shop on Jefferson Street. Well, handmade, anyway."

Freddy shrugged and offered a weak smile. "She insisted. And research indicates they are better for your spine and posture."

Which confirmed they were indeed a couple

"Where's Ted?" Sauder asked.

"In Luckport. Said she couldn't be bothered by such foolishness."

It was just after one. The next session, something about trade routes, didn't start until two. Sauder continued her lecture.

"I think it was about there were Wize found me and drove me to Chicago.

"Where we met," Freddy said mostly to Sauder.

"In a bookstore on Printers Row."

"They have stores for books?" Avery said. But it was polite chatter. He was taking in the two of them: Sauder and Freddy, each with an arm around the other, playfully knocking hips. It was nice.

For nearly a minute, they said nothing. Avery for his part was still awed by the Outside, where the wind blew where and in whatever direction it chose and the sun gave way to violent rains with frightening cracks of lightning. It was wild and chaotic and beyond anyone's control (except possibly, with enough borax, the Weeds). One could easily get the impression that chaos was god. And yet beyond the chaos there was a beauty and a pattern of sorts. It seemed equally as foolish to him to deny the pattern as to think one understood it.

Today, though, was mild and bright, and it took him a moment to realize Freddy was speaking to him.

"I said, 'This Wize fellow, or Stanislaw Pink if you will, was quite a character.'"

Avery nodded. Another example of pattern amid chaos.

"Fascinating idea to co-opt the Wizened Security Guard mythos."

"Mythos or not, he *was* the Wizened Security Guard."

Freddy gave a dismissive snuffle. "Metaphorically, of course." The petty theft, the archaic outfit – "

"You never met him." Avery let it go at that, resuming his surveillance of a family of ducks below him, swimming upstream. He had seen many strange things in the past few months: Weeds and weeds, death and dirt, gigacubes of glass and miles of grass. By comparison, a two-hundred-year-old lunatic seemed prosaic.

"There's a book by him, you know," Sauder said, shifting the topic. From the early 21st Century. *Parables of the Wizened Security Guard.*"

"Not by him. About him," Freddy said." Authored, interestingly, by a Stanislaw Pink."

The ducks had found a calm patch of water in the lee of a concrete piling. "I'd like to read that," Avery admitted.

Ted had no time for foolishness, but her father Alex did. He joined several dignitaries (for lack of a better word) on the podium for the passage of the resolution commemorating the Wizened Security Guard. Others included Mayor Daley, Chief Shabbona, President Adams, Sauder and Avery, who found the whole thing funny and oddly appropriate.

"He was a man who was not just a man but a man," the mayor rambled with enthusiasm. "I mean, a big, giant man. Ya know."

"Wize, or Stanislaw as we knew him," made a big impression on Luckport, Alex told the audience. "No pastry or keg was safe when he was around, but we were still happy to see him."

"Somehow I knew he'd die owing me money," Chief Shabbona said through tears. "I'd cut him a $100,000 marker Canadian just to see that crazy hat again."

Avery himself read the resolution declaring March 15 Wizened Security Guard Day (nobody knew his birthday, or age for that matter, but it was a good spot in the calendar for a day off. He had decided to make his comments extemporaneously. A mistake. Looking out at the hundreds in attendance, all looking back in hushed anticipation of what the great war hero would tell them, Avery was literally speechless. His encounters with Wize flashed too quickly before his mind's eye, and in jumbled order. Stanislaw the poet, Wize the martyr, the exploding chair, the wild cart chase. At last, he blurted, almost to himself, "That man loved his cake."

After an embarrassed pause, they unrolled the thirty-foot banner behind him: a large version of Wize's cap with its signature cartoon mouse. The blue field behind it matched his security guard shirt, down to the random yellow and brown stains. President Adams, wearing the matching cap with cartoon dog, covered his face and shook visibly.

Amid the polite applause, Avery took his seat next to the president, who was by now nearly doubled over with emotion.

"There, there," Avery said, assuming that to be the right thing to say. Then, when that seemed to have no effect, he added, "I'm sure the loss hurts you more than the rest of us."

Without looking up, Adams reached out and grabbed at Avery's sleeve, tugging it violently. The president looked up. There were tears in his eyes, and he was convulsing. But to Avery's surprise, the man was not sobbing but laughing.

"The fat guy would love this – it's all so botched up and ridiculous. There, there are – mustard stains! Oh Prosperity, what a perfect tribute to that thoughtless, lucky, fat bastard."

Avery relaxed. "Thank God. I thought it was just me."

Adams doubled over again and said in a whisper, "Do I really look distraught?"

"Inconsolable."

"Good, then nobody will mind if you pretend to help me off the stage and we go get blind, stinking, roaring, put-us-in-jail drunk."

CHAPTER 30

Were one to visit Illinois today one would find, about ten miles north of the blast site along the old Interstate 59, a large, two-story Victorian house, and, next to it, an unfinished barn. Inside the unfinished barn one would find evidence of several unfinished and failed projects: a finely-carved handle for a non-existent rocker, a sagging, parallelogram-shaped bookcase, several crudely-painted watercolors leaning against a disassembled Kubota tractor, an oak door set across two sawhorses and covered with rags, screws, pencils drawings and tools, including a claw hammer holding open a book titled *The European Corn Borer and Its Control.*

This would be the home of Avery and Ted after the war.

The two had married and lived in Luckport for a time, sharecropping a few acres owned by Rueben the Slack. But it didn't last. Avery was a hero and the Lucks looked to him for leadership. And not just the Lucks: there was talk of nominating him for President. Adams, the outgoing Chief of State, apparently felt that twenty years in the position had been long enough.

But Avery just wanted to farm. Or maybe raise horses. Or craft fine wooden furniture.

Eventually, they decided to try their hand at running an inn. They claimed an abandoned house near Mendota and named it the Earlville Inn, after a nearby ghost town. It was a good location due to its proximity to the new throughway to the South, a throughway that effectively cut Naperville in half.

Ted had done, and continued to do, most of the work at the Earlville Inn. She tended the garden, raised the cattle, slaughtered the cattle and took care of the steady trickle of guests. This left Avery plenty of time for his unfinished projects.

One evening in May, almost exactly two years after the war, Ted and Avery were on their porch, watching the orange sun sink below the trees. They were sitting on a crudely-fashioned bench Avery had made from with an old log and an excessive number of nails.

"I'm pregnant," Ted told him.

This made Avery happy and he kissed her.

But it also made him anxious. Living Outside was one thing, having a baby there was quite another. Also, how would they take care of it? They had just enough to live on as it was.

One week later, Avery was sitting on the same bench, drawing up a plan for a crib on a scrap of paper. He didn't really want to build a crib because he knew by now he was no good with tools, but he was trying to keep his mind occupied. Ted had just told him that his father-in-law would be coming for an extended visit to help with the pregnancy. And Alex still didn't like Avery much.

So he really didn't notice the visitor until it spoke.

"Avery," it twittered.

But then Weeds always just appeared out of nowhere.

"How are things in Naperville?" Avery asked.

After the war, the Weeds were given control of Naperville. The Lower Downs had died in the Grand Atrium explosion and the aliens seemed the most qualified to fill the vacuum. They were given a forty-nine percent share by the board. There was only one condition: that the Weeds promise not to attack the earth. There had never been any indication that they intended to do such a thing, but it seemed best to get something in writing.

"The associates seem to love Casual Fridays," it said. "Who knew?"

"But they still don't want to commute, huh?"

"A few are building homes. Most still fear the Outside."

Avery looked toward the door, thinking he should call Ted. She had never met a Weed. Then he remembered she was visiting their neighbor a mile up the Interstate.

"Thanks for scrubbing the air, by the way," he said.

The nuclear missiles, though small, had released unhealthy amounts of radiation. The Weeds were kind enough to neutralize it somehow. With borax.

"You are welcome," the Weed said. Then it shook in its inscrutable way and added, "Avery is special."

Avery exhaled loudly. He knew he was restless and indecisive and even a piss-poor farmer. But one thing he was not in any way was special.

"What the hell does that mean?" Avery said. "Just how am I special? Do you mean I'm smart? That I'm lucky? That I'm destined for greatness? What?"

"No. Avery is just – how does one say – as in special education?"

Avery nodded slowly, three times. A nail popped out of the bench.

"So how can I brighten your day?" he said at last. "A room, perhaps?"

"We want Avery to be Lowest Down."

Avery's head jerked up.

"We want Avery to run Naperville."

"But you run Naperville."

"Yes. But it's boring. And we have other plans."

"But you just basically called me retarded."

"The current Lowest Down, you may know him as Professor Bob, requires too much – babysitting? He has too many ambitions for himself."

"Doctor Bob." If anyone had survived, it would be him. "Yes, I could see where he'd need watching."

"The corporation runs itself," the Weed buzzed. "All Avery has to do is sit in an office and, on occasion, put on a necktie. We can teach you the Windsor knot."

Avery folded up his piece of paper. The Weed had said that last bit more slowly than usual. Maybe they did think he was retarded.

"What if there's trouble?" he asked.

"Then Avery calls the Weeds."

"I'd get a salary, and benefits?"

"And stock options."

Avery looked out at the uneven prairie grass he never seemed to get around to clearing. A job would fix a lot of problems: indoor health services, security, even an excuse to get away from his father-in-law. So what if the work was boring? He was bored now. And stock options, whatever they were, sounded impressive.

The Weed waited, motionless. Avery shifted in his seat. The damn bench was so uncomfortable: too low, too hard, no arms or lumbar support.

"I'll take it on one condition," he said.

* ON SUCCESS *

The Wizened Security Guard was perched on his stool at the front desk. An aura of wisdom lay about him, along with several candy wrappers.

A young woman entered and slowly approached. She was attired in a conservative business suit, accessorized with a floral scarf that signified her position of middle management and lack of fashion sense.

"How," the young woman asked, "do I get to the Executive Suite?"

The Wizened Security Guard nodded sagely and leaned back a little to stifle a fart.

"Many seek the Executive Suite, where wishes are granted and restrooms are well-maintained," he said. "But the journey to that place is not like other journeys. Intelligence will not help you. Integrity will not aid you. Hard work will not avail. The seeker must abandon friends, family and dressing down on Fridays. Only then might they reach the Executive Suite."

The woman looked back at him with an expression of awe. Or impatience.

"What's wrong with the elevator?"

- Parables of the Wizened Security Guard
  Tinley Park Codex, circa 2028 A.D.

APPENDIX A OF A

Literature, Legend and Legacy: The Wizened Security Guard
(notes for a graduate thesis by Sauder Douglas)

Historical journals are awash with solid treatments of the fall of the American democracy, the rise of geocorporations and both Branding Wars (Original and Extra Spicy). There simply doesn't seem to be anything a scholastic neophyte like myself can add to the "big picture." And while I have access to many fine firsthand accounts – even firsthand knowledge – of the Naperville Conflict, the subject is too popular among master's and doctoral candidates to offer much promise. On a personal note, the events are also too recent and personal for me to feel confidence in having the required objectivity to give them their due. Those interested in a full and, I think, fair treatment of the subject should read *A Grand Failure: Mergers, Mayhem and the Melting of the Transcontinental Corridor, V I, II*, Frederick Douglas VIII, PhD, JD, MDiv (Pill Hill Press, 2184).

For now, my work has led to an interesting and parallel literary study that informs, at least in a small way, the last two centuries of United States history. Specifically, the work and life of Stanislaw Pink, or the Wizened Security Guard. He was a presence, both in reality and folklore, from the 20th Century right up to the current one. My work intends to separate wherever possible, the man from the myth – and Pink the poet and author from Wize the low-level employee, dupe, warrior, corporate subversive and, ultimately, unlikely leader and martyr.

My historical research is ongoing, and I hope to have more to add as I mine both corporate and "Outside" archives and collections. For now, and for the purposes of justifying this topic as worth pursuing as a graduate thesis, I want to address a few literary pieces I have recently uncovered.

Most of Pink's work, or work attributed to Pink, are the brief fables known as *The Parables of the Wizened Security Guard*. Most familiar are those titled On Happiness, On Success, On Teamwork, *et al.* There are also scraps of verse, primarily snippets of performance pieces written for occasions in Luckport and Joliet. These pieces provide a window into both recent and 20th Century corporate and Outsider culture and, therefore, merit study in and of themselves.

Additionally though, Pink seems to have fancied himself a writer of speculative fiction. This passion was present early on in his life (or Wize's life; again, it is an ongoing challenge to separate the two personae). This is demonstrated by some rather amateurish, or at the very least childish, attempts at stories. I include the longest (and oddest), which I recently unearthed (quite literally) in the site of the original Naperville Corporation along the I-88 Corridor. It is, if not entertaining, as least telling.

APPENDIX B OF A

SPACESHIP BLASTOFF ROCKET TRIP
TO THE MOON OF EARTH C-
By stan Pinkel?

General Taylor admired the towering spaceship that towered two thousand feet above him on the launch pad. Its gleaming titanium-diamond alloy surface reflected the cold, snowy peaks of the Himalayas.

"Impressive, isn't it?" said Professor von Frankfort, who had come up beside him.

"*She's* impressive," the general replied. "In the Navy we always call our ships *she*."

Both men were wearing parkas to protect them from the cold, but they had to yell to be heard above the cold arctic winds of the frigid Himalayas.

von Frankfort took his pipe out of his mouth and laughed. "Well, is *she* ready for take-off?"

"All the food and water and weapons and scientific stuff is loaded. And we're pumping in the high-octane gas fumes now. I'm just worried about the hull."

"Bah!" von Frankfort said. "As head rocket scientist on this project I can assure you that nothing is stronger than titanium-diamond alloy —

except the supermegatanium we used to make the capsule. Why, gamma rays couldn't even penetrate that!"

"Look out!" cried General Taylor as a giant ball of fire erupted and hurled toward them. He pushed the scientist to the ground just as the flames reached them.

"You really should be more careful with that pipe!" he said. "You set off the gas fumes."

The professor got up and brushed himself off. "Lucky I ordered these inflammable parkas!" he said.

"Well, we better get back inside Earth Base Pronto," the general said. "The sun's going down and it's going to be a dark night."

"Hopefully we'll put an end to that," the professor replied.

The light from the setting sun shone on the side of the massive rocket ship, showing the name on the side: UNS Blastoff!

At that same moment a small, V-shaped jet hurtled over the Atlantic Ocean. There were four people inside, including Rex the dog, who sat alertly in the copilot seat. It was piloted by Lt. Billy Desmond. In the back seat sat his younger brother, Capt. Wes Desmond, and, beside him, Dr. Yuri Yokomoto.

"*Sank* you so much for ride, Captain *Les*," he was saying.

"No problem, Yuri," Capt. Wes replied. "After all, we can't go on our moon mission without our geology expert. I'm just sorry your jet broke down."

"Yes. Japanese jet not so good as *Amelican*," Yuri said sadly.

"Well, they're pretty darn close," Wes said to be polite. "Not so low, Billy!"

"You're not the boss of me!"

"Actually, I am, Billy," Wes said. "I'm the captain, remember?"

"Big whoop!" Billy pouted. But he nosed the jet up just the same.

As kids, Billy used to push Wes around. But as soon as Wes became as big as his big brother, that all changed. Wes got better grades, was a better pilot and, most important of all, could beat Billy in a fight. Wes only hoped he wouldn't have to prove it again on this mission.

Rex barked suddenly.

"That's right, Rex. That's the coast of Europe," Billy said.

Wes checked his watch. They'd have to speed up to get to Nepal by bedtime.

"Hit the gas, Lieutenant," Wes said. "Just don't break the photonic barrier."

"I know how to drive!" Billy replied.

"Excuse *preeze?*" Yuri said, bowing slightly. "What is photonic barrier?"

"It's like the sound barrier, except with light," Wes explained. "As you know, when you break the sound barrier it creates a sonic boom. Well, when you go faster than the speed of light, it creates a blinding flash of light."

"Speaking of light, it's pitch black outside. And the headlights aren't helping much," Billy said.

"They won't this close to light speed," Wes noted. "Turn on the radar beams."

"I know!" Billy said.

"This darkness is a heck of a thing, Yuri. What do you make of it?" Wes asked. "By the way, would anyone like a cocktail?"

"Yes, *preeze*," Yuri said.

Rex barked.

"Rex would like some milk," Billy said.

Wes pushed a button and a portion of the back seat folded down to reveal a complete bar.

"No one know," Yuri said. "All we know is moon get weaker and weaker for past few months, and now it go out *compreetery*."

"Could it be the Russians?" Billy asked.

Yuri shrugged. "It could be air *porrution*. We won't know until we, *ah*, get there."

"And if we don't get to Earth Base Pronto by lights out we'll put the mission behind schedule," Wes noted.

"I know. I'm speeding up now!" Billy said, hitting the accelerator.

"No!" Wes cried. "You'll create a photonic boom!"

But it was too late. The speedometer had already passed light speed and a photonic burst lit up the countries below them.

"We just blinded everyone in Turkey," Wes sighed, taking a sip of his cocktail.

"Turkey sounds good," Billy said.

The Desmond brothers got up at precisely 6:30 a.m. (or 06:30 in military talk). They had a lot to do before the 3:00 p.m. (or 15:00) take-off. Billy didn't want to get up, but Wes (with help from Rex), managed to wake him.

They rushed downstairs to the cafeteria. Cookie the cook had promised to give them a nutritious breakfast of pancakes and orange juice.

"Here ya go, boys," Cookie said as soon as they sat down. He put two big plates of pancakes in front of them, with the butter already melting on top. "There's syrup on the table and a pitcher of chocolate milk if you want it."

"Woof," said Rex.

"Come on, Rex" Cookie said, wiping his hands on his apron. "We'll find something for you in the kitchen."

Wes and Billy both tore into their breakfasts, which also included sausages and bacon. It wasn't until they were almost finished that they noticed three people had joined them.

"Good morning, Yuri!" Wes said. "How did you sleep?"

"*Velly* good. I dream I *froating* like *snowfrake*," he said smiling.

"I say, these are golly good pancakes!" said a skinny Englishman next to Yuri. "Of course, in England we call them kippers."

"*Oui*, they are *magnifique*," said the girl on the other side of Yuri. "But in France we call *zem* crepes."

Wes, remembering his manners, stood up to introduce himself.

"I'm Capt. Wes Desmond of the United States Air Force," he said. "And you must be Prof. Dudley Picklesforth." He shook hands with the Englishman.

Picklesforth raised one of his bushy eyebrows. "*Sir* Dudley Picklesforth, if you don't mind. Foremost authority on aliens. And I must say, old bean, that you needn't crush my hand."

"And I am *Meez* Simone Bridgette," the girl said, holding out her hand. "I am Prof. von Frankfort's assistant."

Wes noticed she was very pretty, with big eyes and long dark hair. Billy noticed too, because he jumped up and shook her hand before Wes could.

"And this is Lt. Billy Desmond, my brother," Wes explained.

"*Magnifique!*" Simone said to Billy in a sweet voice.

Wes then shook her hand. "*Bonjour, mademoiselle. Je m'appelle Wes.*"

Simone's eyes widened. "You speak *zee* excellent French, *monsieur*," she noted.

"I-ay eak-spay ig-pay atin-lay," added Billy, who was always jealous of his younger brother.

Just then the young Navy Corporal Jimmy Benson entered and announced it was time for their mission briefing. The team returned their plates to the kitchen. Wes figured he'd have just enough time to brush his teeth before the meeting.

Wes and the others took their seats in the large briefing room. Gen. Taylor and Prof. von Frankfort stood in the front near a large projection screen. There were donuts.

"I'm sure you've all watched your briefing videos," the general said. "We'll make this quick so you can prepare for blastoff. Professor?"

"Thank you, general. Simone, will you please dim the lights?"

A large white globe appeared on the screen. Wes immediately recognized it as the moon.

"This is the moon at its normal brightness," von Frankfort explained. "But over the past few weeks, the moon has gotten dimmer and dimmer..."

The image faded.

"...until it has now gone out altogether!"

The room went black.

"Where is everybody? I can't see!" Picklesforth cried in a panic.

"Don't be such *zee scardee-cat,* Sir Dudley," Simone said. She brought up the lights to reveal the Englishman was clinging to Wes.

"Sir Picklesforth – are you afraid of the dark?" Wes asked.

"I was just protecting you! You *are* the mission captain."

"Getting back to the briefing," von Frankfort said. "We have to find out why the moon went out."

"Excuse *preeze,*" Yuri said. "Does not moon go out each, ah, month?"

"Yes, but as a scientist I can tell you this is different," the professor explained.

"Your mission is to fly to the moon, find out why it has gone out, and fix it," the general said.

"I say," Picklesforth said, "what happens if we can't get the blasted thing lit back up?"

"The moon effects the tides. If we don't fix it, the oceans will stop moving and all the fish will die," von Frankfort noted. "Also, our lighting bills will all go up."

"Arf!" said Rex.

Gen. Taylor sighed. "I thought we agreed there would be no dogs."

"We promised my mother we'd bring him along for protection," Billy said.

"Yes. She's getting old, and our dad's kind of a goof-off," Wes added. Their father was very undependable and didn't like Rex at all.

"He would be jolly good at warning us of approaching aliens," Picklesforth admitted.

"All right," the general said. "But you pay for his space suit – and food!"

"Don't worry. We make lots of money as test pilots," Wes said.

"It's settled, then. You blast off at 15:00 hours. The team will consist of Capt. Wes Desmond, Lt. Billy Desmond, Dr. Yuri Yokomoto, Sir Dudley Picklesforth, Rex the Dog, and my assistant, Simone Bridgette – "

Everyone rose to their feet at once.

"Simone!" Wes said. "Pardon me, but this is no mission for a girl!"

"I know as much about rockets as any boy!" Bridgette said, glaring up at Wes.

"Now, now," von Frankfort said. "I'm too old to go myself, and Simone is more than capable."

"She would be jolly useful if we encounter any aliens who speak French," Picklesforth noted.

"Besides, you're taking your dog," the general said.

Billy slumped back into his chair. "It's not the same!" he said.

And for once, Wes agreed with him.

At a quarter to 15:00 hours the team assembled at the door of Earth Base Pronto, ready to board the shuttle that would take them to the rocket. They were disappointed to find out that Cookie the cook wouldn't be making the trip. But he did pack them all a nice lunch.

"No soda cans, though," von Frankfort told them. "They'd explode in space."

A dark blue van pulled up to the door.

"Godspeed, gentlemen," the general said. "And ladies."

The team ran out into the bone-chilling cold and jumped into the waiting vehicle.

"Excuse *preeze* – stop shoving!"

"Sorry, old chap, but it's freezing out here."

To their surprise, the van was warm and toasty, thanks to their driver, young Navy Corporal Jimmy Benson.

"Next stop – the launch pad," he cried as they drove off.

"And *zen* – *zee* stars!" Simone added.

As they approached the ship, they could see steam rising off its surface.

"That was my idea," Billy told Simone. "I had them turn up the heat so the ice and snow wouldn't stick to it. I'm also piloting the Blastoff."

"*Zat iz* impress-*eeve*," she said, fluttering her big eyelashes.

"Wes is actually our ace pilot," young Navy Corporal Jimmy Benson called back from the driver's seat. "But he's going to be pretty busy being the leader and giving orders."

"Who asked you?" Billy said.

The van pulled up to the spaceship and the crew packed into the elevator.

"I say – quit shoving! You're crushing my pipe," Picklesforth said.

"So *solly*."

"It was also my idea to launch the ship from a mountain so we'd be closer to space," Billy told Simone, who was stuck between the two brothers.

"Billy wanted to launch from Mt. McKinley, but I suggested the Himalayas, which are taller," Wes added thoughtfully.

"I *sink* you are both *tres* smart," Simone said.

As soon as they were all inside and the double doors were sealed, the crew strapped in for takeoff.

"Fire up the rockets, Billy. There's only thirty seconds to liftoff."

"I know what I'm doing!" Billy grumbled as he turned the ignition switch.

The engines fired up and the ship shook from the vibrations.

"By Jove, I hope we're not going to blow up!" Picklesforth said, swirling his moustache.

"This is von Frankfort in Earth Base Pronto," a voice said over the intercom. "Takeoff is in exactly 15 seconds."

"Remember," General Taylor added, "the fate of the earth's fish depends on you all."

"Arf!"

von Frankfort counted down the seconds: "10-9-8-7-6-5-4-3..."

"Hold on everybody!" Wes ordered.

"2…1…liftoff!"

Rocket ship Blastoff fired into the sky like a bullet from a gun. The exhaust was so hot it melted the snow off all the mountains in the Himalayas. Wes and Billy, who were used to flying, let out whoops of excitement. The others closed their eyes and gritted their teeth. In a matter of seconds, they were hundreds of miles into the atmosphere, the clouds far below them.

"I believe I can make out Jolly Old England down there," Picklesforth said, looking out the porthole by his seat.

"Excuse *preeze*. That is Africa."

"No time for sightseeing," Wes called out. "We're approaching the ionosphere, and if Billy doesn't hit it at exactly the right angle, we'll bounce off it and fall right back to earth."

"Exactly 36.7 degrees," Billy added, clutching the control stick.

"Thirty-seven point *six* degrees," Wes corrected.

"You think you're so smart just because you're good at math!"

Simone looked at her instrument panel. "Four seconds to impact with ionosphere."

Seconds later, there was a loud *pop*, followed by a *whoosh!*

"We've done it!" Wes said with relief. "We've punctured the ionosphere."

"By jove, what was that *whoosh?*" Picklesforth asked.

"That is air escaping into space," Yuri said. "But the hole will seal itself in a few seconds."

"Nature is truly wonderful," said Wes.

"Well, what do we do now?" Simone asked as she unstrapped herself.

Wes thought for a moment. "Well, the moon is a quarter of a million miles from Earth, so we won't get there until after midnight. I think we should all take a nap so we'll be wide awake for the landing."

Just then Billy ran up to Wes and started yelling.

"I'm tired of you telling me what to do, and acting smart and everything just to make me look bad in front of everybody else!" he said, with his face all twisted up the way it did when he was mad.

Wes, who was always fair with is brother, tried to explain. "Billy, I'm the commander – "

"I don't care! You can't tell me when to take a nap like you're dad or something. What are you going to do next – give me a spanking?" By now

Billy's face was all red except for a squiggly line on his forehead. Wes knew there was no arguing with his face when it got like that.

"That's it! I order you to go to your room."

"No!" Billy said, pointing a finger in Wes's face. "I'm the older brother and you can't make me!"

Wes looked around at the crew. They were waiting to see what he would do. He knew he couldn't back down. With lightning speed, he used the red python leg sweep to knock Billy off his feet. Then he used the sleeping bear headlock to render him unconscious. When they were kids, Billy used to make fun of Wes for spending $1.25 on the Crimson Dragon Jujitsu Kit he had seen in the back of an Archie's comic book. But the skills Wes had learned from the book and accompanying full-color chart had helped him in many a fight.

"I'm sorry I had to do that," Wes explained to the others. "But nobody points a finger in the commander's face."

Yuri and Picklesforth carried Billy off to his room.

"*Zat* was brave," Simone said. "But now *'oo eez* going to fly *zee* rocket while we are sleeping?"

"I've thought of that," Wes said. He pushed a few buttons on the console. A closet door slid open and out stepped a large mechanical man. He was all silver, with a dome-shaped head and antennas for ears.

"*Sacre blue!* It *eez* an alien!"

"No — it's just Obort," Wes said. "The name stands for Operational Buddy Of Robotic Technology. Me and Billy built him out of old car parts dad left laying around."

Simone stepped closer to examine the robot. Sure enough, its belt was a chrome bumper, its shoes were old tires, its eyes were headlights and its mouth was a car radio.

"*How may I be of assistance?*" Obort asked through his mouth speaker.

"Obort can do anything we need him to do, including pilot the ship," Wes said.

"But *misseur*, how can *zis sing* fly *zee* ship when it *'as zee* laser beam guns for hands?"

"Don't worry. Obort — switch out of fighting mode."

"*Yes, Capt. Wes,*" the machine replied. It stuck its arms into its metal pockets and, when it pulled them out again, they had metal hands.

"Obort, please pilot the ship so we can all take a nap, Obort," he sighed.

"*Yes, Capt. Wes.*" Obort stepped toward the pilot seat.

"Let's get some shut-eye," Wes told the crew. "And no television!"

They all headed for the doorway, but stopped when Rex started barking at them.

"Oh Obort – don't forget to feed Rex."

"*Are you there, Capt. Desmond? This is General Taylor at Earth Base Pronto! Please respond!*"

Wes rushed down the hallway toward the control room.

"Darn! I was having such a nice dream too!" he groused. It was his favorite dream, the one where he wins the Indianapolis 500 by two laps. Only this time, girl who gave him his trophy (and a kiss) was Simone.

"I say, I believe we have overslept," a groggy Picklesforth said as he wobbled into the hallway in his tweed pajamas.

The two entered the control room and were quickly joined by Simone and Yuri. Billy, who had arrived before the rest, was talking into the intercom.

"This is Lt. Billy Desmond, Earth Base Pronto. We're here. We, uh...." Seeing Wes, he handed him the intercom. "You think of something to tell them, Capt. Smart Guy."

"This is Capt. Desmond, general. I apologize for the delay. We overslept, plain and simple. I hope we are still in position to land."

"*This is Prof. von Frankfort,*" a voice replied. "*You've already landed!*"

The crew cried out in surprise.

"*Take a look out the window,*" von Frankfort said.

Yuri turned on the outside lights and Simone threw back the curtains. Sure enough, the ship was in the middle of a crater – on the Moon.

"*Rooks rike* Obort really good *pirot,*" Yuri said.

"We must have landed on the dark side," Billy said. "I can't see anything beyond the crater."

"It's all dark," Wes noted. "That's why we're here, remember?"

"I know – I was just testing you!"

"*There's no time to lose – you'd better start exploring right away,*" von Frankfort said. "*And reset your watches – you're on Moon time now. Earth Base Pronto, out.*"

"But first, we eat, *oui?*" said Simone.

They were in the galley, eating the delicious bacon, lettuce and tomato sandwiches Cookie had packed for them, when the rumbling started.

"By Jove, what was that?" Pickleforth cried, dropping his teacup.

Simone and Billy ran to the window.

"It's probably just an earthquake," Wes said as he joined them.

"So *solly* to disagree, honorable Captain," said Yuri the geologist, "but earth-*krakes* only happen on earth."

The shaking got stronger and stronger

Simone's eyes widened as she looked out the window. "Captain, it's a stampede!"

"Where?" Wes asked.

"Over to *zee* right. It looked like...*beeg* pussycats!"

"A spacecat stampede – this is horrible!" Picklesforth cried from his hiding place under the table.

"Picklesforth, I thought you were an expert on aliens," Wes said. "Now you're afraid to meet one?"

"Well, really, my good fellow, I hadn't the foggiest notion I'd actually run into one. I thought maybe we'd find some footprints or something."

Billy started making fun of him. "Picklesforth's a fraidy cat, Picklesforth's a fraidy cat!"

"You take that back, you poppycock American!"

"Make me!" said Billy.

The two started wrestling. Rex started barking. Finally, Yuri and Wes broke them up.

"I could have taken him!" Billy said

"By jove, you popped a button off my nightshirt!"

Simone had crossed to the window and was looking out. "You silly boys, *zees ees* no time to fight each other. Look!"

Wes was the first to notice a glow coming through the window. "Douse the lights!" he ordered.

They all crowded around the window and looked out. The light was actually many smaller lights – strange torches strung around the necks of the cat creatures. They had arms and legs like men, but furry bodies and faces like cats. They even had long whiskers on their noses.

"Perhaps *zay* know why *zee* moon has gone out," Simone said.

"Let's go out and talk to them," Wes said.

They started heading for the door, but Yuri stopped them.

"*Preez!* Don't forget breathing mask!"

"That's right!" Wes said, smacking his forehead with his hand. "If we breathe pure space air we'll suffocate!"

They went to the cabinet and removed the masks, which were red and had stretchy loops to hold them in place.

"Surely we're not going out there unarmed!" Picklesforth said.

"You can take your laser sprayer if you want," Wes said. "But don't shoot unless I give the command."

Billy, who was putting the specially-shaped breathing mask on Rex, added, "Let's take Obort too. He should scare them."

"*Coming, Lt. Billy,*" the big robot said.

As soon as they stepped outside, the cat lights went out, though they could still hear and feel the rumbling of the stampeding aliens.

Rex sniffed the space air and let out a howl.

"Easy boy," Billy said.

"*Rook* out, *preez!*"

Just as Yuri cried out, they heard a metallic creaking, followed by a loud bang.

"We need light!" Wes commanded.

"Luckily I brought some flares," Simone said.

"That's good thinking for a girl."

Simone blushed.

"Light those flares!" Wes said.

Simone handed out the flares and the others lit them and tossed them into the darkness. In the red glow, they could see the few remaining cat aliens running to the east.

Simone looked examined the UNS Blastoff. "Oh no! *Zee* ship is *tres* dented," Simone said.

"Yes, *preez.* We may have to do repair before we can *brast* off again," Yuri added

"First things first," Wes said. "Billy, let's check for alien footprints."

But Billy didn't answer. He was gone!

The crew wandered around the ship, calling out for Wes's older brother. They stayed in the light of the flares so they wouldn't disappear themselves.

"It's not just Billy," Wes noted. "Rex and Obort are gone as well." Wes Desmond was always very observant.

"I guess we should – *gulp* – go look for them," Picklesforth said at last.

"Some of us, yes," Wes said. "But we can't forget our mission. I want to contact those cat aliens – "

"Mooncats!" Simone said. "Let's call *zem* Mooncats."

"Yes. Good. Anyway, we'll have to split up into teams."

"But, by jove, wouldn't it be safer if we all stick together?"

They talked about what to do for a while, but couldn't reach a decision. Finally, they all went back into the ship and Simone made them hot cocoa.

"The marshmallows are a nice touch," Yuri said.

After more discussion, it was decided that Wes and Simone would track down the Mooncats while Yuri and Picklesforth repaired the ship.

"We'll take the moonbikes and follow those paw prints," Wes said as he and Simone put on their breathing masks.

Once outside, they opened the hangar door and rolled out Moonbike 1 and Moonbike 6 (which was a girl's bike). They looked like dirt bikes except that they had big, wide wheels so they wouldn't sink into the moondust. Each bike had a headlight on the handlebars powered by a generator on the tires.

"Let's synchronize our radio watches," Simone said.

Wes checked his. "Band 1.076. Mark!"

Wes took out his radio. "Blastoff, this is Moonbike 1. Do you read me? Over."

"*Roud and crear, Moonbike 1,*" a voice replied.

"We'll check back in at 01:30 hours. Over."

"*Over.*"

"You and Picklesforth get started on those repairs – and no TV until you do. Over."

They started pedaling, which caused the headlights to come on. The trail led straight east, toward the lip of the crater.

As they approached the lip, they saw that it was about twenty feet high.

"Oh no – *eet ees* too high!" Simone said.

"Don't worry," Wes said. There's no gravity here on the moon, so all we have to do is get a running start." He pedaled furiously and the moonbike spit dust out behind him. Simone, getting the idea, also sped up. Wes hit the crater lip at top speed and his bike went almost straight up in the air.

"Yahoo!" he cried. The bike came down and he fishtailed to a stop just in time to see Simone's jump.

"Wee!" she yelled. Her bike came down right next to Wes's. But she fell off and knocked down Wes, landing on top of him. They lay in the dust, laughing.

"*Zat* was fun! We should do *zat* again!" she giggled.

"You're pretty cool for a girl," Wes said.

Simone, still lying on top of Wes, turned and looked at him. She was very pretty.

"*Sank* you," she said. Then she kissed him on the cheek.

Wes hurried to his feet. "We better get a move on," he said.

Suddenly they heard hissing all around them. Hundreds of torches lit up and they saw they were surrounded by Mooncats.

Simone said. "Look behind *zem!*"

Wes looked up and saw many homes perched on posts. They were just like regular homes, except made for cats. They had round doors and were covered with carpeting.

"Wow. We've found the Mooncat City!" Wes said.

He slowly raised his hand to give the universal peace sign, and so did Simone. Seeing this, the Mooncats retracted their claws.

"Greetings," Wes said. "I'm Capt. Wes Desmond of the United Nations Ship Blastoff."

The cats looked at him and shrugged.

"Do any of you speak English?" Simone asked.

The cats shook their heads. Then after a moment a weak catty voice said, "I speak English."

An old Mooncat hobbled up to the front. He had mangy black fur and walked with a cane.

"I am called Shadow," the cat said with a weak hiss. "Why are you invading the moon?"

Wes and Simone looked at each other in surprise.

"We aren't invaders," Wes said. "We come in peace."

Shadow plopped down on a moon rock. "That is what the other man said. But he is very mean."

"We don't know any-*sing* about another man," Simone said. "*Eez zat* why you were running?"

"He is a big, mean man. He says he does not like cats."

"Actually, we are here to find out why the Moon has gone out," Simone said.

"Yes," Wes added. "It's affecting our tides and raising our electric bills."

Shadow translated this information to the rest of the Mooncats. They shook their heads sadly. Some of them hissed their answers back to Shadow.

"The lights have gone out because of this man," the old cat said.

Wes was surprised. "Because of one man?"

"Yes. Because of one very stupid man."

Shadow took Wes and Simone to his house. It was one of the highest in the crater. Even though he was old, the Mooncat was able to climb quickly up the pole. It took Wes and Simone a little longer. Inside, they met his wife, Fluffy, and their seven kittens. Since it was dinner time, Fluffy invited them to eat. The food was a round vegetable that looked like brussel sprouts and tasted like tunafish. Simone, being French, liked it a lot. Wes ate one to be polite, then just drank milk (which was served in a saucer). After dinner, they sat around and talked.

"I don't understand," Simone said as she played with the kittens. "Who *eez zees* man and how did he put out *zee* moon light?"

"And what lights up the moon in the first place," Wes asked. "That's one of the things we came to find out."

Shadow let out a tired meow, then sat down.

"I guess you could say that we light the moon," he said. "With our lump-lumps."

"What *ees* lump-lump?"

"It's a vegetable. It's what we eat."

"Ah!" Simone said. "We just ate *zees* lump-lumps!"

"Yes," Shadow said, licking the back of his paw. "We grow them. We start planting them on one end of the moon and continue till we get to the other end. Then as we harvest them we plant more, so we always have fresh lump-lumps."

"But how does that light up the moon?" Wes asked, confused.

"Lump-lump plants glow in the dark until they are ripe. When they go out, we know it's time to harvest them."

"I get it!" Wes said. "So they light up the moon! And as the riper ones go out, less of the moon is lit up."

"Yes!" Simone added. "*Zat eez* why we get *zee* phases of *zee* moon! *Magnifique!*"

217

"The whole process takes about a month, in earth days," Shadow said. "Excuse me."

The old cat rose stiffly and crossed to Fluffy, who was standing in the hallway. It was time to put the kittens to sleep. Wes crossed to one of the round windows while they waited. Outside, he could see torchlights all across the crater. Beyond that it was dark.

"Now we know what lights *zee* moon," Simone said.

Wes set his big jaw in thought. "Yes, but we have to know how to turn it back on."

Soon Shadow and Fluffy returned and curled up together on the couch.

"What can you tell us about this earth man?" Wes asked.

"Oh, he's big and he's mean," Fluffy said. "He kicked my poor Shadow just for being in his way."

"Well, he didn't start out mean," Shadow said. "Like I said, at first he just wanted to be left alone. We gave him a big crater all to himself. And he built a house out of moon rocks in it. He brought furniture with him in his rocket. We didn't see him much for a while. He stayed indoors, watching hockey games on his *tee-vee* and drinking *earth juice*."

"He'd only come outside to work on his *baby*," Fluffy added.

Simone was confused. "*Eee* works on a baby?"

"It's some kind of machine. But he calls it his baby."

"What is this man's name?" Wes asked.

"We just call him the earth man, since he was the only one here. Until your ship came." Shadow scratched Fluffy between the ears and she started purring.

"Anyway, things were fine until he decided to clean up his crater. He had this idea that it should be perfectly flat and level inside. He tossed all the moon rocks out, then raked the dust until it was smooth. He was crazy about it."

"And if anyone left a pawprint in the crater, the earth man would get all mad," Fluffy said. "He'd wave his arms and say horrible words. You could hear him clear on the other side of the moon."

"And he didn't stop there. Soon he was trying to smooth out the whole planet – and that included the lump-lump plants."

"He said the glow kept him up at night!" Fluffy said angrily. "As soon as they'd spring up he'd come by with that big metal stick of his and whack them down."

"And that's why the moon is dark," Shadow said.

"But...why did he become so mean?" Simone asked.

"Who knows? But you don't want to cross him," Shadow said.

"I think it's that *earth juice*," Fluffy added in a whisper.

Wes nodded knowingly. Cocktails made most adults very happy, but it made others very sad and mean. "Where can we find this man?"

Just then loud meowing echoed throughout the crater and kept repeating.

"Goodness — it's the alarm!" Fluffy said, jumping up. "He's coming right now!"

They turned out the lights, and the cats in the other houses did too. Only a few torches at ground level remained lit. Wes looked out and saw a large man staggering toward their pole. He was weaving back and forth and grumbling to himself. He had a golf club in his hand and, wandering near a pole, he whacked it. Finally, the man stopped, doing his best to stand straight up.

"I'm looking for Wes Desmond!" he yelled. "Capt. Wesley Desmond! Get out here right now!"

Wes stepped out on the balcony.

"I'm Capt. Desmond," he called down.

The man looked up and almost fell over.

"Well, lookee here. A bigshot captain. Hey, why don't you go back to earth, bigshot captain?"

"Not until you stop bothering the Mooncats," Wes said.

"Me bother them?" the man blurted. "They're the ones bothering me, with all their digging and meowing and lump-lumps!" (He used some really bad words, but I didn't write them here.) Then the man took a swing at a nearby pole, but missed and fell flat on his face.

Wes noticed something familiar about the earth man's voice.

The man struggled to his feet. "What are you doing up here anyway?" he asked, slurring his words. "You and Billy are supposed to be home watching your mother."

"How do you know Billy?" Wes called down. As he did, the man wandered near a torch. Wes could finally see his face.

"Because I'm your father!"

It was a long walk back to his father's house, and not a fun one either. Mr. Desmond kept telling Simone embarrassing stories from when Wes was a child. Like how Billy would beat him up and make him cry, and about how Wes used to wet the bed. Wes was now bigger and stronger than his dad, and could have beaten him up, but he knew it was wrong to punch your father no matter how much he deserved it.

When they arrived at Mr. Desmond's crater, it looked a lot like the Desmond home. The front yard was smooth and covered with white rocks. There was a large TV antenna on the roof. And the back yard was filled with junk.

"*Zere eez* Rex, *zee* poor *sing*," Simone said, pointing.

Sure enough, brave Rex was lying in the back yard, chained to a metal post. Even worse, the chain had become so tangled the dog couldn't move. Wes was about to complain when Billy came out the front door, wearing a dirty T-shirt and boxer shorts.

"Hey dad!" he called. "There's a Blackhawks game on, and I made some Banquet chicken! Oh – hey, Wes! I found dad."

Mr. Desmond turned to Wes. He wasn't staggering as much as before. "Come on, Wes – be a man! Watch some hockey and have an Old Style. Unless you're too busy playing dollies with your girlfriend there."

"First, she's not my girlfriend," he said. "Second, I drink cocktails, not beer, and third, where did you get a rocket ship?"

Just then Wes' communicator came to life.

"*I say, Moonbike 1, have you made any progress fixing things out there? Earth Base Pronto tells us the earth's dolphins are swimming in circles and the surfers have no waves. Also, Gen. Taylor can't pay the light bill.*"

"I'm working on it, Picklesforth! Over!"

"*I say. No need to get snippy. Over.*"

"Dad, you can't stay here – "

But Wes' father had wandered off and was now pulling a spark plug out of his *baby*: a junky Ford Mustang.

Wes was shocked. "How did you get that heap up here?" he asked.

"In the rocket ship, of course," Mr. Desmond said while he gapped the plug with a matchbook.

"And where--?"

"The rocket? I'm sort of test-driving it for the Russians." He held a finger up to his lips. "Don't tell them I'm here; I'm supposed to be orbiting Mars."

Billy came back out of the house. "Dad! You gotta see this fight. I think one of the refs just lost a tooth!"

"Be right in, champ!" Mr. Desmond called. He was now puttering around his rock garden.

Simone pulled Wes aside. "Wesley – *zee* moon, *zee* Mooncats. We must stop *zis* man!"

"What can I do," Wes said. "He's my dad." He walked over to his father, who was now hitting moon rocks with his driver.

"You can't stay here, dad. Don't you see you're ruining the moon?"

Mr. Desmond became suddenly angry. "Hey, I'm not doing anything! I'm just keeping things neat and tidy."

"Dad, I found another can of Beer Nuts!" Billy yelled.

"Great," said Mr. Desmond, who was now adding wiper fluid to the Mustang, which had no wipers and no windshield.

In desperation, Billy crossed to his brother. "Billy, please help me. Dad's the reason the moon has gone out. We have to stop him."

Billy pushed his younger brother away.

"Are you kidding? Dad's right. This is the life. So why don't you and your girlfriend just get in your rocket and go back to earth?"

Wes watched sadly as Billy walked over to help their dad replace a headlight. They were siding against him just like when he was a kid. He looked over at Simone, and her pretty eyes were big and sad. It looked like the end for the world's fish.

Then he looked at Billy again, who was suddenly very angry.

"Where did you get that?" Billy, referring to the headlight in his dad's hands.

"What? This? I yanked it off that piece of junk you brought here."

Billy's eyes became wide.

"Obort!?"

Wes noticed a pile of junk near the car was actually the robot he and Billy had spent hours putting together.

"What did you do to Obort!?" Billy screamed.

"Hey – don't take that tone of voice with your father!"

Billy ran over to the once-great robot, which was now a bunch of spare parts.

"You're always breaking our stuff," Billy said, trying not to cry.

"Oh, don't be a baby," Mr. Desmond sniffed.

"I'm not a baby!" Billy said, wiping snot from his nose. "I think I'll take Rex for a walk. Here, Rex!" Billy looked around and saw the dog, who was wrapped up in his chain. He turned back to his father.

"You said he was out playing!"

"I don't want that hound tracking moondust into my house. Now shut up and hand me the ratchet."

Wes watched as Billy's face got red, except for a squiggly line on his forehead. He hoped his older brother would be mad enough to help him. Instead, he exhaled, shrugged, walked over to their father's dirty red toolbox and pulled out a ratchet. Mr. Desmond, who was bent over the hood, gave a quick glance.

"That's a crowbar, lamebrain!"

Billy paused for a moment, then whacked him on the head.

"No!" Wes and Simone both cried.

Simone ran over and checked Mr. Desmond's pulse.

"*Eee eez* okay," she said. "*Eee eez* only knocked out."

Billy shook his head. "He hasn't changed," he said. Then he looked at Wes. "What do we do with him?"

"There's only one thing we can do," Wes said. "Drive him home."

"I'll take him in the Russian rocket," Billy said. "You can pick me up at the Kremlin."

"Will do – big brother," Wes said. And they shook hands.

And that's how the Moon got turned back on. And how the USN Blastoff Team was formed.

(Interesting – but what does this have to do with Abraham Lincoln????   C– !!!)

NAPERVILLE

ABOUT THE AUTHOR

Chris Bittler is an author, copywriter and all-around snappy dresser eking out a meager existence somewhere in Wisconsin. His screenplay, *Raging Angels*, may well be the worst movie ever produced. *The Bad Idea Catalog*, co-authored with the great Dave Markov, may well be the best parody ever published. *Naperville*, a dystopian corporate novel, is a quarter-finalist for the Amazon Breakthrough Novel Award 2013. His favorite author is G.K. Chesterton and his favorite color a sort of drab green.